CELADON

Other works by this author:

Fiction:

Sunsets of Tulum

Nonfiction:

In The Sunlight of Sakurajima:
My Two Years in Southern Japan

A Writer's Roadmap
Make your writing dreams come true

Best-selling travel guidebooks include:

New York City
Japan
New Orleans
South Korea
Mexico
Yucatan
Guatemala
Tanzania
Indonesia
USA
Canada

Look for these other titles by Barrel Fire Press:

Summer to Fall, by Albert R. Waitt

CELADON

a novel

RAYMOND AVERY BARTLETT

Barrel Fire Press
Kennebunkport, ME
©2020

First Edition

ISBN-13: 978-0-9889390-6-6

Library of Congress Control Number: 2019906706

Cover design by J.Benitez,
99designs.com/profiles/1463359

Printed in the United States of America

"There are no foreign lands. It is the traveler only who is foreign."

— Robert Louis Stevenson

In many ways, for Jim.

PART I:
HOME

Chapter One

Pottery is like love: a form of impossible perfection. I had been in the studio most of the afternoon, escaping from the thousand duties a loved one's passing requires by mixing a fresh batch of Celadon No. 147, when the girl interrupted me. Celadons are the *filets mignon* of ceramic glazes, the best of the best. Yet they are also difficult, temperamental; no two turn out exactly alike. Some celadons are as extinct as the passenger pigeon: the recipes lost, the potters who made them long since passed. Thus, in certain parts of Asia a single cup the size of a cereal bowl can cost as much as a luxury car. Assuming, of course, that it was authentic to a certain potter in a certain place in a certain time, and that the potter is dead. The paradox of most fine art is that the best thing the artist can do to increase the value of his or her craft is to expire. If there are teacups that cost as much as a car, a large vase known to be from a dead potter — such as one with a particular type of long-extinct celadon — can be priceless.

While I can't complain of the modest living I've made with clay and am honored my work is prized enough to be part of more than a few museums' collections, the truth is that I am rarely happy with the pieces I produce. My glazes in particular have never been what I envision them to be. Specifically to the hundreds of celadon recipes I've tried over these years, only No. 147 has come close to what I have striven for, and it has taken me a lifetime to arrive there. Even so, where others see the beauty, I see the flaws. But it is useful at times to have an impossible task, as one can always find a little more to do when seeking to avoid something. And my wife's passing away has been as difficult to accept as it has been to deal with. Making 147 is as good a thing as any to fill the void.

This glaze is, I admit, spiteful, even schizophrenic at times, and if fired incorrectly, if the cone melts at a temperature even slightly different than the 2300 degrees Fahrenheit it requires, it comes out looking muddy, often with a moiré of bubbles that screams failure to me, or to any other potter who knows what a true celadon should be. Despite the crazing, those fine cracked lines within the melted glass, the surface should feel as smooth as silk stockings on thighs.

I always hold my breath when I'm opening the kiln, hoping what's inside has burned itself into beauty. Celadon No. 147 *can* be perfect. If the temperature is just right and the wood fire reduces the perfect amount of oxygen and the additional firing ingredients come in at just the right time and the moon is rising in the House of Saturn, it turns a truly otherworldly green, as iridescent and mesmerizing as the inside of an abalone shell. A peacock's tail shimmering in the sun. No other glaze on this planet can come close.

I am joking about the moon and the House of Saturn, by the way. The magic in clay is entirely terrestrial. But in all the years that have passed, I can count on one hand the number of times a firing has gone perfectly. In mixing this batch of 147 I am well aware that it is my last chance to get it perfect. But in pottery — as in life, as in love — it is not the end that matters, but the process.

The journey one takes, not the getting there.

And certainly not perfection. In fact, the Japanese have a word for the "perfecting flaw." *Wabi-sabi.* A frog jumping into an otherwise still pond. A blemish on a girl's porcelain skin. A mar on otherwise smooth glaze that shows understanding of just how imperfect we all are.

A potter I once knew, when I was young and just learning the art, used to say that in clay there are four joys: the joy of shaping it, of firing it, of glazing it, and of giving it away. In my own career, I have stuck to those four joys. But what motivates me, drives me, pushes me to my limits, is the motivation that comes from the impossible pursuit of perfect celadon.

With the mask on and the drill going it was impossible to hear the girl knock, if she had, so she had to come all the way in and she surprised me. I have potter's deafness anyway, a product of years of accidental inhalation of the glazing powders. A constant ringing in my ears like a little brass bell. *Tinnitus.* I might not have heard her even without the background noise, but I hadn't expected a person there, and in flinching I lifted the drill too high. A stream of glaze spun out across the room, hitting the tiles and the table and some reached the ceiling, leaving a spot of drab mud the color of a wasp's nest. Amazing that the brown blotch might, seared at 2300 degrees, turn impossibly iridescent green.

"What is it?" I asked, trying my best not to light into her.

"I'm so sorry," she said, in Spanish, and began trying to clean the mess up.

"Stop," I said. "Please, I'm working, just tell me what you came here for and then leave me alone."

She answered, still looking terrified that I was going to fire her. Or perhaps she was worried that I'd fire her grandmother, whom she was helping while we put the house in order and prepared for the estate sale. It was a mammoth job, as Marinne was a bit of a clutterer and had filled the house with trinkets from our five decades of trips together. Every ceramics conference I visited, every art show, every business trip she tagged along for, she came back with some souvenir — never a piece of pottery, not once — but something else to remember the trip by: a stuffed bear that would sit in a corner forever; tiny glass pigs that she arranged on a windowsill, thus preventing it from being opened as surely as if it had been painted shut; the clothes — racks and racks and racks — most worn once, if at all. To me the souvenirs all blurred together, but for her the trips were as clear from these items as if she'd taken photographs. The bear from Poland. The pigs from Toronto. This blouse from Brazil. That one from Hungary.

Writing this makes it sound as if I'm upset with her, or angry, but they all seem infinitely dear now that she lies under six deep feet of earth at New Saint Mary's Cemetery. I can't touch those things, can't move them, certainly can't watch them be put into boxes or tossed in the trash. For several weeks after she passed away I walked around the house feeling as if I — not my wife — were the ghost, unable to sit in chairs that she had sat in or to sleep in our bed. If it weren't for my situation and what that will mean in a few years, I would keep it all, like a personal museum of her bric-a-brac. Marinne's Museum. Even the dust on the windowsill pigs is hers, in a strange way. I couldn't so much as dust them.

So I was very happy to have Lupita Villarosa, aka *mi Señora*, aka my housekeeper, handling it. Her taking over freed me to mix glazes and throw pots for a little longer. Accepting as I am that all things, even art, must come to an end, I plan to have one more firing before moving on. Perhaps it will be my best yet. My swan song.

"Calm down," I said to the girl, all the while trying to remember her damn name. She had told it to me more than once and yet I couldn't ever seem to keep it in my head. Age, I believe. It robs you of those things that you used to take for granted. I was always good with names. Now I couldn't even tell you the syllables. It could be anything from Flor to Angelique. Tinnitus doesn't help. You just don't remember things well when a thousand hornets are buzzing inside your head all the time.

Not Lupita, though. I know she has a different name than her grandmother.

"Please ignore the mess," I said, filling a Dixie cup with ice water and handing it to her. "Here. Sit. Calm down."

For the first time, she smiled. Just the barest flicker but it was enough.

"I know you don't like to be disturbed when you're working," she began. "My grandmother tells me all the time. All the time."

"Your grandmother knows me well."

"I know we're supposed to … to put everything, no matter what, into the trash bags. But I found something—"

"Just throw it away," I interrupted. "If you stop to ask me each time something seems vital it will be twenty years before the house is empty."

"It's something important."

I smiled. "Yes, of course everything is. But—"

"Not just *what* I found. It's where I found it."

I stopped mopping the floor and looked at her. The poor thing still seemed terrified, wanting to comply with my wishes yet not be blamed for tossing something priceless. I relented.

"Go on."

The empty Dixie cup had been sacrificed to the stress gods. She crumpled its corpse in her hands. "It was in her closet. Your wife's. A box. I know that kind of box. I've seen those boxes when I've looked in my aunts' closets." She paused, twisting the crushed cup, her knuckles white. "Her wedding dress. I knew it was that kind of box. And maybe you can't understand because you're an old man, sorry, not old … you're a man … but I just wanted to *look* at it. I've seen photos. It was such a beautiful dress and I thought, just thought maybe—"

"Yes?"

"Maybe I could buy it from you. My sister is getting married and we can't afford to have a new one, that's why I opened it up, just to look, see if the size would be—"

I laughed.

"You can have the dress. How's that? Of course. Take it. I am sure Marinne will be happy to know it's making someone else happy." I paused a moment before saying, "She doesn't need it anymore."

I thought that would be the end of it. But the girl looked even more uncomfortable.

I waited.

Still nothing. She just looked at her feet. The Dixie cup, shapeless, lay discarded on the table.

"Just take it. No problem. Is there anything more?"

"When I opened the box," she said, "there was a letter sitting on top of it. The envelope was open, and looked like it had been mailed a long time ago, Señor Chase. From Japan, addressed to your wife—"

She stopped. "Señor Chase? Are you okay?"

My mind had blasted a thousand light years away. We remember exactly where we were, what we were doing, when certain events occur. The death of JFK. The day men walked on the moon. The Challenger explosion. The planes hitting the World Trade Center. That letter and the awful tragedy surrounding it. I fumbled for a chair and sat there, holding my temples. The girl talking all the while, her eyes wide and me staring through her, back through the decades. I couldn't catch my breath.

"You can leave for the day," I told the girl.

Mar. That was it.

Her name.

Mar.

The sea.

Mar. Like my wife's name, cut. A name I should remember and yet, somehow, always forget.

"I'm worried about you," she said. "I'll call an ambulance."

"I'll be fine, Señorita Mar. Please go. I need to be alone."

"Just let me call someone—"

"No!" Suddenly I was yelling at her, holding onto the table to keep my balance. "Take the wedding dress and *go home*. How many times do I need to say that I need to be *alone?!*"

She leaped for the stairs as if I'd hit her. A faint slam of a car door seconds later told me she was gone. I doubted she'd even gone back upstairs to my wife's bedroom.

But I would mail her the dress.

I sat there trying to summon the strength to go up and see the letter with my own eyes, though I didn't need to. I knew exactly what it said; I had written it myself. I stared at the vase that is the centerpiece of my studio, as if to ask it a question. As if it could actually respond. It was eighteen inches tall and just a simple, universal form like a cigar, wider in the middle than at the ends. My one and only keepsake from two years living in a hidden pottery town in southern Kyūshū, the southernmost island of the archipelago that is Japan. An unassuming urn but for the fact that the glaze was an absolute perfect celadon.

It was dark by the time I lifted myself and floated, unbound by gravity, upward, dissolving through walls like the ghost I will be and into my wife's bedroom, where that dress and the open letter on top confronted me. A feeling of dread seeped out from inside my guts. My fingers and toes, tingling and numb, felt like the leaves of a great sprawling vine that's suddenly been cut at the root.

CHAPTER TWO

Perhaps it is a conceit that I have always felt our own lives are as plastic, as malleable, as shaped by the whim of the Creator as my vessels are. Some remain on the wheel, always bending this way or that, being pressed or pinched, trimmed or sliced as the years spin around like a pottery wheel. Others are cut free and bisqued, tempered by a low fire, enough to be rigid. Even fragile. But we can still dress our fragile forms in glaze, wrap a tapestry or a deceit around us and then hurl ourselves into what will shape us forever: The kiln turns us all to brilliant, beautiful stone, unrecognizable from the mud from whence we came.

At least that is my story: a piece of mud, transformed.

As a child I knew nothing of art or culture. I liked policemen and firemen like all little boys because they were big and brave and strong and had flashy lights and always seemed important in a way that my father — a custodian at a nearby factory — never was I would have loved for him to be part of their Fourth of July parades, all the people cheering.

But policeman and fireman dreams vanished the moment I realized there was something called "being an astronaut." A firetruck? A police car? Those were nothing compared with riding in a rocket ship and going to visit the stars like the Little Prince. It was very early on, second or third grade, that I knew with my deepest conviction that I *would* become an astronaut.

"But it's always good to have a second plan," my father said. "Otherwise you end up stuck doing nothing like your old man. What about a doctor? Last year you wanted to be a policeman ... what about that?"

"I don't need to have a second plan," was my answer. "I know what I am going to be."

"But not everyone can be an astronaut," my father cautioned. "You have to be lucky!"

"I'll just be lucky then."

I make it sound as if my father was somehow against this, but he was tickled by it in the way that all fathers are when their sons hit on a dream for the first time. My father did not have money for books we could keep, but the library was free, and he took me to get my library card and laughed when I skipped the children's section and went to the adult shelves, where I spent only a few moments before picking out one book. Just one. An oversized coffee-table-style volume called *The Constellations*.

"There are all kinds of books about astronauts," my father said, shaking his head that I wanted that particular book. "Here, this one's good ... The Little Prince! He's from space. Take that too. You can get a bunch. The ladies love it when little boys get lots to read."

But that was the book I picked. I renewed it over and over until I'd reached the library limit. Then I borrowed it again whenever the hold period ended. Other boys knew dinosaurs and Tonka trucks and played cowboys and Indians; I knew the eighty-eight standard constellations before I was ten years old, and many alternate ones from other mythologies.

I knew the placement of planets, could pick out Venus and Saturn and Jupiter, even, would show them to my father, who by then had seen quite enough of them. At some point he spent most of a day with me adding glow-in-the-dark stickers (probably full of radium, back then) to my bedroom ceiling so that I could look at them when I went to sleep each night. He did it from the book at my direction, so they were accurate. We ran out of space in my room, and the stars spilled out into the hallway, the upstairs study, then downstairs to the alcove and the TV room until every room in the house had its own sets of constellations. I could navigate from the front door all the way to my bed in the darkness, using the stars for guidance as Polynesian sailors had.

"For my little astronaut," he said when we finished. "If belief is all it takes, you're halfway there."

His filling the house with constellations for me is one of those fond memories, one of those places where his love for me bubbled up and became a tangible thing, but for the most part, we were not truly close. My mother died when I was just two years old and my father remained single after that. A head and a half shorter than most men and broad, he never struck me as the type most women would go for unless he were charming or gallant, which he wasn't. I did not get the sense that he was looking for anyone else, either. Whatever magic electricity had happened between him and my mother to bring me into the world, it was pushed into a compartment of my father's heart that he'd chosen not to reopen for anyone else. Or perhaps, back to the vessel analogy, he'd already been glazed and fired. He avoided talking about her; I learned not to ask; there was only one framed photo of her — none of the two of them. Even that photo disappeared, eventually.

Being a single dad at a time when even single moms were not common forced him to make some hard financial decisions. At some point early on, he began working night shifts as well as during the day, and without any money for a sitter, he had to take me with him as he did his rounds in the factory. I say custodian because he was never grouchy about grabbing a mop if someone spilled something and he could fix almost anything with a myriad assortment of glues, cements, tapes, caulks, strings, clamps and so on. But he was a pipes guy by trade, an industrial plumber, an HVAC expert long before that acronym ever became used. He spent most of his time checking pressure and oiling valves on the miles of pipe in the factory's underground heating and ventilation tunnels. His forearms were huge Popeye-style muscles built up from years of working with wrenches and copper.

Having me there at night could not have been easy, but he had no choice. We'd undo the foil on our TV dinners together and watch the evening news, he'd doze for an hour while I did homework, and then we'd go outside. He would pull our dented, rusting Ford into one of the three parking spaces near the service entry to the heating plant, and it was my job to find something to do for the next few hours until I was tired. When I got sleepy, I would open the door of the car and climb in the back seat where he'd put pillows and a blanket and I would stay there until he got off work at four. When I woke up I'd be home in my bed the next morning.

It sounds bleak, perhaps Dickensian, but in childhood, everything is normal. Somehow I didn't feel as if my home life were any different than my peers'. My father was a goodhearted man, not particularly effusive, but I never felt he resented me because my mother had died and left him a widower. A kid doesn't ask for more than love. Until the accident, I felt lucky to be who I was and in the family I was in.

Sometimes he would let me tag along and I would get to explore. While there were parts of the plant that still operated twenty-four hours, the areas where my father worked were often one or two stories below, so he and I had the basement and its labyrinth to ourselves. He had a key ring that probably weighed as much as I did and there was something magical about asking him to let me in here, into this hallway, or that room, or that stairwell, and have him nod silently, fish through his key ring for the right one, and open up the place for me to explore. As each door opened I pretended I was an astronaut heading out through the airlock into a new, unknown planet. And the understanding was that I'd be back in the car sleeping by the time he needed to go home.

He put his energy into work and raising me and by Sunday, his one day off, he was spent. He loved watching television, and perhaps because it was always on I grew up envying the houses where the rooms were silent. I would go over to friends' places and play checkers or a board game, thrilled by that wide, world-opening silence. No *Andy Griffith* show. No *I Love Lucy*. No fake laughter. Nothing but my own thoughts which — like the vacuum of outer space — were silent and vast and infinite.

It's one of the reasons I can make peace with going deaf. I've never minded silence. It lets me get work done.

There were aspects of what my father did that were dangerous, and that impressed me, too: "If there's a leak," he once told me, "the steam will come out so fast it'll cut a broomstick in half. That's how strong it is." He smiled, looking tired, but also proud. Sometimes there'd be oil or soot on his face, and I'd get to wipe it away before he returned to the task of the night.

"I love you, Dad."

He tousled my hair. "Just make sure you get the hell out of here, do something with your life someday. Don't become an underground mole like your old man."

"I'm going to be an astronaut."

Why would the world plan anything else for me?

The factory's giant furnace crouched beneath a chimney that rose up so high you could see the lights of Boston from the top of it. I know this because I discovered that by twisting a paper clip into a shape like a tiny coat hanger, with one of the corner ends open and no hook, then inserting it quickly several times and giving it a slight twist, I could pick the small lock that kept the access to the chimney closed. Decidedly *not* a father-sanctioned adventure. He would have been furious if he'd ever known I was taking advantage of the freedoms he'd given me.

After picking the lock, I could go from that access along a catwalk to a narrow ladder made of iron rungs that ascended up the outside of the tower all the way to a tiny platform at the very top, where the bricks were so hot from the steam and fumes that even in the dead of winter there was never ice or snow. As I climbed up, sweat would stream down my forehead as if I were in a sauna, the bricks as warm to the touch as a live animal. I didn't know that only luck kept me alive, that the ladder was to be used with the furnace off, and that a sharp downdraft of super-heated steam could have scalded or killed me.

That climb mesmerized me. I would go up there and see the world shrinking below me and when the furnace came on I would feel the mass trembling and shivering as if it were a rocket, and I would hold my breath and pretend that I was searching the galaxy for my mother. Aliens had abducted her, you see. She was somewhere waiting for me out there in the vastness of the stars.

The accident happened November 14, 1953. Poet Dylan Thomas left the planet at the young age of thirty-four just a few days before. Cambodia had gained independence. My father had just gotten a small raise and had celebrated by purchasing *The Constellations*, the same book I'd always gotten from the library. It was in the back seat of the Ford that night. I carried it with me everywhere.

I had gone up the chimney often enough to know the heartbeat of the furnace, know its burps, burbles, and roars. I'd never felt so close to the stars. Sometimes on the moonless nights the vast swath of the Milky Way seemed so close I felt I could reach up and stir its vast soup with my hand. I felt safe up there, as close as the "Little Astronaut" would ever get to the cosmos he craved.

At 9:38 p.m., the tower made a noise I'd never heard before. Instead of that awakening and the hum, there was a loud thump and a shudder, deep in the guts of the structure, as if a giant truck had hit the building. Then a violent tremor shook the chimney, so strong that both my feet slipped off the rungs and for a few seconds I was hanging, swaying back and forth as the chimney decided whether or not to topple. Had I not been gripping the metal rungs I might have fallen the 180 feet to the pavement below, dying, (oh, the irony!), on the hood of our very own Ford.

Once I had my feet on the rungs again, I stared down, stunned, not understanding what was happening. For a moment the woods below lit up with orange, every branch, twig, and trunk in vivid detail. Then a strange, odd, whistling howl, a mix of high and low notes, as of someone pressing the upper and lower registers of the world's largest pipe organ all at once. A wail that built insanely to a demon's shriek, followed by a silence just as deafening.

Then everything went dark. No lights. No engines working. People poured out of the building, milling in the darkness, flooding the parking lot. Far away, the thin wail of a siren, soon joined by more.

Anyone looking up might have seen a scared, confused boy looking down like the Smokey Bear cub after the fire. But they were as bewildered as I was: Nobody knew then that one of the release valves had failed to open, causing the steam to build up as it would in a giant pressure-cooker bomb. When it blew, it tore through the building, shrapnel sliced through the walls and ceilings, filling the lower levels with 850-degree steam. They found pieces of the furnace embedded in the oak trees that lined the parking lot.

As I tried to process what was going on, the ambulances arrived, one after another after another. I stayed up there watching, frozen, unable to imagine that my father might be one of the ones who was carried away.

But he was.

One of the last they found, because he'd been closest to the explosion.

He had realized that something was wrong seconds before the blast went off and had been dashing back toward the furnace to manually release an auxiliary safety valve. Had he not had his hands gripping the valve handles he might have been simply tossed down the tunnel, but because he was holding on to the rusted steel ring the blast kept his head up as his body whipped around like a flag on a pole in a typhoon.

It should have killed him.

He was so close, the temperatures so intense, it seems impossible even now that he could have survived at all, but he clung to life as tenaciously as he'd clung to that valve. Perhaps because he knew he could not leave his child alone in the world.

For that, despite what lay ahead for both of us, I was thankful.

He was badly burned, especially his face and hands.

The accident did not kill him, but the steam stole his eyes instead.

CHAPTER THREE

My father, independent and stoic to a fault, now depended on me for even the most basic needs, and the scars — plastic surgery was still in its infancy — were so painful that sometimes, even under medication, he would cry out. Or he would wake up gasping, clawing at the sheets as if he'd been splashed with acid.

I was the one who helped him bathe, who shaved him. I helped him dress, set out his clothes in the morning before I went to school. In class, I'd worry about whether I'd done enough to get him through the day. He succumbed into his blindness and the physical pain that it caused, and could anyone blame him? I was so young that it took me until adulthood to understand the true meaning of how deeply that accident robbed us. I heard him fall once in the bathroom and had to help him, his pants around his ankles, as he found the footing he'd lost and got back onto the toilet. There is a loss of dignity we all feel if we are lucky enough to age, our body failing to control and measure what it once did. Many of us ease into it, with a fall, an accident, some little thing that happens and marks the first of many submissions to the years. What happens to us has happened first to our parents or even our friends.

To experience that helplessness in one's late thirties is a cross I think no one should ever bear. A part of me longed to be free of him, but I loved him. He was my father; he needed me.

Not surprisingly, my grades dropped over the next few years, and while my teachers all knew the reasons behind it and were kinder to me than they might have been, I still went from being an A and high B student to barely passing every class except French, which simply came easily to me, and Latin, which I enjoyed because of its quirky need to decline. Every language requires conjugation. In Latin, however, you must also decline. *Cibus, cibi, cibo, cibum, cibo, cibi, ciborum, cibis, cibos, cibis.* I remember it even now. Languages somehow stuck inside my brain the way a card shark sees what's in a deck. Not that it was perfect, but French seemed more like a dialect of English than something truly foreign. So many roots were identical. My grades in French and Latin (or more likely, the words on my behalf of those two teachers) were what kept me from failing.

Still, with my grades slipping I had yet another reason to call myself a failure. When you're that young and caring for an invalid, the duties overwhelm your sense of who you are. You stop dreaming, like a pig in a pen who accepts that that's where it will always be. Becoming an astronaut seemed as distant and as silly as the stars.

It wasn't until the very end of high-school though that things became dire. I saw my friends with their futures getting brighter. I heard about colleges, about programs abroad. Others dove into relationships, had sex with their partners, and a few got married, and of course, a few became parents, sooner than they'd have planned, but still they had a worthwhile journey all their own.

My darkness was individual. I found that only my French class motivated me, in part because my father would let me recite poetry and read to him, he needed that, though as he grew ever-more-addicted to the pain syrup (a potent prescription mix of laudanum and codeine, long off the market) I suspect he heard the poems less and spent most of the time in his own world.

Still, it was time we could share. My teacher felt I had a true "gift for language" and seemed more upset than I was that I would be unable to attend college or do a study-abroad in Paris or Lyon. "You have the *je ne sais quoi!*" she used to say, shaking her head. "What a shame to not use it!"

I didn't know exactly what I was missing, but just as I had looked at the stars and felt an overwhelming desire for space, now I would imagine the streets of Paris with that same yearning. Yet leaving my father was unthinkable, and despite the daydreams I forced myself to focus on things that were attainable. Just getting by. That was all I wanted at the end of each day, when I'd crawl, exhausted, into bed and see the faint constellations glowing at me: just get through another day. Caring for someone is exhausting in a way that people never understand until they're forced to do it. Some can't. Some won't. Others rise to the challenge like Churchill in the time of war. I was a caregiver.

But on prom night of my senior year I found myself dateless, friendless, alone, staring at the black inky waters of the Charles river from beside the Watertown Dam. Below me, the white froth churned as the water slipped over and I had convinced myself that it was time to leap, one simple leap, over the guard rail and let myself drown. The construction was such that a circling current could hold a boy under for minutes, even hours. Every decade or so a pet or person drowned, caught in the chilling circle of the dam. I stood, my hands shaking on the cold steel rail, trying to will myself the strength to climb over. The hit "Runaway," by Del Shannon, kept spinning in my mind, over and over, an earworm that I had to end even if it meant plunging into the water below.

But at some point my gaze traveled from the churning froth underneath me up the smooth reservoir wall to where the glassy water reflected in perfect clarity the map of the stars. As I looked from the river to the sky, I saw my own house, the stars reminding me of my father and his desperate situation, and that dream I'd had years before of being an astronaut. If I were going to live at all, I had to get out of Watertown. If only to briefly see what the world held.

I went home. My father was sleeping, drugged from the syrup or from exhaustion or from pain, and I didn't have to pretend that I'd been dancing with pretty girls. I changed out of my clothes and lay down in my bed and stared up at those faint, broken stars. That night, I swore that I would find a way to travel … and I chose not to die. Because of that little door I'd created, that promise to myself, Watertown was no longer a cage. Travel would not happen tomorrow, not next month, but it would happen. I would come back, but as soon as I could, I would go away for a while.

Chapter Four

Shortly after my graduation in 1961, my father and I worked out a deal so that I could accept a job that the kind high school French teacher set up for me at a printing shop in one of the larger Boston universities. A neighbor would check on my dad a few times during the day, make sure he was all right, but I'd be free to commute into Boston as long as I was back in the late evening. Each day I made sure his clothes, meals, and medicines were set, and left him sleeping, knowing that he'd spend most of the day listening to the television once he awoke.

I'd take the bus from Watertown to the closest T station, then get the Red Line from there in to Downtown, a commute that took an hour or so if I were lucky and twice that if I were not. The printing press was in a building that has long since been torn down near Quincy Market, an ink-and-roller world that did esoteric or vanity runs for university professors who had to show they had a new book out to impress the administration. My tasks were primarily readying the presses and laying type, if a book, or inking lithographic stones, if there were images. I was the person who cleaned off the dried inks, scraped the wheels, put oils and grease into the moving parts. It was not delicate work, but it required exactitude and precision, and my quick reflexes were needed: Were the press to start suddenly, it would take off my arm as easily as if it were a pinkie. By the end of the day I was sweaty, my fingers covered in ink and linseed oil. In my canvas smock, splashed with the colors of the day's production, I could have been a fishmonger or butcher or any number of men who survive by doing the work that the rich care not to do. But I was making art.

I was also making money, and while the other kids my age who had jobs were out spending their earnings as fast as they made it, I opened a bank account and put aside every penny I could. It wasn't easy to skip movies that came out, to eat at home with my dad instead of at Friendly's or HoJo's, but seeing that balance increase each time I added a paycheck was the reward. When it got big enough, all my shackles would open and I'd be free.

My boss was a taciturn fellow without quick reflexes who had lost three fingers (two on his left hand and one on his right), all victims to presses turned on at the wrong time. His goal was to make sure that the work got done and he seemed both happy and a bit vexed that I did not join the missing-digit club on his watch.

I'd worked there for two years before stopping for lunch at a little French-themed cafe two corners down, the kind of spot that sets tiny tables out with a vase and red-checkered cloth in the summer so people can dine *al fresco* while breathing exhaust fumes. I'd gone in only because there was a rush job for a poet laureate that had to be completed and I didn't have time to walk the extra ten minutes to Faneuil Hall. I was a sub or pizza guy. Tuna salad on rye. Maybe a lobster roll if I was feeling flush and fancy. Expecting to grab a tuna melt, I'd been confronted by a myriad of baguettes, *pain d'* this, *pain d'* that, and odd things with drippy cheese on croutons.

However, as I scanned the menu, the "eureka" light started flashing and I realized those hours spent in French class had taught me something useful after all.

I stood there marveling that I could read much of the menu, feeling in a strange way like I'd stopped off for lunch in Paris. Someone bustled around in the back, behind a little curtain that kept customers from seeing into the kitchen. After a minute or two of standing there, I decided I couldn't wait any longer and turned to leave. My hand was on the door handle when there came a delicate jingle, the curtain parted, and a girl about my age came bursting through. Out of breath, she stood for a few seconds looking at me, her cheeks pink and flushed. Delicate skin, so white it was almost translucent, like skim milk. Curly strawberry-blond hair tied up in a loose pony tail to keep it from dirtying the food. A frilly apron evoked Impressionists and Europe and the Seine.

"*Oui?* May I help you?" she said, following the question with perhaps the world's most perfect smile. Full lips, red lipstick, white, shiny teeth. But it wasn't how the smile *looked* that made it perfect. It was how much it conveyed: A smile that felt like I'd been hugged from across the room.

"Of course," I said. From out of nowhere came French: "*Je voudrais un … un … croque monsieur et un café au lait.*" I felt as awkward as if I were a white-faced mime wearing a beret.

"*Oh, merci!* French!" she said. "But we can speak English."

"Four years of American high school French. I can't even order a sandwich correctly?"

"Your accent is better than most!" With tongs, she placed my order into a paper bag.

"If my accent was good, we'd still be speaking French."

She said something in French so rapid it would have made a diplomat wince.

"Now you're just showing off." A hiss from the espresso machine.

"All I said was that I hope your sandwich tastes wonderful."

She rang the price into the register, handed the bag to me, and for a moment our hands touched when I pressed coins into her palm. The poet laureate would have gone to his lecture without his precious chapbooks had not a bunch of middle-aged women burst in and descended on the poor girl like crows on roadside carrion.

"I'm Marinne," she said, when she got free again enough to chat. "Marinne Pont Claire. And you are?"

"Neil," I said. "Just Neil."

"Nice to meet you, Just Neil."

I took my food, and the smile that she returned kept my heart fluttering for the rest of the afternoon. The sandwiches were average at best, but I would have eaten ten of them to have a smile from that girl and to put a few quarters into her palm.

Marinne Pont Claire.

She was not the only discovery during my time in that printing cellar. As I laid type for university poets (many of whom would stop by in their worn tweed coats and bow ties to check the lead themselves) and my bank account grew closer and closer to setting me free, I often had the chance to commit passages of verse to memory. The same with the art books for which I prepared the lithographs. I found myself flipping through the pages to admire works of Picasso or Bruegel or Klimt and a host of local unknowns, many of them wonderful artists who would never manage to carve a name in the history books, but who devoted their lives to their craft with as much madness as any of the famous do, because they are compelled, driven, even addicted. Books about Japanese potters, hidden ceramic villages, Koreans who had been abducted from their homeland and brought to Japan. It was high drama. School had left me with the impression that art was frilly, something extraneous to real life, something nobody needed. But there in that basement, perhaps giddy with the ink fumes or poisoned by cadmium ochre and linseed oil, I first understood that art and poetry and literature are genuine. They matter. They are as essential ingredients to life as oxygen in the air.

Poems and small conversations with these literati in tweed led me to literature, a dark descent from which no one escapes. I read voraciously, devouring whole bookshelves, one great author at a time. Tolstoy in October, Nabokov in November, Steinbeck before the New Year. Hesse and Kipling (oh, Kipling!) and Orwell. Everything Dickens. On and on and on.

Yet no volume was more fascinating than one by a professor of Asian art who had made an anthology of Japanese ceramics. I could see that it was art, of course, who can stand in front of one of those perfect vessels and not be moved? Yet for me it was something else as well. Something deep and internal. For I saw in those shapes not vessels of clay and glaze, but objects of outer space: burned forms, seared by suns and a hundred years of travel. The scars of impact with other bodies on the way. The shapes reminding me of planets or asteroids or starships. They were beautiful in a way that redefined my concept of beauty.

At some point, a love crosses the line and becomes a need for possession. The more I stared at these pages, worked on the lithographs that would fill the tome with its riches, the more I needed to possess it. To have it. So I began to steal pages, one by one, first by slipping them under my shirt when nobody could see me, then by offering to work late, so I could do entire chapters without anyone knowing I was creating my own volume, page by page. Each day I thought I would be discovered, but never was, and while at the time I felt lucky, I realized much later that it was there I realized one can get away with something dishonest, a lesson that seeped its way into many other aspects of my life.

And why such a love of reading in someone who had cared so little for school just a few years prior? The astute reader will have already spotted the connection between my lust for books and the boy climbing up the chimney to stare at stars and a far-off city skyline. Of course it was not literature per se that I was in love with. With the help of books and paintings, albeit vicariously, I was traveling for the first time.

CHAPTER FIVE

Getting away from Watertown, being able to be "myself" rather than a caretaker, and just understanding that Marinne deserved the best me that I could offer her, helped me. I could breathe, at least. Not knowing that Marinne liked me exactly as I was, I resolved to make myself into a gentleman, thinking that would help win her. I trimmed and combed my hair. I bought not one, but two new shirts, the Oxford kind, with collars that buttoned down. I asked one of the younger professors what scent he used, and bought myself a bottle so I could smell academic.

"Who's the girl in your life?" my father asked, the day I splashed the cologne on at home.

I asked the professors coming into the shop if they knew how to learn French. Really learn it. Forget high school. One of them found me a bootleg copy of Pimsleur's Speak and Read Essential French, which I began to study. The connection of this new interest in French and recent events was undeniable, yet had I been on a witness stand, I would have sworn it was just because I wanted to learn something new. Even now the logic there seems flawed. It wasn't as if I had to speak French to communicate with her. It wasn't as if Marinne expected that or that I would somehow impress her. But there I was, babbling French phrases to myself in Boston Common on my lunch breaks, trying to read French poems and literature. I began greeting people at the print shop with, "Bonjour" until my boss pulled me aside and told me not to make an ass of myself.

The next time I walked into the store Marinne barely recognized me.

"Neil?" she said. "You've changed. New job?"

Something in the way she said it made me worry that this wasn't a good thing.

"I got a haircut."

"You did more than that. Wow, you bathe in that stuff you're wearing?" A delicate hand waved in front of her nose.

I placed my order. There was none of the flirtation that I'd felt before. She rang the register and handed me change.

"Is everything okay?" I asked.

"Yes," she said.

"You seem concerned about something. Or just—"

"No," she said. "I'm fine. Let me get your sandwich."

I waited, my heart in my throat, like a patient about to hear a doctor's fatal diagnosis. She returned, handed me my sandwich, and smiled.

"Well," I said. "*Merci*. I'd love to see you again."

"I'd love that too," she said, with the enthusiasm of someone getting a speeding ticket. Her eyes stayed anywhere but on my own.

So that was that. I left, got halfway down the block, then hurled my fancy sandwich against the wall.

It took me another two weeks before I went back, in the middle of the afternoon when there'd be the least chance of other customers in the shop.

She was at the counter, nodded at me when I came in.

"We don't have the *croque monsieurs* left," she said. "Isn't that what you get usually?"

But I wasn't there to order a sandwich.

"Are you free tonight?" I asked, walking right over to the register.

She still looked unhappy. "What?"

"Can I take you to the movies?"

She took a step back.

"I'm busy."

"Tomorrow then?"

She shook her head.

"Why not?"

The slightest of pauses before answering. "I have a boyfriend. He's coming to Boston for two weeks."

"Oh." My heart in my throat. Long awkward pause. Then: "He doesn't live here?"

"Paris."

"Paris." Any city in the world and it had to be Paris.

"I'm sorry," she said. "You—"

"Don't be sorry. Why sorry? Nothing wrong with having a boyfriend from Paris."

"Neil."

"Really."

"I like you, I do. Just—"

"Just you've got a boyfriend in Paris." My voice was shaking. "So that's how it is."

She gave a little shrug. "I guess so."

"You have any soup?"

"Lobster bisque?"

"I'll have a cup of that, please. Sure."

I sat at a table by the window, sipping bisque and staring at the street outside, my mind running through how he looked, her boyfriend from Paris, the fancy clothes he wore, the smarmy accent. I envisioned him cut like a men's magazine model, a fedora tilted to one side. A thin upper-lip mustache. Paris.

Could I blame her? I was nothing, from a boring nowhere suburb, spoke with an ugly Boston accent, could barely order a sandwich in French, let alone any other language. Why wouldn't she be dating someone worthwhile instead of me?

I finished the bisque, put the tip on the table, and waited until she was in the back room to walk outside, resolving that would be my last time going to that little cafe.

When I saw her again it was winter, 1964, and snowing, and I looked up from the press and there she was in the threshold of the office. A gust blew the door out of her hand, and a draft tore through the busy print shop, scattering loose pages and making everyone shiver. Her curls were longer, down her back, dotted with snow. She looked lost, confused, and then her eyes met mine again and she smiled.

I stopped laying type and went up the three stairs, meeting her at the door and pulling it closed behind us.

"Neil ... Here's where you work?"

I nodded.

"I need these printed," she said, holding out a page. "Is this the kind of thing you do?"

It was a eight-by-eleven inch page with the cafe's name and address and a "Going out of Business" sign.

I swallowed.

"What happened?"

"I'm not sure," Marinne said. Her jaw tightened. "The owner just wants to sell."

"What about you?"

She shrugged. "What about me? They're laying me off is what. I don't know what I'm going to do. She sent me to get these printed. I've got another week to find something else."

"I'm sorry."

"It's not your problem. I'll get by."

"Will you go to France?"

"Why would I go to France?"

"To be with your boyfriend. Wouldn't—"

"I broke up with him. He came and visited and by the end of two weeks both of us knew it wasn't working out. No hard feelings, just ... Some things aren't meant to be."

"What? Why?" I said it as if I were shocked, horrified, though nothing could have made me happier.

"He never touched me," she whispered. "He never even wanted to hold my hand."

"Can I hold it then?" I asked. "*Ce soir?*"

She looked at me. "What time?"

Our courtship was deep and sincere, marked by mittened hands held, by walks and talks as we wandered through Boston Common, by feeding the swans as the springtime willows wept above the shore, and as much touching as she would allow. I abandoned French, not because I was bad at it but because it made Marinne too self-conscious of how different we were, and because I realized early on that just adopting a few words of a foreign language doesn't make you its muse. In fact, Marinne, like so many transplants to the United

States, didn't want her heritage to be the first thing people noticed about her. To me it made her more exotic, more alluring, but we rarely talked about it. She had left too early for France to ever have felt like her home.

Despite that, we had plenty in common. Like me, she too was an avid reader; we spent hours in the public library, talking in whispers about books we'd read or wanted to, and stealing kisses behind the shelves. I had not yet told her about my past, about my father, about how destitute I was and how much I felt like an impostor among these brilliant minds, hers included. I would lie awake at night in my room, the same shabby ceiling, staring at the constellations that now had changed, shifted, as paint peeled away, taking with it Solaris or Alpha Centauri. It pained me that most of the Pleiades was gone. Cassiopeia looked like a parenthesis instead of a W. At some point I resolved to repaint, to replace each and every star, but then a few months passed and I realized that would never happen. The ceiling, like so many other things in my childhood, would not ever come back.

I was sure that if Marinne knew the real me and my situation at home, she'd drop me in a moment for someone with fewer responsibilities. So I cultivated culture, crafted myself in the image of the poets and literati, pretended to be a refined rich kid like the ones I envisioned she dreamed of and hoped she forgot that guy I was when I first walked into the now-closed cafe. Into that fiction, I admitted some of the truth: that I would travel, put Watertown and my life there far behind me.

"If you promise yourself something, you need to keep that promise. Right?"

"You would leave me?" she asked.

I nodded. "But I'd come back."

Later, when she did know my father's accident, my past, she accepted this. But at the time she pulled away, spoke little to me for the rest of the afternoon.

It was in the Boston Public Library that I pulled her into a dark corner and ran my hands up under her sweater to her breasts and down, too, to the slick of wet warmth there between her thighs. I felt her gasp and tremble as my fingers moved, exploring her, her eyes open and intense, watching me as if at any moment I might disappear. We froze, hearts pounding, when a librarian walked toward us, a black man with salt-and-pepper hair and an imposing white beard. He was walking down the corridor toward our little corner rapidly. We could see him through the spaces in the shelves. But if he knew we were there he didn't show it; perhaps he wanted to encourage us to find a more comfortable and private area for lovemaking. He stopped at the very closest rounder at the end of the aisle, but never turned the corner. Had he, he would have seen us together, searching madly for a Dewey decimal number that existed only in our minds.

I hungered to do more, but as the weeks followed it seemed she was adamant to not have things go any further, which seemed all the more cruel given that she was from the south of France, a land that stereotypes taught me was far more free than we were. I imagined women rutting on topless beaches and protesting only enough to seem "proper" before giving themselves over to passion. Yet ironically, Marinne, not even Catholic, would not budge from her view that everything should wait until after marriage.

This was still the early sixties. The tsunami of free love hadn't yet hit America's prudish shores, and this is not to say that she was unwilling to do anything at all. She loved kissing and would lift her lips to mine at the slightest provocation. Her eyes would close, she would tremble in my arms almost as if she were having orgasmic spasms. In the subway stations. In the park. She would kiss me anywhere. Every time we met, she would claim a kiss, long and slow and shivery, and another one before she'd let me leave. I loved the sensation of her warm body pressed to mine, her breasts against me as we embraced, and I loved that feeling of being needed. But it was a daily agony to know that she did not want to go further with me than we had already gone.

I cannot blame her for being who she was, for feeling what she did about sex before marriage, for wanting and not wanting me exactly as she did. We are who we are, and it would be cruel of me to exact from her memory an apology I do not think I deserve.

We were happy together. I had a job with some prospects for advancement. My father was stable. I should have felt a contentedness I'd never had before.

But it is human to hunger. Our biggest achievements and most spectacular failures all come because humans have the insatiable ability to dream. My account balance, though I spent some of it for dates with Marinne, continued to grow, and with it the knowledge that I would have to leave.

CHAPTER SIX

The docks have changed so much over these past decades that they barely resemble the port I knew from my childhood. Now Boston's harbor belongs to the rich man. The fishing trawlers have been pushed out by yachts that cost more than houses. One can perambulate the Rose Kennedy Greenway, dine in black tie at any number of waterfront restaurants, shop for brand-name goods at a Quincy Market and Faneuil Hall so different from mine it angers me they've even retained the name. Then why not retire to the multi-million dollar yacht and ease the tensions of the day with a fine cognac and a massage? The water below no longer has the refuse that it did in the 1960s: It looks clean, thanks to a new pipe with which they pump the sewage out into Massachusetts Bay to wash ashore on other beaches and fill the Stellwagen whales' feeding grounds with raw, untreated sludge.

Out of sight, out of mind, but at least the rich don't have to look at it now.

Marinne and I had been steady for a winter, spring, summer, fall, and another winter again, so it was 1965 when I began to yearn for real travel with an intensity that I have difficulty putting to words. My father no longer played a large role in my life. He was there when I'd get home and there when I left, and if he were sleeping or the bottle had tipped I knew what to do.

Had anyone stopped me on the street that spring, I would not have hesitated an instant if asked if I were happy.

In early March, 1965, as we walked through Boston Common arm in arm, the willows had again turned that unique shade of greenish yellow, as true as the crocuses an indicator of warm weather on the way. A few white clouds, high up, looked as if a cat had scratched the sky. Marinne and I were just walking and a dread hit me, something cold and ugly: The time had come.

I wanted to leave.

I didn't have all the details of how to make it happen, but I did by then have a good deal of money saved, money that I thought should buy me at least a year of wandering. Going to Europe had long lost its appeal. Now the wilds of Asia burned inside me, and nowhere more exotic and fascinating than Japan.

Up to that moment my journey had always been a fiction, something I kept inside myself, a hand warmer if you like, for those cold days of being so lonely and desperate to see something beyond the Watertown walls. But I'd saved to the point that I had to call my own bluff: I would either take the leap and travel, or admit to myself that for all my yearnings, I would never get away. I would be one of those people who stays in his hometown his whole life, always wondering what might have been if I'd done things differently.

I had no reason to leave, either. How do you tell someone it's not them, when it isn't? When it's you. When it's not even you. When it's something you've chosen to try just because you always wanted to

"You're thinking about something," Marinne said, a few minutes later. "I can feel it."

I shrugged. "No. Nothing."

"Your eyes. They get that way sometimes." She stared at me. "Are we breaking up or something?"

"No. Of course not."

She stopped. "You don't have to lie to me, Neil."

"I'm not lying."

"Don't patronize me either."

We walked hand in hand down Summer Street to the imposing edifice of South Station. The street vendors were hawking hot dogs and nuts; the cold spring air smelled of caramel and trains. We bought some butter-roasted cashews and I poured the hot candies into her palm.

"Isn't it amazing," I said, looking at the steel rails that spread out like a delta. "Those tracks go anywhere. Follow them south and you can end up in New York City. West all the way to the California coast."

"Well they can't go everywhere," Marinne said. "Trains don't run underwater. You can't get to Japan."

We laughed. But the truth of what she said seeped into me. Trains don't go everywhere. And she had mentioned that word: *Japan.* I hadn't said it. She had. It was as if she'd already read my mind. As if she'd known.

And I might have told her. It was so long ago, the memories have blurred a bit. The tinnitus distracts me from reaching too deeply into what conversations we'd had. I don't know. But it surprised me, that she'd pop out that country, as if plucking it from my own mind.

"You could hop on a ship when you reach California."

"And go where?" I asked.

"Keep going. Hawaii. Then Japan." She looked at me. "Because you need to know. I need to know. We need to know."

"Know what?"

"To know if I'm the right girl for you."

If she had punched me I would not have been more surprised. My chest felt as if she'd put a loop around it and pulled it tight for a half a second before letting me breathe again. She'd defined what had been there in my mind, unsaid and even unformed, and it scared me to think not only that I was so readable, but also that she knew me that well. I didn't have an answer formed yet, but for her it had been there for a while. How the hell did she know that about me?

Japan.

A country that had risen like the phoenix from the ashes of World War II. Many Americans still hated the Japanese, thought of them as caricatures with round, bottle-bottom eyeglasses and Hitler mustaches. Yellow teeth, the yellow menace. Japanese cars hadn't even arrived in bulk on the American market. The idea that cars might be Japanese was as laughable then as the thought that California might in the future produce drinkable wine.

Yet Marinne's comment cemented the fascination, a need that grew stronger every day. The Japanese spoke a different language and had different customs and they slept on futons and wore kimonos instead of Western clothes.

To me that country's name sounded almost as musical as Marinne's had been.

Japan.

Yes. I rolled the name on my tongue. Relished the syllables.

That was what I needed. Travel, the need to leave, had a direction now. It would be a voyage to Japan.

Stubborn and pride-filled that I was, I couldn't bring myself to tell her then that I did plan to leave. I got angry at her instead, then we walked in silence from South Station north, along the waterfront. There was no Greenway, no Big Dig back then. The Central Artery, hailed as a modern miracle, had opened a few years earlier, winding through Boston like a giant green boa, decapitating Boston's North End and the waterfront. Nice girls didn't walk with their boyfriends in the shadows there. Our fight petered into silence as we realized how easy it would be to get mugged or worse in the darkness cast by those new steel girders. We stayed together, arm in arm, until we got to the bridge on Congress Street, where we watched the fishing boats unload seafood near what would one day become the Barking Crab restaurant. The water below smelled of drowned rats and fish death and sewage. We still didn't speak. I saw Marinne stealing glances at me several times, but if she had questions, she kept them to herself. I knew she was uncomfortable and yet, almost as if testing her, I kept us walking, silent, along the docks.

As we neared the North End I saw an oil tanker, so mammoth that it seemed rooted in the sea, sluggishly cut through the water on its way out through the channel. The white wake was all that hinted at motion. I inhaled as if I'd caught a beautiful woman's glance from across a room. We stopped and watched it.

"You want to be on that ship," she whispered. "I can tell."

"Just stop."

"What are you so worried about?" she continued. "What do you lose if I know what's there in your heart?"

"Why are you so fixated on this?"

She looked up at me, her lips small and pressed together. She opened her mouth to say something and then thought better of it.

"What?" I asked.

"What's bad is you wanting to travel and never doing it. If you want to leave, you should go."

I paused. I have never been good with speaking on the spot, and if I had not become a potter I think I might have been a writer, if only to give myself the endless option to revise what I say.

"Why would I want to leave?"

She formed her words with care.

"Because if you don't leave now," she replied, "then you'll never stay."

She was still looking away, east, toward the freighter. It took me a moment to realize she was crying.

"You *want* me to go?" I said. The monumental topic we were addressing felt like a train rushing over my head. She was *letting* me go?

She turned back. Each cheek had a shiny pathway down it. "I want you to be happy."

"We can go together. You can come with me."

Marinne pulled my head to hers and gave me a long, slow kiss. It seemed softer, deeper, more true than anything we'd ever shared before.

"Never make promises you can't keep," she whispered, her lips in my ear. "If I go with you, who will be here to take care of your father? We both know you can't leave him, what ... to rot?"

That was the moment I knew that I would ask her to marry me. I had no clear vision of what the future would be or bring, nor did I even know if she'd say yes. We were so young, anything could have happened. But that was the moment I stopped thinking of Marinne as my girlfriend and began imagining that she'd be my wife. She would stay, be his caretaker. That she'd do that for me seemed an impossible debt, but one that I couldn't say "no" to.

We ate lunch at a teacup-sized cafe on Hanover Street, two tables and a menu scrawled on sheets of brown paper that they pasted up on the wall. We hardly said a thing. Toward the end of the meal she asked whether I was angry with her. I shook my head. Seconds later she burst into tears, and she rushed out of the restaurant into the street. I tossed a few dollars on the table and caught up with her, grabbed her, and crushed her to me.

"I love you," I said.

She dried her eyes with her sleeve. I held her in front of me and then licked a tear that was glistening right on the very tip of her nose.

She tried to laugh. "I like the thought of you getting to see the world. I just don't want you to see so much of it that you … that we … lose what we have."

I held her, pressed her body into mine.

"Lose what we have? How could we ever lose what we have? Just a year, that's all it is. One quick year."

"And what about your dad? How will you tell him?"

"He'll understand. He was always the one telling me to be an astronaut."

We held each other so intensely and for so long that people stopped what they were doing to stare at us and we didn't notice. A small crowd gathered. Tourists thought we were Italians. Italians thought we were tourists. Eventually, the owner of the pastry shop we were in front of came out and yelled at us in a thick accent, handing us a cardboard box tied with red and white twine.

"Here's a box of cannoli. On the house! Now you two lovebirds go get a room, why don't you? You're distracting my customers because when they see you, they realize they don't want pastries, they want to be young again and be falling in love."

I fumbled in my pocket for some cash but the owner thrust it back.

"You keep that for the room. Right now, I need to sell cannoli. Scram!"

CHAPTER SEVEN

Marinne showed her love for me by purchasing a going away present that she gave me the week after we'd established that I was going to make the voyage to Japan: a set of Japanese language textbooks, with extensive vocabulary lists and flashcard boxes.

"You don't want to arrive without speaking the language!" she told me, as I stared at the gifts open-mouthed. That she would have found such a supportive gift even now still strikes me as so typical of Marinne.

My father, however, did not take my travel proclamation the way I'd expected.

"What?!" he yelled at me, launching himself out of his chair so violently that I thought he was trying to strike me. "You're going to, to what ... to abandon me? And your country? Be a draft dodger? A rat?"

I didn't know what to say. I didn't have an answer. Not a good one.

"Maybe they won't find out."

"Of course they'll find out. Hell, if I could I'd turn you in myself. I don't want my son to be a draft dodger. A weasel. A coward."

"You always said I should be an astronaut. Reach for the stars."

"When you were young. Little boy dreams. Oh, and also, that was when I had my eyes." He sank back in the chair and reached for the pain syrup. "What about me?"

"I have part of that covered," I said, and told him about Marinne's idea.

He listened as he poured the dose, his hands shaking so much that the liquid spilled on the coffee table. Putting the spoon in his mouth, he leaned back, his body relaxing.

"And the draft board? How do we explain it to them?"

I had that covered too. I wasn't going to explain it. I was just going to go.

"I'll think of something."

"I can't believe you'd abandon me."

"I can't believe you'd make me stay. It's just a year."

"Worthless piece of shit."

And then he sank back into the chair and closed his eyes. I stood there in the threshold between the kitchen and the television, listening to it blaring, watching my father slip behind his eyelids to a place where he could still see.

I went outside, staring up at the night and wishing I were already up there, journeying at light speed to places no one had ever discovered and planets no one had ever seen.

Marinne and I got engaged, but unlike so many of my peers, we held off on marriage. Kids I'd gone to high school with had been getting married left and right to avoid serving in Vietnam under the "peacetime draft." LBJ would eliminate the marriage exemption in August, 1965. The irony for me was that because I was needed at home to care for my father, I was actually allowed to stay home on a 3-A deferment no matter what. Yet I was leaving anyway. Heading to Asia, no less. If I'd had any close friends, they might have been angry at me for treating the war so flippantly when so many of them, conflicted or courageous or both, would never come home.

I used some of the money I'd saved to purchase a band of gold decorated with a diamond that was extravagant enough to ease whatever qualms I had about leaving and about becoming engaged. The lady at the jewelry store had this advice for me about the ring.

"Young man," she said, nodding grave approval. "Remember that whatever band you give her is a symbol of your faith in her. So it's a good investment if you care about her. She'll never question how much you love her." She winked. "And you'll have peace of mind.

She might see a nicer man while you're away, but she'll know the nicest ring is if she stays with you."

That Marinne would be fickle enough to care what ring I left her with seemed absurd, but I didn't want to argue with the saleswoman. "I'll take that one," I told her, and hurried out of the store.

I placed the token in my coat pocket and invited Marinne for a walk in Boston Common. Pretending to show her some of the spring's duckling hatch I pulled her into the welcome seclusion provided by the boughs of one of those weeping willow trees, the same trees that had chilled me earlier that year when I'd realized the time to leave had come.

That stand of willows does not exist today. For security reasons, most of the low-hanging branches on these great trees have been trimmed away, and anything there by the pond has been removed. It is difficult now to imagine that on a walk around the perimeter of that small, muddy puddle was a spot beneath the branches where one could feel alone despite people walking by on the paths just steps away. The leaves were so dense that they prevented all but the most brazen peeper any glimpse of what was going on inside.

"What are you doing?" she asked, giggling, as I swept her underneath the shroud of green.

"I saw some ducklings here the other day," I whispered. "If we're quiet, we can see them."

I stalked toward the edge of the water and then pointed down.

"They're right here!" I mouthed, pretending not to wake the imaginary ducklings. With my left hand I motioned for her to come over to me. With my right hand, I readied the ring.

As she craned over me in hopes of seeing the sleeping nest, I turned and went down on one knee. I felt this was not optional, though in retrospect it was more like comedy than romance.

She stared at me.

"What are you doing?"

"Marinne, this past year you have made me the happiest man alive."

"What are you—"

"Each day that passes I feel lucky to have met you, to know you, to have had this time together." I pulled out the ring, my fingers trembling. "Marry me. I want to spend the rest of my life with you."

"Yes?" she asked. It was a question, as if she were asking herself permission.

"You will?"

She nodded. Her lower lip shook. "Stand up, silly thing. Stand up before you get yourself all muddy."

"You'll marry me."

"I will, of course I will." Her voice quavered.

I reached for her hand, pressed the ring onto her finger.

"It's lovely," she said, holding it up so the sun could hit it. "It must have cost a fortune."

"My fortune is you," I said.

She kissed me. "We're getting married?"

"We are."

"I'm a bride-to-be?"

"You are."

But instead of looking happy, Marinne was quiet and then sighed. Her hand went to her eyes for a moment. "At least you're not going to war."

"I'll be back in a year."

"The longest year of my life."

CHAPTER EIGHT

I left for Japan on June 24, 1965, on the *Pandora*, a rusted, world-weary, diesel freighter bound for Hong Kong via Panama and then to Japan. My hope had been to take a leisurely voyage, stopping at ports every few days, but the cargo (I never discovered its exact nature) was needed for the base in Sasebo, presumably for the Vietnam war. The route was thus anything but leisurely, with only one stop — for provisioning and fuel — in Panama.

Marinne saw me off at the wharf; my father refused to come. I could not have picked a worse day to embark on a voyage. A summer squall opened up as we were nearing the docks and flooded the roads. Our taxi went on Broad Street and then tried Milk and still couldn't get around because of the downpour. Only by backing up all the way to Tremont and circling around on Boylston could we reach the destination. The vessel loomed, dark and ominous, its bridge disappearing into the fog as if the ship itself were being dissolved. We were late to the point that there was no time for anything but the briefest of hugs and the torrents of rain were so heavy that there was no sense in even using our umbrellas.

"I love you," Marinne said, touching my face. The rain made it impossible to know if she was crying, but I knew she was. Her skin was puffy and her eyes were red and they looked up at me with such desperate sadness that I might have stayed on the dock and watched the ship pull away.

As I opened my mouth to tell Marinne I'd write her daily, a deckhand with forearms the size of my thighs and a pink turtleneck rushed over and indicated that cargo had to go with him. My suitcase was sturdy, but I'd treated myself with wild abandon to the downtown bookstore and by the time I was done packing them there was barely room for my clothes. I had a few pairs of slacks, shirts and underwear, and a warm, wool pea coat. That was it. No, not quite: Marinne had slipped a pair of her silk panties into my hand the day before I was to sail. Beautiful lacy turquoise, the color of sea foam. That she would do something so brazen for my goodbye gift was both erotic and torturing, and they contrasted with the practical, useful, anything-but-sexy language set.

The deckhand picked up the heavy suitcase as if it were filled with paper towels.

"Get your ass on board. Now!"

I ignored him for a moment and turned to my betrothed. I love you, Marinne, I tried to say. It was there, half-formed, when a foghorn opened up with a series of blasts so loud that it made us both flinch and cover our ears. I picture the captain and first mate up on the bridge staring down at the little farewell and timing their toots for maximum effect on their passenger.

"Last chance," the pink-shirted crewman yelled, his voice far off, our ears still ringing. "Or we leave you ashore."

"Go," Marinne said.

That vision of Marinne in the rain imprinted forever in my memory. I go back to it on certain days when the rain is falling that same way, in downpours, and with fog. She stands, lips full and glistening in a half-pout, one lonely, wet girl, raising her hands at a vanishing boat. Her hair was sopped yet beautiful, clinging to her cheeks and skin. Her eyes were fixed on me with an intensity that I would only see from one other person, one other time, my entire lifetime, searing into me, as if our gaze were a physical thing that could pull her on board with me. I should have simply stayed there with her, stayed forever in her arms.

Marinne, how gorgeous you were that day, some perfect rain angel sent to protect me, perhaps, and I slipped out of your grasp without even "I love you," in return.

The clanging of the gangplank as it was untied brought me to my senses, and with a last look I turned myself away and ran toward the *Pandora*.

Minutes later, on the cold, galvanized deck, I made my way to the starboard rail in hopes of calling out to her. She was still standing there, but my "I love you," was drowned, this time by a renewed downpour. The *Pandora*'s giant screws whipped the putrid water below us into a green-brown froth, and the dock and the yellow taxi and the forlorn figure still standing there melted away into the fog.

Part II:
Voyage

CHAPTER NINE

The *Pandora*, aged and rusted, was a freighter that — according to the captain — had at various times in its long career at sea carried everything from cars to tea to a million and a half worth of Turkish hashish (though what happened to the money was never explained). Not a penny had been spent on maintaining the vessel, and even a cursory tour of the deck showed cleats that were badly in need of replacement, railing sections that were loose, hatches that refused to batten down. Rust had turned many edges into rough sickles that could, were one to slip, cut to the bone. I did not know it at the time, but the *Pandora* would make only a decade and a half more voyages before being sold for the scrap metal and cut apart in Hong Kong. As the vessel glided into the fog, my guts writhed in deep, gripping fear that I was making a terrible mistake.

No one could have looked the part of a ship captain less than Asbjörn Solomonson, from somewhere in Northern Europe. Sweden, I believe. The captain stood almost seven feet tall and couldn't have weighed more than 180 pounds. Were he muscular and in a jersey he might have passed for a basketball player, but his face was so gaunt that his cheekbones stood out like hatchet blades, and despite a lifetime on the sea his skin was so pale that even Death himself might have looked sunburned in comparison. His posture was poor thanks to decades spent in terror of banging his head on iron thresholds and ceilings meant for midget crewmen. He even shuffled his feet when he walked, giving him the haunting impression of a zombie.

Then there was the pink-shirted crewman, who turned out to be the first mate. Larry (I never got his last name) was as swarthy, barrel-chested, and broad as Captain Solomonson was thin. Whether his garish choice of wardrobe was derived from a handicapped fashion sense or a desperate attempt to bring color to the pallor of the bridge, I will never know.

My cabin was clean and tidy, and when I saw my suitcase had been placed in the brass-rimmed luggage receptacle I relaxed. Though small, the room had everything that I thought I needed to be happy: a tiny private washroom, a reading lamp on gimbals, a berth across the far wall. The mattress was firm and comfortable, and a green velvet curtain offered additional privacy if for some reason I forgot to lock the door. It took only a few minutes inside the chamber though, before I began to feel nauseated. It grew stronger by the minute, until, one hand at my mouth, I dashed out to the nearest railing and hoped the fresh air would keep me from hurling my meal into the sea.

I tried to clear my head and look out to the horizon, which is supposed to help landlubbers get their sea legs, but in the thick fog I could make out only a few indistinct shapes, and after squinting to try to discern them, I vomited over the side. When I grabbed the railing to steady myself a piece of the salt-flake iron sliced my palm. Scarlet drops of blood splashed onto the hull. A kind of christening.

My throat tightened up, my bowels felt loose and watery. Making my way back to my cabin, steadying myself with the uninjured hand, I thrust open the door. Placing the wastebasket in preparation for what was to come, I collapsed into bed and curled into fetal position, holding my stomach. I felt cold and alone and sorry for myself. Then angry, for it was my own damn fault. I had asked for it; I had insisted on it. Before the *Pandora* had even left Boston waters I was wishing I were home.

I would like to say that things improved, that in a few days I got my sea legs and that I made friends with the crew and learned the ways of the sea. That's how it's supposed to work in all the fairy tales. How different the romance from the reality. I was queasy every single day I was on that ship. The sight of the ghostly Captain

Solomonson never ceased to scare me, and the garish Pepto-Bismol-pink garb of the first mate seemed all the more offensive when any moment might find me dashing in haste for the rail. And readers will have guessed at the irony of my bringing all those books with me: The moment I tried to open one the nausea worsened, and I soon gave up any hope of reading anything at all.

That is not to say that I didn't eventually adjust, as anyone does, and accept some things are going to be. At certain moments the ocean, the shimmering sea surface, the tatters of clouds, the sun plunging down to disappear at the end of the day in a tapestry of pinks and golds, would for a few seconds make me feel that somehow it was worth all the discomfort and miseries to be there, experiencing that moment, and bearing witness to the wonder.

What creation on this planet is more powerful than the sea? What is more temperamental? More fickle? More majestic? More wrathful? In some ways, this incredible ocean saved me. Staring off at the vast blueness and that thin horizon where the cyan of the sky met the staggering deep, the glimpses of fish as they jumped, as silver as mercury, visits from dolphins and the far-off spouts of whales, grounded me in what was real and what was not and taught me — almost as soon as the fog of Boston had lifted — how insignificant my own life was.

That can be a useful lesson for a young man.

The water didn't care a bit how miserable I was or how much I missed Marinne. It didn't care that I could fall overboard and be swallowed up in something overwhelming. My job at the print shop, my father, Boston Common, and even Marinne: Nothing mattered when you held it up against the vastness of the sea.

And if we speak of vast, on the *Pandora* I could look up at night and see the stars in their full undimmed glory for the first time. Without the light pollution of the city they seemed to hang nearer than I'd ever known before. Unbroken, beautiful night for 360 degrees.

Stargazing eased my bouts of nausea, perhaps because it focused my eyesight on far away objects or because the chill of the night air refreshed me. If Captain Solomonson haunted the bridge during the day, I haunted the decks at night, often meandering up and down the enormous, empty vessel for hours. At times the stars were so dazzling that I found myself wanting to leap off into the night toward them and disappear. A kind of seafarer's madness, perhaps: If life means nothing, what a temptation to journey onward to the stars.

It was on these night walks that I made my first friend of the crew, a Japanese man who was an assistant to the cook and the only person on the boat approximately my own age. I say that laughing, because while he looked ten years my junior, in fact he was almost thirty and had spent almost a decade at sea. He was small and wiry, with nary a wrinkle to show for all those years of sun, salt, and spray. I discovered him on the deck one night staring up at the barest fingernail of a new moon, his face filled with pride and awe, as if somehow it was his own creation up there, his own newborn child.

He was blocking the narrow gangway, so I paused, not wanting to be impolite by brushing past him. I would have had to push him out of the way.

"It's beautiful," I said.

He nodded, then put out a hand. "Japanese," he said. "Kagoshima."

"I'm Neil," I answered, shaking the firm fingers. "Neil Chase."

"Kagoshima," he said again. "From Japan." He smiled, a gold incisor absorbing light like a black hole, making it look as if he were missing a tooth. We leaned on the rail together beneath the crane tower and Kagoshima held up a can of beer. I took it. We pulled off the tabs and dropped them into the cans and said "Cheers" and sipped in silence, watching the sky and the darkness below them. When I'd finished, he offered another and I shook my head. I had a low tolerance for alcohol and my stomach needed no more excuses to torment me. I continued my walking, and when I reached my cabin again I found I was sleepy and went to bed.

Kagoshima was there the next night too, sitting in the same spot, looking up at the same sky. It was cloudy that night, but there he was, enjoying his own personal meditation as religiously as a monk. Just him, a few beers, the exhaustion of a good day's work, and the night sky. He seemed happy to see me and offered yet another beer, which I accepted. This time Kagoshima was more animated, or more drunk, and he threw his arm out at various aspects of the sky.

"Moon!" he said.

"Moon," I replied. "Tsookey."

"*Tsuki!*" he corrected, shortening my vowels. I had learned this early on from Marinne's vocabulary books, but hearing the pronunciation was critical.

"*Tsuki,*" I said, trying again.

He nodded. "*Tsuki.*"

His finger shifted to Venus, the evening star.

"*Hoshi.*"

"Venus."

"*Hoshi.*"

Meeting a new friend cheered me, and I went back to my cabin hoping he'd offer me another language lesson soon.

I fell into a routine of feeling nauseated and irritable during the day, napping if I was able to, and then roaming the deck at night until I met up with Kagoshima, who would share a beer with me and teach me Japanese. I soon graduated from vocabulary to grammar structure, and from nouns to verbs. Japanese is not difficult to pronounce and my mind was so otherwise unoccupied that it soaked up these little lessons like a sponge on a floor spill. It seemed providential that he was offering me language lessons, too, since my intention was to spend time in Japan sightseeing before finding a return voyage. The required stops in Tokyo and Kyoto, plus, time permitting, a few visits to pottery towns. As often as I could, I studied the books Marinne had given me, though thanks to Kagoshima I was fast moving beyond their level.

That is not to say that we were communicating the way we would in English. I should underline that these conversations with Kagoshima and the others are how I heard them, felt them, understood them. They are my memories, as true as I can recount them, but they are not the actual Japanese language transcribed. Japanese is nuanced and I — even after living there for months — found times when I only understood a fraction of the conversation. Thus, if a dialog sounds too Anglicized, know that it is my aging memory, nothing more, that has warped the words over time.

As I would learn, while we grow up thinking that humans are all the same, what's valuable and what's not can vary so widely that people can be doing what seems natural, or be trying to help, but actions are misconstrued. With Kagoshima and me, it was rather funny at times. I had been pointing out Venus for a week, for example, before he made it clear that I'd learned the word incorrectly. Because *"hoshi"* means "star," not "Venus."

A simple mistake, but a telling one.

Not long after that, I learned something else. While for the most part I did my thing on the ship and the crew did theirs, on Sundays I was invited to dinner with the captain. For most of the journey from Boston I was too seasick to attend, much less enjoy it, but as we entered the latitudes of the Caribbean I seemed healthier. A day before we refueled in Panama, I told the captain that I had appreciated Kagoshima's taking me under his wing.

The captain paused, his skin seeming even more pallid as he contemplated.

"Kagoshima?" he replied. "We have no member of the crew named Kagoshima. You mean Ken?"

I felt my cheeks redden. "I've been having a Japanese lesson every night with him for most of the voyage."

"Kenji Matsuyama. Works in the galley. Helper to the cook?"

I told the captain how we'd met and how he'd introduced himself as Kagoshima.

"He's from Japan," the captain said. "From a place called Kagoshima. He must have just realized you got it mixed up and then been embarrassed to hurt your feelings. Japanese are like that. They'll stay silent a long time before risking embarrassing you."

That night, with the lights of Panama glowing on the horizon, I met up with Kenji — or Kagoshima — Matsuyama. He had only one beer left but he refused to drink it himself. We passed it between us and sipped while watching the indigo ocean roll and stir.

"Your name is Kenji," I said. "I've been calling you Kagoshima."

"I'm Kagoshima," he replied, laughing through his teeth, a kind of gentle "tsk tsk" sound.

"You could have told me."

He looked at me.

"What does it matter, the name? Not so important."

"How can we be friends if I don't get your name right?"

"Name not matter. Beer, we drink, talk. That what's important."

CHAPTER TEN

We waited twenty-eight hours before the canal captain came aboard and piloted us through the Panama Canal. Being that close to land should have made my stomach calmer. Howler monkeys hooted from the trees, their demonic roars protesting the injustice of a ship passing through what had once been jungle. The water was glassy, not a ripple save for the wakes of the many freighters lined up for passage, yet I threw up twice during the crossing: once shortly after the ship began its ascent in the locks at Gatun, once as we leveled off on the Pacific side of the Miraflores. I had hurled so often that the enamel on my teeth had gotten soft from repeated exposure to bile.

Only after we'd dropped anchor in the calm breakwater surrounding Panama City did my queasiness fade, supplanted by the excitement — no, joy — of knowing that for the first time in more than a week my feet would be on dry land. As soon as I felt I could stare at a page without vomiting, I wrote Marinne a letter.

> *My Dearest,*
> *If only you knew how awful this trip*
> *has been, how much I have longed to be back*
> *there with you, holding you, off this ghastly*

> *boat and on dry land again. You were so right: If ever there were something that would make me want to stay, it was leaving.*

I recounted the various tortures, then went on:

> *The only small good thing is that I have made a friend, a Japanese man named Kenji. We do not do much other than look at stars, but he's trying to teach me some of the language and I am learning as best as I can.*
>
> *I miss you more than anything. Counting the days until we're in each other's arms again.*
>
> *Love forever, mon amour ~*
> *Your Neil*

As the ship paid canal fees and was inspected, Captain Solomonson approved a shore leave for Kenji and me with the severity of a séance, cautioning us to return no later than midnight, as we were to embark again at three in the morning. This curfew gave me no cause for alarm as it was only four in the afternoon. It would be long enough for me to mail the letter, and Kenji "Kagoshima" Matsuyama agreed to help me find a postbox and a stamp. He had dressed up for the excursion: spotless white slacks, black shoes polished to a shine, and a gaudy Hawaiian shirt that still had creases in it from where he had ironed the fabric. His hair, slicked back with pomade, smelled of orange peel. Though he was a full head shorter than I, he had transformed into a different person from the recluse I'd shared beers with on board.

"Are we on a date?" I joked, as we waited for a skiff.

"I always look good for the ladies," was Kenji's reply. At the time I thought perhaps he knew a cute postal worker he was hoping to impress.

A water taxi came out to the boat and we flagged it down. The sun was hovering behind us as we neared the docks, the light was thick, clinging like paint to the pilings and fishing vessels and pelicans and gulls. My heartbeat quickened as I thought about getting ashore, if only for a few hours. The air was a mix of smells, some universal to any port, like shellfish, seaweed, salt, and ships' diesel, and some unique to Panama — banana and sugar cane and jungle vapors.

Kenji laughed as I clambered up the barnacle-studded ladders to the dock and planted my feet on the ground. A strange sense of vertigo made me feel as if the dock were swaying like the ship had been, a dizziness that took almost an hour to fade.

"You no sailor," my friend joked. "You stay here."

When Kenji had joined me I asked him where the post office was and he nodded. "I know post office in town," he said. "We take taxi. We go have beers at bar, go to post office."

"Can I make a phone call?"

"No," Kenji said. "No time. Too expensive. We on shore, make every moment count!"

We hailed a beat-up Volkswagen beetle with black fenders and a small cardboard "taxi" sign taped to the windshield. Kenji haggled in Spanish over the price (this was new to me — Kenji's English was next to nothing, but his Spanish seemed fluent, at least to my untrained ears).

We hopped in.

As news to me as his Spanish fluency was the discovery that the so-called "bar" Kenji was taking me to was in fact a brothel. Had I known this up front I would have excused myself and tried to mail the letter on my own. As the taxi drove, the streets grew darker and more narrow, and the dapper gentlemen and well-dressed ladies were replaced by seedy youths and women with high skirts and low necklines. I assumed that we were passing through a "colorful" section of town en route to the post office. In fact this district was our final destination.

Kenji was my friend and he'd never been outlandish in any way on the ship, so when the taxi came to a stop outside a gaudy building with red lights in the two front windows, I realized far too late where we were, and why my friend had taken such pains to dress "for the ladies." The pale blue building had a few of the shingles missing, and its lacy trim must have once been white but now it was a dull, unpainted, gray. The red lights in the windows on either side of the dark door made the house look ghoulish, like a giant skull with glowing embers for eyes.

"I can't go in there," I said, as he opened the door and hopped out.

He laughed.

"You can't stay in street. You get robbed. Inside you just get raped."

He was already crossing to the house, and the neighborhood, if I could even call it that, was not the kind of place where anyone other than beefy sailors or saucy women wanted to walk around alone.

As soon as the vehicle left we were surrounded by women who clearly knew Kagoshima. They cooed and strutted and he went to the door of the brothel like a proud rooster surrounded by beautiful hens, purring in Spanish and saying things that caused the girls to laugh and giggle. One even slapped his face, and he responded by grabbing her behind and squeezing it so hard that she jumped. I hung back, not wanting to go in.

"And did Señor Matsu bring us a friend?" asked one of the women who had stayed with me. She hooked her arm around mine. She spoke in English, almost unaccented. "I don't believe we've met before."

"There's been a misunderstanding. I'm not ... This isn't what I—"

"You don't have to explain anything," she giggled. "There's nothing I haven't heard before, if you know what I mean." She walked me toward the building.

"I'm Mariposa. It means Butterfly." She laughed. "I guess that means you can call me Madame Butterfly!" Then she exploded into a fit of laughter that ended in deep coughing. She took a moment to regain herself, holding onto the railing. Another girl rubbed her back as we stood outside on the wooden porch.

"Are you okay?" I asked.

"I'm fine," Mariposa said, recovering. We opened the door. She was not unattractive, perhaps in her early twenties, plump, her ample cleavage heaped onto a green corset, the darkness of the areola just visible. Her obsidian-black eyes were accented with heavy aqua eye shadow and long fake lashes; her coral-pink lips were turned into a pretend pout.

"Don't you want me to be your playmate tonight?"

"I'm engaged to be married. My friend didn't tell me this was a brothel—"

I tried to disentangle my arm from hers and realized I would need a crowbar. She escorted me toward the hallway. "Let me teach you some lessons for your wedding night," she whispered, breathing into my ear. "Secrets. Of. Woman's. Pleasure." Despite myself, I found the sensation of her lips at my ear delightful. But I was too taken aback, too terrified to have the slightest perk of an erection. My penis cowered, limp as a baby bird.

Sensing my desire to slip away, Mariposa called for backup and two more ladies of the night came out and surrounded me. "I'm Flor," said the one on my left. Had I tried to embrace her I doubt I could have even tucked my arms around her sides. Her breasts seemed to float, unapologetic, around in a bustier that must have had construction scaffolding inside. "If you like 'em large, I'll be in room fourteen."

I nodded.

"Waiting for you!" she said, as if it were a command.

Then they ushered me into a small courtyard in what (had the owner had a different concept of venue) could have been an attractive boutique hotel. A cement fountain burbled in the middle. Several fruit trees rose up, their branches brushing the iron railings of the balconies. An office was at the back, lamplight spilling onto the terracotta tiles. A few girls came out from their boudoirs and waited, most looking scared or sullen or just bored, a few others primping or pulling up their skirts to show sexy, caramel thighs.

Kagoshima had already disappeared, devoured in a sea of sinful pleasure that he no doubt had waited months for. A regular, he enjoyed the favors of the best of the ladies for less, and from their treatment of me — at least initially — it seemed everyone expected that I was a Kagoshima *protégé*.

If they expected me to promptly choose someone and head upstairs after parting with cash, they were disappointed. I wanted nothing more than to be allowed to leave, but when it became obvious to them that I was not going to choose a girl myself, Flor rolled her eyes and then pushed me over to a woman dressed in green satin. The girl slipped her arm through mine, and I followed her up the narrow stairs wondering what happens to someone who doesn't want to and how to extricate myself from all of this as quickly as possible.

The first thing I noticed when I entered was the giant wall-length mirror that hung opposite the door. It was heavy, framed in faux gold that had worn off in places, revealing wood grain below. A lone crack divided the mirror into a right half and a left, each pane off axis, such that when I stared at myself in the looking glass it served up a me that was cleft in two. My left half seemed to stare straight back at me. I looked young and frail and timid. The right-side reflection was staring off, not back at me, but at some place to the right. I had an eerie premonition that this other me was watching the future, while the me making eye contact was a me already in the past; that this present to me was in fact, the one that mattered least to anyone. I froze there at the door, trying to catch my breath.

"Hello there, Sailor," the girl cooed. I confess that I found her beautiful, perhaps because she seemed the least outlandish of any of the women here I'd seen. She had a slender figure and perky breasts that (compared to Flor's vast bosom) seemed almost petite. There was a shyness about her that I found comforting, as if I'd been lucky that night and was with a girl who also was here for the first time. I couldn't help wonder what series of misfortunes had brought her there in front of me instead of on a ballroom dance floor.

Excluding the mirror, her room was stark and devoid of luxury, with a lone twin-sized mattress against the far wall, a yellow feather boa curled up on the pillow like a sleeping cat. A free-standing clothes rack held a variety of costumes, some with sequins, some leather. A triangular sink and seatless toilet were behind the door but there was no curtain for privacy — one could only wonder if for some that was part of the attraction. The air smelled of sex thinly masked by a heavy, cloying perfume.

Having closed the door behind me she put her hands on my shoulders and began to press into the muscles. "Oh, you're so tense. Don't you worry, I'm going to take such good care of you—"

"I can't," I said, cutting her off. "I'm so sorry."

"Honey," she whispered, her voice confident syrup. "I know exactly how to fix a performance problem—"

My face was so red even my ears felt on fire. "I thought my friend was taking me to the post office." I opened my coat and took out the letter, showing her that I wasn't just making it up.

She looked, took a half step away from me to assess the situation, then let out a laugh that died into a whistle. "Honey, no matter which uniform you want me to put on, I can tell you that it ain't going to be stamps getting licked here or letters that get put into the ... mail slot." Her expression changed to boredom. "And I'm not just here out of the goodness of my heart. I have a daughter waiting at home who needs food on the table and I don't have time to—"

"It's to my fiancée. Whatever your fee for tonight is, I'll pay it. All you have to do is mail this letter. Just promise me that you'll mail it. It's very important, and my ship leaves tonight."

She looked at me from head to toe, then sighed.

"I was thinking you'd be a john that I enjoyed, for once. Not a fat, sweaty, sailor." She held out her hand. "Sure. Give me the letter."

I handed it to her. "Promise me you'll mail it. And tell me your name."

"I'm Daisy," she said.

"Your real name."

"Just Daisy," she repeated.

"I'm not … not your customer. I won't tell anyone."

She folded the letter and then tucked it in between her breasts. Like a dinosaur trapped in a tar pit, the envelope sank, inexorably, out of view.

"My fee. Five dollars, American."

I knew the probability was that she'd just take my money, no matter how much I gave her, and deposit the letter in the brothel trash. I gave her three five-dollar bills. A lot of money back then.

"One for your time, one to give the house, and one to make sure that letter gets mailed."

She took the money, felt it, then nodded. "Plus postage."

I gave her another five.

"I'm Yvette," she said, pointing to the door. "I'll mail your letter. You can go now if you want to."

I waited more than an hour downstairs for Kagoshima, sitting on a cement bench in the courtyard near the fountain, slapping mosquitoes. The water smelled foul enough to make me wince. I felt sorry for the goldfish trapped there, felt sorry for the girl in green. I felt sorry more than anything for Marinne, who would surely never receive that letter.

The lady running the show was in many ways the classic brothel madam, only slightly shorter than Yvette, with a cigarette dangling off her lower lip and a red satin bathrobe that offered up her breasts for the world to see. I am sure the madam thought I'd had a premature experience as I was out of the room upstairs in minutes. In deference to the male ego and its disappointments, she left me alone. But when I'd waited long enough for Kagoshima I began to worry that we might not make it back to the dock in time.

Going to the reception desk, I asked the woman if there was any way of interrupting Kagoshima's fun upstairs to get him the message that our ship, literally, was going to sail.

"Señor Matsu?" she asked.

"Yes, I'm worried that our boat is about to leave without us."

She shook her head. "You were waiting for him? Sugar, he left here already."

My knees went cold.

"He left? When? Why?"

She looked at me. "Señor Matsu had a debt to pay with some … businessmen."

"A debt?"

"He was always generous with my girls, but I think he was robbing Peter to pay Paul. Or Paula, in this case." She laughed at her own joke.

"How did they know where to find him?" We'd only just gotten off the boat. He hadn't stopped for anyone before coming here. The madam's eyes flickered to the telephone, then back to mine: All I needed to know that she'd been paid to rat him out.

I swallowed, imagining him going quietly, that explained why I hadn't heard anything: True to his culture, he wouldn't have wanted to upset anyone or cause a scene. I had no way of helping my friend, and it dawned on me that perhaps if they didn't get money out of Kagoshima maybe they'd try to get it from me instead. My knees felt the adrenaline first. The ice was gone, replaced by a heaviness and a dull pain.

"Can you give me directions to the docks? I have to be there soon."

The woman stubbed out her cigarette in the ashtray and laughed. "Hire one of my girls to take you."

I stared at her. "Will I be safe?"

Madame leaned back. "Safe?"

"Walking in the dark, with just a girl … ."

"With just a girl? One of my girls?" She stood up. "What's your name, Sugar?"

"Neil."

"Neil, let me tell you something about me and my profession and the girls who work here. We know these streets better than anyone in the city. Better than the taxi drivers. And there isn't anything safer than walking around with one of my lovely escorts on your arm. Do you know why?"

I'd assumed she was being rhetorical but she waited for me to reply.

"No," I said. "Why?"

"No other whores are going to cut in on another girl's action, and the thugs know that if anything happens to one of my johns then they'll have to deal with me. They won't be getting laid in this city ever again." She straightened herself up, the bathrobe slipping open even wider than it had been, unconcerned, perhaps even proud, about revealing her heavy breasts and a paunch that drooped toward her graying pubic hair. I looked away.

Quick as a snake strike, she reached over and grabbed my chin, pulling my face toward her, eyes intense and blazing. "You get that, Sugar?"

I nodded. "Sure. But can someone show me how I can get back to the dock or not?"

"Depends."

"On what?"

The madam smiled. "How much money you got left?"

CHAPTER ELEVEN

Yvette, whether by her choosing or no, was the one to escort me to the docks, which were so close that we didn't even take a taxi. I thought we were miles away from the port but the driver before had just been detouring through the city to inflate the fare. And as the madam had said, no one gave us any trouble. At one point a gang of five surly-looking youths spilled out of an alley and started walking toward us, blocking our path.

My escort didn't hesitate.

"Hello, boys," she called, her voice low and sultry. "Need a good time?"

Where I had prepared myself for an altercation, instead, one of them yelled "Whooo!" and the shortest of them, wearing a brown porkpie hat, said something in Spanish that was lost on me. She replied again and they stepped aside as if we were royalty, and we met no one else until we reached the docks.

"I told them they'll have to wait," Yvette explained. "That I'd get them later. All of them."

"Will you?" I asked.

She shrugged. "Not all at once."

The empty wharf, dark and shadowy, frightened me, but I need not have worried. My damsel in green took me to the harbor master's booth and we rapped on the glass until he woke up. Rubbing his eyes, he stood and unlocked the door.

"This young boy needs a launch," my friend explained, in Spanish.

"Wake a guy up for that?" the harbor master said. He pointed. "Over there."

We walked toward where he had indicated and saw nothing. Yet just as we were about to turn around, the girl in green stopped me. "Hear that?" she asked.

We paused And then, faint but distinct, the sound of voices. Almost at the same time, I caught a whiff of a cigarette.

We went to the edge of the dock and looked down. Whereas the dock had been almost at eye level when I'd arrived, now it was a good eight feet drop to the waterline below. Relaxing in some small launches were three young boys. A cigarette glowed as someone inhaled.

"Hey," said Yvette. "My friend needs a lift."

"Where to?"

"The *Pandora*," I answered. In the darkness I could just make out the silhouette of my vessel. "Over there."

"Hop in."

I turned to the girl.

"Thank you," I said. "Here, I want you to have this." I pressed ten dollars into her hand. With the twenty I'd already given her, surely that was more than she would make the entire night.

She didn't answer. I realized she was looking at me strangely.

"Take me with you … ," she said. "Please." She reached out and put her hand on my arm, her touch hot as a branding iron.

I remembered what she said at the "hotel."

"What about your child?"

She laughed, then pulled a kerchief from her sleeve and dabbed her eyes.

"Don't be so naive," she said. "Every hooker in the world will tell that to a john who doesn't want to pay … ."

"I can't," I said. I felt as if I were pounding the nail in the coffin for the letter that, presumably, still suffocated somewhere there inside her cleavage. She would hate me now. Hate the world of men who could drift in and have their way with her and then leave. Hate me more because I had been above her, too proud to partake of her pleasures.

"I'm sorry."

"Just remember me," the girl whispered. "Yvette."

I paused, trying to think of what to say, and she realized what the outcome would be; before I could say anything else, she turned around and walked back toward the streets. Her head was up, her stride purposeful. With her long black hair cascading down her back, she brought to mind some spurned yet haughty debutante at a ball. As the boys below called out at me to clamber down to the skiff, I watched her disappear into the night, staring after her until she'd turned a corner. It would not be until I reached Japan, wrote Marinne my new address, and received her first reply months later that I would learn that Yvette, poor girl, did indeed mail that letter after all.

The entire skiff ride I thought about her, furious at Kagoshima for taking me there, but sad for Yvette and all of them too, forced to work in something so vile. I tried to think of how to tell him how angry I was using simple words he'd understand, playing our fight out in my mind. There would be no beer drinking with him; he was no longer my friend. He had taken advantage of me, left me somewhere that might have been dangerous.

Shame on him for the betrayal; shame on me for trusting him.

As soon as I was on deck, I went to the bridge and told the captain what had happened, minus a few of the details. For once I saw the captain animated.

"What?! He's not with you? Where the hell is he then? That's not like him at all. Japanese are punctual as a clock. He's never been late from shore leave, never. Not once."

Kagoshima had not yet even boarded the *Pandora*.

"Get a search party together," he yelled at the first mate. "Find him. We'll hold the boat."

The sun had risen, casting long early morning shadows by the time they returned. A trash picker had found his beaten, broken body, face-down in a small gully near where the brothels were. There was no question that he was dead, and the first mate said there was no doubt that it was Kenji. Despite the bruising, his face was recognizable, though they'd pulled out his gold tooth.

There was no way to bring the corpse with us, so the first mate returned to shore to give the police permission to cremate the body (which the undertaker expedited), though our sailing was still delayed.

By the next day, Panama was a thin lavender line on the horizon, the ship was churning its fume-filled way across the Pacific, and Kenji "Kagoshima" Matsuyama was aboard in a small cardboard box, sealed with tape. The captain told us that we would have a ceremony once we were underway, and the Japanese sailor's ashes would be scattered to the sea.

The sun, bright and warm, cast its light on gulls and pelicans, on ships in the bay, sent fingers down through the water hitting glinting fish there. The green of the forest on shore seemed calm and quiet. Everything reminded me how pitiless and devoid of sentience Nature was. Whatever transpires in a fragile, quick life, things just go on. The sun will rise the next morning. The moon will wax and wane. The waves will pound onto shore.

Numb, I watched the sea, a perfect deep blue, and the sky, azure and as clean as a silkscreen. That mesmerizing line they make when they meet, the sea touching the sky. It struck me that those who have never traveled never understand that each voyage changes you, shifts your perspective indelibly, causes you to never again assume that the people and structures present in your current life will always be there. It makes you love them more for their transience, but it makes you love them less, too. You learn that somewhere in the horizon is another world, another parallel set of friends and lovers, another life one could live just as easily as the experiences one feels right now.

I longed to write Marianne, yet when I returned to my cabin and sat down at the little writing table with its gimbaled kerosene lamp I could write only a few sentences before I ran out of things to say. I curled up in my bunk and tried to take a nap, but sleep wouldn't come, even though I felt less nauseated than when I'd left Boston. Wondering what Marinne was doing and wishing I could hold her in my arms, I lay in my bunk and stared up into the darkness, listening to the deep hum of diesel and feeling the wash of the waves.

When sleep came, it took me by surprise.

Chapter Twelve

W e scattered Kagoshima's ashes as planned in a short, solemn ceremony. No land visible, several days out. Hats came off, the captain read a short prayer, and the first mate tipped the box over, scattering the kitty litter-like dust into the sea. I still felt detached from it all, as if these events were happening to someone else.

We were well into the middle of the Pacific when two things happened to suggest that I should part ways with the *Pandora* as soon as we reached Japan. The first was that Captain Solomonson, eager for me to take them, gave me Kagoshima's personal effects: A box of books left in his cabin and a portrait of a woman I took perhaps to be his mother. Though black and white, it had been colorized with a skill that made it almost look real. The subject had streaks of gray in her hair and was gazing out at the camera with a peculiar sadness that caught my attention. She wore a traditional Japanese dress, known as a kimono, decorated in autumn reds, browns, and golds. Her eyes stared not directly at the camera, but just off to the side, as if she were looking at the photographer for the last time. Curious, but also shy.

In the grainy background was an old apothecary's chest, the kind with a multitude of small square drawers, and atop it, a large green vase. Though the piece was small in the photo, I recognized it as the same kind of vessel shown in the book of prized Japanese pottery that I had made copies of back in my days in Boston. It seemed a long shot to assume this vase was that exact style and not some look-alike, but I recalled the characteristics well: cigar-shaped tubes with clean lines, and an unmistakable green glaze that — according to the book I'd read as it was printed, the ink still drying — was found nowhere else in the world, a version of celadon. Made from a tiny village somewhere in Japan.

I had not had the foresight to bring even one single photo of Marinne with me, a ridiculous goof. In her place then, I got a photo of a dead crewmate's mother, and a strange premonition that things with Marinne and I were going to change. Kagoshima's death made me feel that Marinne too was gone. I didn't even feel I could tell her what had happened. What point would be served by writing her in detail of my friendship — if it could even be called that — with a dead Japanese man, or how he had taken me to a brothel the night he died. Could she ever understand, when it was difficult even for me to process my own emotions about the trip so far?

I would go to the spot where we'd shared beers so often and sit, listening to the engine's hum far below, feeling the soft rocking of the ship as the prow sliced through incoming swell. The moon and the stars and the night were all there. Just part of what had made it special had vanished.

In Kagoshima's books were a number of eight-track cartridge tapes, suggesting he had been trying to master the English language. Or at least had intended to. Though these were meant for people who already spoke Japanese, they were not impossible to learn from. I was able, with the aid of several dictionaries, to pull a bit of learning from these pages. Combined with the tapes, which often featured English words or sentences and their Japanese equivalents, the reverse, in some ways, from what I'd done with the course Marinne had given me. Not that I was fluent, no, not by any means. But I had enough of the language under my belt already that I felt I could function.

As I leafed page by page through the books this acquaintance of mine had owned, as I stared at the photo of the woman I took to be his mother, I had a growing notion that if I didn't relay the news of his death, this poor mother would never know what had happened to her son. While it had nothing at all to do with me and I would probably not ever reveal the full details, I felt, as the days progressed, that it was my duty to at least try to find her. Going to Japan hadn't had a purpose before this, it was originally travel for travel's sake, but a mother should know about the death of her son.

And who else would tell her if not me?

Perhaps in some ways, the sum of our answers to that single question is what balances the scales when the day of reckoning comes.

Who else if not me?

There are people who will shrug off accepting responsibility and claim they can't solve the world's problems or can't change what can't be changed. But the death of someone in a foreign land matters. Or it mattered to me. I didn't care what culture, what country, what race or color or creed, any mother anywhere grieves for a lost son.

As I write, I cannot think but how so much of this might not have happened if this story had taken place today, in modern times, with the internet and good phones and email. I would have kept in touch with Marinne the way the young people do: video chat in internet cafes, naked selfies, emoticons that kiss and little hearts that beat and all of that. I would have had a cellphone and could have talked or sent emails fifty times a day. Today, the idea of spending even an hour without a text or SMS seems like an eternity to wait to hear from loved ones, no matter where on the globe they are.

But in 1965 none of this was possible. Letters still had to travel days or weeks to reach a person, and telephone calls were so expensive that they were only used for dire emergencies, holidays, and were not well-set for international calls. My mistake, in embarking for Japan, was not realizing how one can lose oneself when everything familiar is left behind.

CHAPTER THIRTEEN

The second factor in my departure from the *Pandora* was the night I woke up shivering. I was so drenched in my own sweat that I thought one of the crew members had played a practical joke on me with a bucket of water. I could barely stumble to the door and unlock it before another paroxysm hit me and I fell to the floor, shaking, grasping for anything to hold on to. This was so much worse than any of the nausea I'd had that I worried it was a kind of airborne form of venereal disease that I'd gotten from the brothel.

"Do you want the good news or the bad news?" asked the ship's doctor, a man I'd not seen once the entire voyage and who may not have even been a doctor, despite the white lab coat. He was gaunt enough to be the captain's brother, though he had some color in his cheeks that I suspect may have resulted from taking too many sips of the codeine syrup in the medicine cabinet.

"The good news," I said.

"You have malaria."

That was the good news?

"It means you're probably not going to die, and we're close to Japan."

"What's the bad news?"

"We have no chloroquine tablets."

"The treatment?"

The doctor nodded. "You're going to be pretty miserable until we can get you on shore."

In a way, I likely caught it from visiting the brothel after all. Airborne, to a degree: The hours spent sitting near the fetid fountain in that courtyard where the mosquitoes congregated. I will never know for certain; in truth, it could have been anywhere along the journey, but sometimes you just know.

The gaudy, pink-shirted first mate took great care that I drink large quantities of tonic water, because — he insisted — it contains quinine.

"It will cure you," he cajoled, emptying bottle after bottle into my glass and waiting, staring at me, until I'd lifted the cup to my lips and drained it in front of him. Whether this had any effect on my symptoms I do not know, but it put me off tonic water for the rest of my life. Even now, more than fifty years later, I feel my throat constrict just thinking about it.

The first mate would sit at my bed, holding a glass of the awful stuff, always dressing in pink bright enough to put a clown to shame. How I got through that final week I do not know, but when we arrived in Japan it was obvious to everyone that it was time for the *Pandora* and me to go our separate ways. If we hadn't been heading for port I might have hurled myself off the ship and swum to an island, or just let the sharks devour me.

Here too, another odd coincidence: I was put ashore in Kagoshima City, not in Sasebo, our original destination. Our route just happened to be passing by and that was the nearest large port, located at the southernmost tip of Kyūshū, one of the four main islands that comprise Japan's archipelago. Rather than wait two extra days, they detoured into Kagoshima Bay and dropped me in Kagoshima City.

Was I that sick? Or were they just desperate to get rid of me, hoping to avoid the curse that superstition claims descends on a vessel on which someone has died? I refuse to call it destiny, but that decision reshaped my entire life. None of this would have happened had I stayed aboard until Sasebo.

I do not remember disembarking. I remember the approach and a few of the islands, and I remember that long before land was visible I could see a thin streak of gray in the sky.

"Ash," the first mate told me. "From Sakurajima, the great volcano. Here," he said, twisting off the cap of a bottle of tonic water. The hiss of escaping CO_2 sent shivers through me. "You need to drink more tonic."

Perhaps it was merciful that I do not remember anything else until I woke up in the Kagoshima City hospital.

Part III:
Japan

Chapter Fourteen

Though this has changed somewhat over the past few decades, at the time I was in Japan it was normal practice for doctors to keep from a patient exactly how ill he was. Cancer victims would often be "spared" the chill of a prognosis. This even extended to families, so it was not uncommon for someone with metastasized tumors to think that in a bit he'd be returning to his job, his life, and his home. This withholding of information sounds dishonest to the Western mind, but the Japanese see it as kind. Whatever the truth or outcome, patients needed rest and sleep and to be happy. If someone were close to death, why offer only the terrifying finality? Why not let him think that all of this was a turn for the worse that would resolve itself soon? Young doctors who told the truth would be shunned, lose their patients, and be sent out to tiny rural hospitals. The belief was just that certain people did not want to know the truth, and many didn't.

But for someone who did want to know the truth, this sense of "it's for your own good" was maddening. I was in Kagoshima City hospital for two weeks before I was discharged, and not once did any doctor tell me how serious my condition was. As I was not on any insurance plan, the hospital kept no records of me even being there. So I have to piece together the gravity of that illness from memory alone.

Two weeks of hospital care is in itself a useful detail. I believe that I had contracted the most deadly of the malaria strains, *Plasmodium falciparum*, which is often fatal. At one point I remember having a lot of difficulty breathing: Perhaps the parasite had infected my lungs, or I'd contracted pneumonia. Perhaps the extended stay was all due to the near constant flow of tonic water through me while on board the *Pandora*. Or withdrawal from said tonic water once I was put ashore. If charts were kept I could have translated them when I returned home. As it was, all I can say is that I was perhaps near to death during parts of my lengthy recovery. I remember being so weak that at one point while attempting to cross the small room to the attached toilet, I collapsed on the floor.

I should have been making immediate plans to return home, I should have booked passage to Boston or better yet, exhausted whatever savings I had left and spent them on plane fare. Any thoughtful person would have felt sick to imagine his sweet beloved pining for him at home while he undergoes torment after torment.

"Enough," would have come for some people far sooner. A different person would not have made it past Panama. I could have ridden a bus to the Mexican border if I'd wanted, from there hitchhiked home and given Marinne the surprise of her life by walking in unexpectedly, the way soldiers do on the local news sometimes.

But I was not that person.

As I lay in my hospital bed, I began to feel that the hard parts of the journey had ended and that some new adventure was just about to unfold. I attribute this optimism in part to the unfortunate events aboard the *Pandora*, my utter inability to enjoy the romance of being on the open sea, a dread of the return journey (be it by plane, train through Russia and Europe, or ship) and all the misery that might befall me, like Odysseus, on the journey home.

But it was also a stubbornness: I had resolved to travel, to see the world, and as miserable as I had been, something kept pushing me on. Arrival in Japan was, in so many ways, like a spaceship's landing on a distant planet. To turn back would have been admitting — to myself and to the woman I loved — what a failure I would always be.

Luck had put me at the bed nearest to the window in a small, otherwise empty ward, and as the hospital itself was on a hillside I had an eagle's-eye view of the city. By turning my head just a little

I could see the expanse of low buildings and rooftops, many of them made with exotic-looking tiles. Bamboo groves grew out of narrow gardens, green and lavender and yellow, prehistoric-looking filigree, as if someone had stuck giant feather dusters randomly about the buildings. Further out, the orange cranes and steel structures of an industrial port, then the bright blue waters of Kinkō Bay. Sakurajima, the volcano, seemed to loom up ominous and angry behind this serene backdrop, its belches of ash shooting high into the sky, billowing up and outward, to scatter hundreds of miles away in the sea. Periodically the windows would rattle from the boom of the explosions deep within the earth. This vista was so exotic it was impossible not to feel as if I had stepped into the pages of some adventure novel. Who back in Boston could imagine a thundering, live volcano at one's back door?

The nurse who was assigned to me was kind and spoke some broken English, so I was able to inquire about my things, and she assured me that my belongings were waiting for me in storage downstairs. She was also my caretaker long enough to teach me some more Japanese, which would prove vital once I'd left the hospital and was on my own. Shizuka was her name — a tall, slender girl with a short bob cut and single silver band around her left ring finger. She had almost no chest at all; sometimes when she leaned over while attending to me I could see clear down her shirt to the dark purple nipples, large as grapes on a chest as flat as mine.

I was young. Nipples in their myriad variety were impossible to ignore.

A particular bond grows between a patient and a nurse, in part because — as with a lover — one can have no modesty. When I was too weak to even stand she washed me, paying the same attention to my penis, anus, or underarms as to any other part of my body. I got hard sometimes, and she saw it as a body function, never once commenting or even seeming to notice. She dried me with a thin cotton towel and sometimes massaged my legs or shoulders. She was the only woman to have seen me naked. Marinne and I had been going steady, but never done anything beyond what one does in public places. Never once had we lain together skin to skin. Despite the fact that Shizuka was plain looking, with a prominent misaligned tooth that pierced the upper gum, I fantasized about being with her

Marinne, too. Sometimes I'd start imagining being with one woman and by the climax be envisioning another.

I was young: Women in their myriad variety were impossible to ignore.

There in the hospital bed, with the kind attentions of Shizuka-san, I first began to fall in love again, long before I met the person I was destined for. One has to be ready to fall in love, and with each day that passed, Marinne seemed farther and farther from me. Or the reverse: My changes were pulling me farther from her. The life I had there seemed less and less tangible. It would be impossible to tell her even the day-to-day events, the simple joy of looking out from my hospital window at the amazing cityscape before me. I didn't even mention the platonic attentions of Shizuka-san for fear that it would be something she couldn't understand.

When I showed Shizuka-san the photograph of Kagoshima's mother it took a few minutes before I could make clear, in my faltering Japanese, what I was asking. When she understood, she brightened.

"The vase? You're interested in the vase?"

"Yes," I answered. "I want to find the person it belongs to. Maybe this woman? In the photograph? And also find out place, place where vases come from. Where vases are made."

She laughed, and then told me to wait a moment. She left the room and returned with a wheelchair.

"Get in," she said.

I had a wild vision that she was going to wheel me throughout Japan in search of this mysterious mother, but our journey ended just a few moments later, in one of the hospital lobbies. There, in a recess on the wall behind the receptionist, on a black velvet stand, was an enormous green vase, large enough to embalm a young child. A single spotlight shone on it, highlighting every nuance of the vessel's beauty.

"Push me closer," I asked.

"*Hai*," she said. Yes.

When I was near enough, I pulled myself up into a standing position by bracing my arms on the receptionist's desk. The girl behind the counter looked at me in astonishment and then laughed, her hand over her mouth, the Japanese signal of discomfort.

That vase.

It was the first time I had ever understood why people could pay millions of dollars for a piece of art. Never before had I felt — it sounds odd to say it — a lust for anything material. From far away the vase merely looked green, not just any kind of green but a particular shade of green, a kind of deep celadon, like forest moss fresh from a heavy rain. Dark jade. Yet closer and the color began to dance, to shift, to melt around the vase as if the flickering of the aurora borealis itself had been trapped inside. Move closer still and the colors changed yet again, from these intoxicating greens to other shades, even reds and oranges, browns. An eye in detail, revealing the iris as a fabric of dots and splashes. The glaze seemed to trap the light from the spotlight and contain it, releasing it in a flickering rhythm as if the piece of pottery had a pulse. It felt that alive.

"Where is this pottery made?" I said, sinking back into my wheelchair. "I have to go there."

Shizuka-san frowned.

"It's better that you not go," she said. "I thought you would appreciate the vase, but you should not go." Apologizing to the receptionist for the interruption, she began wheeling me back toward my room.

"What do you mean?" I asked. "Why shouldn't I go?"

Shizuka-san did not answer until we were back at my bedside.

"It's difficult," she said, her voice hinting that this was all she would say.

When she had helped me rise from the wheelchair and tucked me into the crisp hospital linens, she stood at the window for a long time. With the afternoon light softening her features and the dramatic shadow behind her, it was the closest she ever came to being beautiful.

Finally she spoke.

"In Japan," she explained, "people know not to push too deeply for things. I cannot tell you what to do or not do. If you want to walk into there, you can walk there and drown in the sea or burn in the volcano." She was pointing across the bay at distant Sakurajima. "You could go. But if you were Japanese, you would understand that would be foolish. So why go at all if it won't end well?"

I remember sitting up in my bed. I would have laughed at how grave she made it sound, how melodramatic, had I not caught her eyes. They were intense and earnest.

"I don't understand, Shizuka, how a vase can be … ," I had to pause. "How it can be dangerous?"

Perhaps my ears had played a trick on me. Perhaps I used an incorrect word and said one thing while meaning something different? Another part of me wondered if there was some kind of superstition surrounding this that I'd stumbled on.

She looked at me.

"To ask too many questions," she said, "is also very foolish."

She might have slapped me.

"Shizuka-san, I didn't intend to offend you. If you didn't care to answer questions about the vase, why not just shrug and say you knew nothing of it? Why take me there? Why show me at all?"

She was silent.

I waited.

"There are certain places in Japan where people do not go. These villages, some are hidden away for very good reasons. I know the vase is beautiful. I thought if you saw it you reached your goal. I didn't know your goal is to reach the village. To meet those people."

She laughed again. I knew it meant she was uncomfortable.

"I have other patients to attend to. I'm sorry. I must go."

That was the last time I saw Shizuka-san. Several hours later I was greeted by a doctor and a different nurse, my vitals were checked, and I was told that I was well enough to leave the hospital. Not well enough to travel, the doctor added. But well enough for some bed rest and quiet relaxation at a home.

"I've nowhere to go," I told him. "I came by ship and was taken ill."

The man nodded.

"Unfortunate, but we do not provide recuperative boarding houses."

"So, I'm out on the street?"

He had almost left the room, but stopped and seemed to take pity on me.

"Chase-sama, perhaps someone will trade you room and board for some English lessons. English is popular with the ladies these days."

Discharged, I was still barely strong enough to stand. I had nowhere to go. I had a packet of crisp American Express travelers checks, but not a clue where the nearest bank to cash them was, so I had no money, not a single yen. I would find out later that banks were closed on weekends anyway, so it would not be until Monday that I could get actual yen. I wanted to ask Shizuka-san for help but she either wasn't at the hospital or had been trying to avoid me. I stepped out of the building and the Kagoshima heat hit me. I felt dizzy. After lugging my belongings behind me for an agony of minutes, I stopped at a low wall that enclosed a flower bed and sat down. I tucked my head between my knees and vomited. Thin and colorless, it pooled on the hot cement for a moment, then evaporated, leaving only a stain behind. I pulled from my pocket an envelope of medicinal powders they had given me on checkout, opened one, then realized I needed water or some liquid to wash it down with.

Still feeling nauseated, I looked around and realized that I had still not even left the hospital grounds. A different entrance was only a few steps away. Surely they could not refuse me a sip at the drinking fountain.

As soon as I pushed open the door, I realized that this lobby was the same one that I'd visited earlier that day. That mesmerizing vase stood like a haughty movie star on its carpet of black, chin in the air like a supermodel ignoring a crazed fan. The glaze seemed almost iridescent from where I stood at the door. It was minutes before I realized that the young receptionist, a different girl from before, was looking at me.

I showed her my medicine packets and asked for a glass of water.

"Over there," she pointed, showing me a men's bathroom door.

In contrast to the rest of the hospital, the little washroom was filthy. A bright yellow urinal mint hung suspended on a piece of rusting wire, overpowering the small room with the scent of ammonia and fake citrus. Yet somehow it failed to mask the stench of unflushed urinals and stale shit. I held my breath, turned on the faucet, and splashed cold water on my face. Then, my hands trembling, I shook the contents of a packet into my mouth and scooped a palm full of water in to wash it down. Still holding my breath, I pushed the door open and went outside. Only then did I exhale.

The receptionist was prim and cute, with tiny lips that seemed pursed in a perpetual peck. She had no makeup, but long eyelashes and high cheekbones made it seem as if she were wearing mascara and blush.

"Thank you," I said.

"Where are you from?" she asked.

"America."

"Oh, I'd love to visit there someday."

There was a short pause.

"That's a very interesting vase behind you."

She smiled. "Yes, this is a kind of traditional Kagoshima pottery. It's not found anywhere else in the world. Only one family."

"It must make people here very proud."

She seemed to think for a moment before responding. "I guess so. We appreciate its value. This is so expensive. Japanese people like expensive things."

"Yet, it seems people are uncomfortable when I mention it." I told her about Shizuka-san bringing me to see it and what had happened afterward.

She laughed. The laugh of nervousness. Hand at the mouth.

"You know a lot about Kagoshima."

"Please," I asked, leaning over the desk. "Tell me where these vases are made. I promise I won't tell anyone you told me. I just ... I just find them beautiful."

She looked around at the empty lobby.

"I'm sorry. I don't even know the name myself. But please don't try to go there. It's not ... not healthy."

"What do you mean? Did something happen there?"

She laughed.

"Is it, is it a place that the Americans bombed? I would be unwelcome?"

She shook her head. "No, nothing like that."

"What?"

"They're a very special kind of vase. They are urns."

"Urns? You mean for funerals?"

"It's because they're connected to death that we Japanese don't like to talk of them. It's considered unhealthy. I really, I shouldn't be saying this to you either. Maybe something bad will happen to me."

I had a feeling there was more to what she was saying, but at the very least, she had offered me something. Shizuka-san, had she been more forthcoming, could have said the same. Superstition bound them to silence.

"Hold on a moment," I said. "I need to show you something." I ran out to the street and returned with my heavy suitcase in hand. I pulled it over to the desk and undid the clasp and zipper. At the top, wrapped in shirts so that the glass would not be broken, was the photo of Kagoshima's mother. I took it out and placed it in front of the receptionist.

"I was on a boat with this woman's son. He passed away, in a faraway land, and I'm the only person in the world who can give her the news. Look at the background. See? She has one of these vases. I don't know her name. Her son's name was Kenji Matsuyama."

The girl looked at the picture.

"Matsuyama is a common name. Could be from anywhere."

"But the vase. If I can find the potter who made this vase, I might be able to find out whom he sold it to? Perhaps he would know."

She laughed. "You're like a persistent detective. The kind who makes himself annoying."

"That's me. Mister Annoying."

"I'm Miwako."

"I am Chase. Neil Chase."

"If you wait for me, Chase-san, I'll show you the Kagoshima Prefectural Museum. I think they might have someone working there who can help you."

"Of course I can wait."

"Take a seat?"

"Thank you," I said, as happy to be able to continue staring at the vase as to bask in the chill of the air conditioning.

At five minutes past noon, Miwako came out from the desk looking as if she'd stepped out of the pages of a magazine. Her tiny pursed lips widened into a smile.

"You look awful," she said, as cheerfully as saying "it's nice outside."

"I don't feel great."

"Let's take a taxi. I feel sorry for you."

The taxi had white antimacassars on the seats and clear vinyl on top of the dashboard, seats that looked brand new, and paint that shone. The door opened automatically with a lever. I slid in next to Miwako, close enough to smell her perfume. She looked at me.

"You have nice eyes."

"You do too," I answered, feeling my cheeks go hot. "Thank you for doing this for me."

"It's better than eating my lunch by myself on a bench."

"Do you like living here?"

"In Kagoshima? It's okay. I'll be moving to Tokyo soon. Once I can save a little money."

"Can you tell me more about the village where the vases are made?"

She looked at me. "You're not going to leave this alone, are you?"

We arrived at the museum. The building was smaller than I expected, shaped in a simple rectangle, like a three-story tissue box. Narrow windows made it look more like an office complex than a museum, and had I not been able to read two of the five characters above the door, I might have walked right by were Miwako not guiding me.

As I still had no money, she paid for the taxi while I lifted my belongings out of the back of the car. It shut with another lever; the driver never had to come out from behind the wheel.

"I know they have an exhibit about Kagoshima ceramics. Maybe a curator will be able to help you."

Miwako assured me that nobody would steal my bag if I left it near the door, and I was glad to forget about it. I pushed it off to one side of the walkway, then opened it up and took out the photograph.

Inside, the museum was so silent it felt funereal. The small windows let in little light. The exhibits seemed forlorn. There was no one at the door but admission was free; a few pamphlets suggested a route for a self-guided tour.

Miwako looked at her watch.

"I'm so sorry," she whispered. "I have to go back to work soon. Will you be okay?"

"Sure," I said. "I'll be fine. Can I see you later?"

"I'd like that."

"Except, I have no money. Terrible way to ask for a date."

"We can walk in the park. No money needed for that, right? You'll have all afternoon to get the information you need. See you here at this door at six."

"Next time we'll go to an expensive restaurant somewhere."

She laughed. "I'd like that."

With that, she turned and pushed open the door. After it closed and she was outside she turned around once and waved. It was a girlish goodbye for someone who was in her early twenties, yet endearing. I found myself staring after her as she walked back to the street. Only when she had hailed a taxi and disappeared inside did I turn back into the gloom of the museum.

While up to now I'd been pleased with my rudimentary command of Japanese, when I tried to read the placards or tags next to the ceramics vessels, I found that the characters were too complicated, too specific to history, for me to read anything but the basic gist. In the description next to a kimono I might recognize the word for cloth, for silk, for shogunate, and a few numerals.

It took all of ten minutes to pass through the entire museum. I'd been hoping to find an exhibit of these beautiful vases but instead found only a small corner on the second floor that had a collection of small vessels, many from other parts of Japan. Among them, from what I could make out from the labels (and I could have been confused) were a few examples of a type of pottery known as kuro-Satsuma, black pottery made for commoners that had become en vogue in the twentieth century, and another style, called shiro-Satsuma, which was fancier, with an ivory-colored base glaze and then colorful overglaze decorations.

As I stood there, from the far end of the long corridor I heard the click of a latch. Turning, I saw an old man appear out of a side door. He was bald except for a thin circle of cropped, white hair that circled his head from one ear around to the other, and his face was that kind of ageless Asian face that could be anywhere from fifty-five to eighty. One leg seemed shorter than the other or perhaps he was arthritic, for he had a noticeable limp, yet he did not use a cane. In one hand he carried what looked like the remains of a convenience store sandwich, wrapped in white wax paper.

He seemed to not notice me at first as he made his way across the dusty tiles. I scuffed my feet as I shifted my weight, so as not to startle him.

He looked up.

"May I help you?" he asked. As he took in the fact that I was a foreigner, his eyes grew wide.

"A friend of mine said that perhaps you could help me."

"You speak Japanese!" he exclaimed.

"A little."

He approached me. It was indeed a sandwich in his hand.

"We don't see many foreigners here. You're American?"

I nodded.

"Thought so. How may I help you?"

I showed him the picture.

"I'm looking for the town where I might find more information about these." My finger went to the vase in the background. "I also need to find this woman. I have news about her son."

"What news?"

I paused. "There was an accident. He passed away."

The man looked in my eyes, scanning them until I somehow passed his test.

"Come with me."

He led me back across the corridor to the door where he'd come from, which led to a stairway and from there we ascended to the third floor. This was off limits to anyone other than staff personnel, and a jumble of artifacts were in haphazard storage, dotted with dust and cobwebs. Close to the entrance was a small desk of gray steel, with a bright green piece of blotting paper on it covered by a tattered sheet of transparent nylon that had gone yellowish from age. Piles of papers and books shrank the writing surface to the size of a single sheet of paper. A rotary telephone occupied a chair.

"Please," the old man said, putting the phone on the floor and indicating that I should sit. "Wait just a minute."

I sat. He shuffled back through the cobwebs to a bookshelf and spent a minute searching, then pulled out a tome, which he gave to me.

Hidden Japan was the title. I leafed through the pages. There were no pictures, and my Japanese was not good enough to understand much from the text.

"You may hear about the discriminated people," he said. "They are a part of Japan's history that most Japanese do not want to talk about. They are the lowest people. You know Japanese feudal structure? Yes? Shogun. Noble. Samurai. Merchant. Farmer. Peasant. Below all of them the lowest class."

The man sighed before continuing. "Hard to define today, in these modern times, than before. Some were butchers. In Buddhism, it is sinful to kill another living creature. All life is sacred. Yet we Japanese eat meat. We must kill to survive. So butchers were necessary, but also unclean. But they were a class created to appease the farmers, so that they'd have someone beneath them, someone lower in the pecking order."

"So, these people did the tasks nobody else wanted to."

"Yes," he nodded. "But other groups were treated poorly too. Not only those who cut meat or worked with dead things. In the sixteenth century we stole potters from Korea and brought them here. Yet we never treat them the same as Japanese. Not for centuries. Even today there is some bias against non-Japanese." He paused. "I believe in America there is no sense of birthright. People all supposed to be equal, yes?"

"Supposed to be, yes. But there's plenty of racism in America. America has a long way to go before it can claim that its citizens are equal."

The old man smiled. "If you are a realist, if you can see Japanese culture with an open mind, maybe you fit in well here. Maybe we are similar to America then. But these people and others ... they are like untouchables in India. The paradox is that we Japanese treat them badly, but because we treat them badly we don't want to talk about it. It's uncomfortable for us. Reminds us of our own failures as a people. We are ashamed."

"Why are you the only one who will talk about this?"

He smiled. "Because I've traveled. I spent many years in India, South America, even the United States. Travel is the way to open your mind. I see many things, I come back to Japan, nothing ever the same."

"It's nice to find someone who can answer some of my questions."

"Many young people," he went on, "don't even know about these things. Older people know, but they won't talk about it. You're lucky to come here and find me. I talk about it." He laughed. "These vases, this style of pottery, it comes from one small village high in the mountains over there. Across the bay. On the other side. Even I haven't been there. Moon Island. It's not marked on maps."

"Why is it not on the map?"

"Because the potters who lived there were originally Korean. Centuries ago, but even now deep suspicions remain. They were shunned, treated differently than other native Japanese. Many years ago the village was hidden entirely. Only the vases came out, a few priceless pieces each year."

"My friend thought you had a vase here in the museum."

The man laughed. "Here? Oh, we are just a small museum. We couldn't afford a piece of that caliber unless it were donated."

"Why does the hospital have one?"

"Because the man who built the hospital, he was very rich, rich enough to build his own hospital. Then he played a joke on the city. He insisted to have the urn there. With his own ashes inside."

I looked at the old man, trying to see in his face if what he was saying were true. His milky eyes stared back at mine until I looked away. The room seemed cold and eerie. I wished Miwako was still here with me. She'd been friendly and kind. I needed someone like that, someone to tether me, moor me, keep me from floating off and away.

The man's knees cracked as he lifted himself out of the chair. He went to a bookshelf, drew his hand across the volumes. The dust hung in the air like ash.

"These burial urns, they are prized even today. Three centuries ago, when Japan was still closed to trade, a Kagoshima noble traveled secretly to Korea by ship. He had seen ceramic vessels from a tiny Korean village that were beautiful. We don't know the date exactly, but around the time the nobleman died, within several decades, this kind of Satsuma ceramics, what's known as Tsuki-no-Satsuma, first appeared. It's believed that he may have brought — possibly against their will — Korean potters to work for him here in Kagoshima, producing the first Tsuki-ware.

"*Tsuki* means moon," he went on. "We can look at a particular village near Busan and see that there are many connections between the vessels produced there and these magnificent works of art that are still made in Kagoshima today. Ceramic historians might tell you more. I only know what I've learned from this book," he patted it, "and from curating this museum. But the mystery is the jump in the glazing. Almost overnight, it seems, this tiny village began producing stunning vases that went so far beyond anything the world had seen before that they were prized by almost everyone. The village produced — even in its heyday — only a few dozen vessels a year, as I said before. And to have one's ashes within one was the mark of the highest, nearly unattainable wealth. Each vessel is distinct and different, yet unmistakably the product of that place. You would not know it by a glance, but some of those potters were the wealthiest men in the art world."

"But do you think it will lead me to the woman in the photograph?"

"I think the only way to find her is to go to the village. Ask if someone recognizes that *genkan*, that entryway. Or perhaps a potter will recognize the vessel. Know who purchased it."

"Moon Mountain?" I said. "That's the village's name?"

"Moon Island," he corrected me. "Yes. I think people will know you come with a sincere heart. They will answer your questions. They will try to help you. But in Japan answers don't happen overnight. If you wish to understand anything, plan to stay there longer than you think. And many people may not want you poking around."

Chapter Fifteen

The generous curator paid for my Moon Island-bound train. I still had no money; the old man led me to Kagoshima Station, less than a block from the museum, and bought the ticket. I had wanted to have time to say goodbye to Miwako, to get a rain check on our dinner date, wanted to have her telephone number, but the old man had been so kind that I did not want to seem ungrateful. The train was modern and comfortable; I was the only blond person in its ten packed cars.

Evening was gathering, and the sky to the east was a deep purple color. The west was as pink as a girl's cheek in the cold. Already behind a jagged range of mountains, the sun backlit them in amber. Shadows lengthened. Students rode home on their shopping bicycles or laughed with their friends in groups of threes and fours. Bamboo thickets, cypress stands, and quaint rooftops whizzed by.

Much of the ride skirted the shores of Kinkō Bay, where fishing boats bobbed and wooden aquaculture cages floated on water that was as silvery as glass. Sakurajima still lurked, seeming to be present no matter which direction I traveled in. As the train veered north, breaking from the water and going parallel to a small river, there was a rattle and I saw a cloud of ash billow up into the sky. My heart raced again. How amazing to be here! How astonishing that volcanic eruptions could be part of the everyday.

By the time the train pulled into the village of Moon Island, I could see Venus as well as a fingernail clipping of the town's namesake. I stepped onto the platform and shivered, realizing it was colder here than in Kagoshima City, yet the air was refreshing and clean. The tiny station seemed to be closing. A sign in English read "Tourist In-formation" above an empty desk, and hanging on the wall were some curious masks that I remembered seeing in books: long-nosed, demonlike faces in crimson lacquer. The person inside the ticket booth looked at me as if my being there were making him uncomfort-able. He was a young man, perhaps still in his twenties, and as I moved toward the window he moved away from it as if I were plan-ning a stickup.

"Excuse me." I said, in my politest Japanese. "Are there any banks open at this time?"

"You speak Japanese!" he exclaimed. "I'm sorry I don't speak any English."

"Banks?" I reminded him. I was speaking Japanese.

He shook his head. "No, I'm afraid there's nothing open at this time."

"Tomorrow?"

"Yes, tomorrow."

"I'm afraid I don't have a place to stay," I said. "Can you suggest anything?"

He sucked in air between his teeth in an "I'm thinking" hiss. Then he seemed to forget about me, dashing out onto the platform to greet an oncoming train. I realized I was intruding. The train came and several people got off: a few high school students, someone who might have been a doctor, a few elderly women in earth-tone outfits who were as wizened as garden gnomes. In ten minutes the little sta-tion was quiet again.

Leaving my suitcase just inside the entrance, I went outside, not knowing whether to turn right or left. Nothing seemed open. A soli-tary cat darted across the road, stopping once to look at me. "What are you doing here?" it seemed to say.

The air smelled of pine and mist. Far off down the street I could see the lights of a tavern spilling out through wooden slats, throwing a pattern on the pavement like jail cell bars. A door opened and two people stumbled out, arm in arm. Laughing, their backs to me, they walked for a short time before turning.

The scent of cooking meat wafted to me and I realized how hungry I was. I stood outside the door and was about to enter when I remembered I had no way to pay for anything. My stomach was growling, but I turned around and walked back to the train station. The lights were off, the door locked. The young stationmaster had moved my luggage into the street. On top of it was a thin blanket and a small note, written in neat English script, which I could barely read in the dim light cast by the exit sign.

"Please sleep here. No one will harm you."

Wrapping the blanket around me, I lay down on a concrete bench. It was so short that my legs draped down over the side, but I utilized my suitcase as a footrest, the first time that it had served as anything other than dead weight for me to lug around. I adjusted an arm beneath my head as a pillow and fell asleep, listening to the crickets and field frogs.

Chapter Sixteen

When I woke up, dawn had begun to pierce the lavender of the morning sky. I lifted my head up from the bench and looked around. The street was still empty, not a single car passed, and the warm earth sent ropes of steam off the pavement that hung in the air like ghosts. A flock of sparrows descended onto the blacktop, hopping and chirping until they realized that something nearby was alive. One looked at me before emitting a sharp warning chirp, and the group departed for the cover of a nearby bush.

Now that it was light, I could see there was a shrine on the other side of the station parking lot. With nothing else to do until the banks opened, I crossed the street and took a closer look. The entryway had a giant orange gate in front that was dwarfed by two of the largest trees I had ever seen. It would have taken at least ten people holding hands to encircle the trunks, which were as warped and twisted as something in an enchanted forest movie. Rich layers of moss had built up on the base, melting away into a shaggy brown bark. Standing there looking up, I felt as if the tree kept on going, that I could climb from its branches and grab hold of the moon.

As had happened when I'd been on the *Pandora* looking up to the stars, I was overcome by awe and a sense of smallness, of how little a human life matters when compared with the life of a tree. This being before me had lived through World War II, World War I, even through the Meiji Restoration that paved the way for modern Japan. It had been here no doubt when the nobles brought Koreans here to make pottery. If the tree could talk, it would point the way to the hidden village that produced the most beautiful vases in the world.

I walked beneath the gate and entered the shrine grounds. Everything was silent, as if even the animals knew to respect the sanctity of this place. It was still quite dark, even eerie. My footsteps crunched in the gravel.

The temple was an ornate compound made up of several buildings, all bright reddish-orange, with the largest in the center. The roofs were made of copper plates that had turned a beautiful delicate green over the years, curved up at the edges. Little demon figurines adorned the eaves. To my right was a fountain constructed of a stone tank encircled by a fierce, very realistic dragon that seemed poised to strike anyone who neared. Water shot out from its fanged mouth into the pool. Someone had placed three bamboo ladles on a rack near its tail.

As the sun slowly transformed the violet sky to blue, I wandered through the deserted grounds. Everything was spotless, yet I saw no one, nor any sign of monks who might be living there. I took my time, going anywhere I could without stepping over gateways or disturbing areas that seemed untrodden. Hidden behind the smaller right-side building was a bonsai-filled garden with a tea-green carp pool, ancient stone lanterns, and a miniature bridge so beautiful that it would have made Monet send for his paints and easel. I found it very calming to stand there and imagine that this temple, this garden, this place, had been the same for centuries. When I approached the water two giant fish emerged, their whiskers twitching, as if they were trying to speak to me.

I decided to make my way back to the train station. As I was retracing my steps I noticed a girl standing in front of the main temple. Her bag sat several paces behind her like a waiting dog. Though I could not see her face, her posture indicated she'd been weeping.

I froze, not wanting to intrude on what she had intended to be a quiet moment at the temple. She stood in front of the main structure, tossed a coin into the wooden receptacle, then rang the curious bell rope that hung down above it, sending a jarring, incongruous jangle ringing out through the compound. As if summoned, a black raven croaked once, then lifted itself from a perch in the cypress grove and swooped off into the dark forest.

The girl clapped her hands, then bowed her head. She stayed looking down for several moments, then abruptly clapped her hands again. Her body shook for a moment as she choked back a series of sobs. Then she turned and went to her bag. From it she took a small wooden board and I watched her tie it to a row of similar ones next to the temple door.

As near as I remember I was motionless. I may have even been holding my breath. Yet something made her notice me, and the moment her eyes met mine I would remember my entire life: Her irises were bright green, as emerald as the garden pool I'd been standing by moments before. They blazed at me from beneath the ink of her glossy black hair.

Just writing about it, half a century later, I have to push back from the keyboard and pause. Never in my life has any girl approached the beauty of that vision there in the quiet temple. I had been hit by a rush more powerful than anything I'd felt before, a pulse through my veins, a symphony and an agony that I would never stop chasing. Just from that lone, almost accidental glance.

As soon as she saw me she took off down the path at a pace just short of a run. I followed as far as the gate and saw her turn right at the street. Forgetting any sense of decency, I galloped after her, bursting onto a different street, one swollen with a sea of students and office workers. A few boys in white starched shirts and jet-black slacks stared at me as I craned my neck trying to spot her. One girl in a knee-high skirt and sailor blouse asked in singsong as she passed me, "May I help you?" to the explosive titter of her friends. A few salarymen gawked at the strange foreigner as I pushed my way through the crowd. But the girl from the temple was gone.

I walked back to the train station and sat on my suitcase until the clock above the entrance read nine a.m. Then I went inside, thanked the stationmaster for the use of the blanket, and asked where I might find a bank. He pointed down the street away from the temple, toward where I'd smelled the delicious barbecue the night before. Drawing a little picture of what the bank logo looked like so I'd be sure to find it, he sent me on my way.

In a few minutes I'd exchanged some of my traveler's checks for crisp Japanese yen, and shortly after that I was at the little barbecue pub with the wooden slats on the windows. Though nobody seemed to be inside, I could smell the same delicious aroma coming out into the street, so I parted the curtain and called a hello into the darkness.

"*Konnichiwa*?"

"Come in," called a voice. "Come in."

A hunched over man with wrinkles around his eyes and deep dimples appeared at the back. He'd wrapped a strip of dark cloth around his forehead. He took no notice of my being a foreigner and walked straight to a long, shallow barbecue, where a bed of even coals glowed beneath some skewers of meat.

"What would you like?" he asked.

"Anything," I replied. "What do you recommend?"

He nodded. "Chicken thighs, very tasty. Chicken thighs with scallion. Pork with scallions? Or … chicken hearts? Very tasty. Everything tasty."

"Chicken thighs with scallion. Two."

"To drink?"

"Beer."

"Bottle or draft?"

"Draft."

My stomach growled. I waited as he filled a mug and placed it on the counter, along with a small bowl of boiled soybeans.

"Ever had those?" he asked. It was the only nod he gave to my being a foreigner.

I shook my head.

"Eat them like this." He took one and put it up to his lips, then squeezed. The shell split and the two beans popped into his mouth. "Don't eat whole thing."

I tried one. I was so hungry that he could have put anything on a plate and I'd have chewed it happily, but these soybeans — seasoned with just a hint of salt — were spectacular. In moments I finished the entire bowl, and as soon as it was empty he refilled it. Almost as quickly, the bowl was empty again. By this time the skewers were ready, and he brought over the chicken *yakitori*, which he'd seasoned with a sweet soy sauce. The owner let me eat in silence. I drank my beer, ate chicken skewers, ordered some with pork. I thought about the beauty of the girl at the temple.

When I had eaten my fill, I paid the proprietor and stepped outside into the bright sun. Somewhere down there, to the south, was

Kagoshima City and the hospital and museum. I looked for anything resembling a metropolis but saw only the quaint swath of village rooftops, electric wires, and farther off, down the verdant valley is green rice fields. Then a splash of bay, and Sakurajima's beautiful ash burps climbing thousands of feet, so high that day that they were sheared off into a thin horizontal line at the top by the trade winds. Squinting, I could see all the way to the horizon where the water merged seamlessly into the sky.

I walked back to the train station and sat down next to my belongings, which no one had touched the entire time I was eating. I took out the photograph of Kagoshima's mother and the beautiful urn behind her. Returning inside to the stationmaster's window, I tapped on the glass.

"Yes?" he said.

"I'm wondering, a long shot, I know, but do you happen perhaps to know this woman? Or the vase behind her?"

I held it up so he could see.

"Sorry," he said. "She doesn't look familiar."

"What about the vase?"

He bent toward the glass and then sprang away as if I'd held up a snake.

"I don't know anything about that," he said, waving his hand at me to shoo. "Sorry, this station is a busy place. We can't have lingerers. Please leave."

"But surely—"

"Please. I give you place to sleep. You go now. Go!"

"I have to tell this woman news about her son. He passed away."

This made the stationmaster pause.

"I was the last person to see the man alive," I continued. "I've come a long way to find her."

The man looked at me, then back over his shoulder at the two other people in the office. One of them, an older man, gave an almost imperceptible nod.

"Try at the police box," the young man said. "You go ask there."

The station was a small black building about a five-minute walk past the little barbecue shop. Just passing made me hungry again, but I kept on going, my suitcase behind me, the hardened metal corners leaving little trails on the clean cement as I pulled. By now I was used to the idea that no one would go off with it, so I left it at the door and approached. A man who looked to be in his early forties was already watching me as I came up to the double glass doors, and as I reached for the handle he opened it for me.

"Thank you," I said. The waiting room was unadorned by anything save a large and detailed map of Moon Island, some parts of it colored in shades of pastels. On it I could see the train station, the tracks, and a nest of roads. Also the temple, some mountains or hills that were yet undeveloped. At one side, entering the map like a large serpent, was a wide six or eight lane highway that abruptly ended several inches from the edge. A dotted line marked its future path, cutting across from the lower left corner, swooping around the center of town, and exiting to the right, near the top.

"Can we help you?" another policeman said, standing up from a desk cluttered with notebooks and files. I'd always thought of Japanese as meticulous and tidy, but one look at the police station dispelled any generalizations.

"I'm very sorry to trouble you," I said, showing the photograph. "But I have some news about this woman's son. Do you know where I might find her?"

The two men studied the photograph. One of them put a finger on the green vase and the other nodded. Then one of them seemed to notice something else and they both leaned in close. I thought at first they were studying the woman's face, but then I realized they were looking at a small placard that was resting on the top of the medicine cabinet, near the vase. Almost the same color as the wall, it blended in so well that I hadn't noticed it was there before. As it was in the background, it was not even in focus. One went to another room, returning a few minutes later with a magnifying glass, large and round, that seemed pulled from a Sherlock Holmes mystery.

Even then it was not easy to read the characters, but it appeared to be the sign-in placard of an inn or rooming house. Of course there was no reason to assume that this photograph was taken here in Moon Island. It could have been anywhere in Japan. But after several minutes of careful scrutiny, the kind policemen wrote down the name of a small *minshuku* on the outskirts of town.

"I don't believe it's been used as an inn for years, but they have a day-use bath there. It's possible that this is the place you're looking for," the younger of the two cops said. "Here, hop in and I'll take you there."

We drove for some time through the beautiful landscape. Part of it was along a road that followed a river that was a translucent, luminous, milky blue. It was porcelain silt suspended in the water that gave it that beautiful opaque shade. Here and there I spotted the iridescent flash of a Japanese kingfisher. Once I saw one plunge into a pool after a fish, a jewel plummeting out of the sky. Then the route diverged from the river and began winding up through a series of alternating rice fields and green tea plantations. Bright flowers that I couldn't recognize lined the edges of the road, which had deep sluices on either side to channel water to the paddies.

The driver was silent, absorbed, perhaps in the absurdity of a policeman acting as taxi driver to a strange foreigner and his luggage. Or perhaps he relished the task as a break from office paperwork. In any case, he did not speak until pulling the car over at what looked like someone's driveway.

"It's down there," he said.

"Thank you," I replied.

He nodded, then pulled a sharp U-turn and accelerated away, leaving me alone, looking at a foreboding, overgrown driveway that led — I hoped — to some answers.

CHAPTER SEVENTEEN

So it was that I arrived at the Kawasoba-sō, which translates as "Inn by the River," a low building marked by a mossy wooden sign that was overgrown and hidden by a tangle of weeds and azalea bushes that hadn't been trimmed for decades. Beyond the cypress trees the August rice fields were already beginning to turn from green to tan; in a month they'd be a rich, deep ochre, the sheaves ripe for harvest. Here though, at the inn, it seemed as if the seasons couldn't seep through beneath the cypresses. The driveway was slippery from layers of moss that coated the pavement except in twin tracks where the tires wore through. Pine needles had piled in the center of the cracked asphalt, giving the impression of an unpaved, two-track lane. I could hear in the distance the sound of water rushing over rocks, all muffled by the fragrant cypresses and bamboo.

I took my suitcase and began pulling it down the drive. Twice I slipped, recovering without a fall. When I turned the final corner and could see the building, I stopped. It was an L-shaped structure with large, rank weeds that covered what must have once been a sizable garden in front of the house. A cement fountain, dry, peeked out above the grasses and unkempt plants. Patches of vibrant green moss coated the rotting thatch; it was hard not to imagine that the roof barely kept out the rain during downpours. The short side of the "L" was facing the driveway, and I could see one of the panes in the front door was missing its glass. Were it not for the thinnest wisp of smoke climbing up from the stovepipe, I would have assumed the place was abandoned.

I stood there wondering what to do until I heard the unmistakable sound of a car slowing down on the main road. A few moments later it passed by me and parked at the circle by the front door of the inn. A pair of slender women got out and rang the bell. Each carried a small bag and towel. After a short wait, and presumably after hearing a "come in," they opened the slider and disappeared inside.

I had no interest in pulling my bag all the way down to the door just to find out I'd have to pull it all the way back up the hill again. Hefting it over the drainage sluice that also served as a curb, I placed it at the base of a large cypress tree, then opened it and took out the photograph. I closed the lid, then placed a fallen tree bough over the top as a kind of simple camouflage — not that I expected anyone to take it. In Japan one can drop a cash-filled wallet in the street and expect it to be at the police station, not a bill missing, the next morning. Nobody would bother with a heavy piece of luggage stashed out of the way behind a tree.

As I approached the Kawasoba-sō, my cheeks began to flush. What if this were not the place? What if bringing up this sad topic would be seen as an insult instead of the welcomed closure I'd expected it to be? What if they hated foreigners? This whole area had been bombed in World War II, of course, so hatred might be very natural.

I stood at the door and pressed the button, my heart in my throat.

"It's open," came a woman's voice. "Just leave 500 yen at the door."

I cracked the slider. There, as in the photograph, was the antique medicine chest, and atop it, the very vase that had lured me halfway around the world. It was smaller than I expected, eighteen inches tall or so, but the colors were more intense and vivid than even the one on display in the hospital. Here too, the aurora borealis seemed to be trapped and glowing within the layers of glaze.

I do not know how long I stared, silent, not seeing anything except this stunning vessel, the second most perfect ceramic piece I have ever seen. It was, at the base, a kind of steel blue-gray, like woodsmoke rising from a forest after a heavy rain, then turned to a green the color of jade. Translucent, the green swirled up and mixed with lighter yellows, saps and ochres. But if I shifted my weight even slightly, the colors shimmered, changed, as if the vase were watching me instead of the other way around. A zing went through me as I realized that — if the curator was right — there was a dead person's ashes inside this one, too.

"May I help you?"

I turned around and was face to face with the woman I knew so well from Kagoshima's photograph. It was the same face, the same hair, though now gray, and even the kimono the woman wore might have — but for the passage of time — been identical. But two things were different from what I expected: This woman seemed at least ten years younger than she did in the photograph. She had smooth skin, few wrinkles, and the gray in her hair was not unattractive. At the time, a young man in my twenties, I didn't realize her beauty; now, however, I know that she would have turned heads even at her age.

And I saw, also not in the photograph, that the eyes now scanning the room were as clouded as cream.

The woman was as blind as my father.

I stood there, my brain processing the coincidences and the strange connections and the threads here in this alien land that were so similar to what I knew back home. A prickle of — of what? — not fear, but something like it, hit the base of my neck.

"I'm," I began, not knowing what to say. "I am American," I started, in English. Then switched to Japanese. "I was on a ship with a young man named Kenji."

The woman sucked in her breath. "Yes?"

"I'm very sorry to bring some news. There was an accident. In Panama."

"He's hurt?"

"He," I started. My mouth felt like cotton. "He passed away."

"Oh," the woman said, so quietly that I almost thought I had imagined it. She made a sound, a kind of slow exhaling, like the air escaping from a tire. And then, as if summoning the strength from a reservoir of pain deep within her, she let out a wail of agony like nothing I have ever heard and sank down to the floor.

"Please," she moaned. "Please, please ... please ... ."

"I'm so sorry for your loss." I bent down and reached out, thinking to comfort her. The moment I touched her she pulled away as if my hand had burned her.

"Get out of here," she screamed. "Leave!"

From down the corridor, I saw the two women who had arrived earlier appear, their hair wet, hurrying toward us. I expected them to stop or help, but instead they both nodded at me as if embarrassed to be there, ducked beneath the hanging curtain at the slider, and were gone. A few moments later their car's engine revved and faded as it left the driveway.

I stood, wishing there was something else I could do. The vase seemed like a mantelpiece cat, watching everything, almost without being seen. The woman writhed on the tatami floor, her fingernails tearing at the fragile reed mat.

"I'm so sorry," I said again. Turning, I pushed through the screen to the outside and began to walk toward my suitcase. I was panting and felt lightheaded, as if what had just happened weren't real.

I was nearing the end of the driveway when I heard the soft sound of footsteps on pine needles and turned around. The inn owner was there, hurrying up the steep hill, a long bamboo stick in her hand that she used to orient herself with the edge of the road. Her eyes were red and puffy, her cheeks glistened with tears. She seemed to know I was there, whether because she could hear my breathing or because she did have some sense of sight left, I didn't know.

"I'm so deeply sorry," she said. Then, she said in English: "My grief made me rude. Can you please excuse me?"

She was — as is still customary in Japan — bowing with each word.

I was taken by surprise at the oddity of finding such a fluent English speaker in this tiny, remote place. As if I'd landed on the moon only to have someone stop by and ask for a cup of sugar.

"I was," she continued, not giving me the chance to reply, "not myself. Such a shock. I didn't mean to be like that. You came all this way. Please come and accept some simple tea." She wiped her eyes with a tiny kerchief she took from a pouch in the sleeve of her kimono.

"I don't want to impose."

"I insist. Please."

I remembered that I had brought some of Kagoshima's, Kenji Matsuyama's, effects.

"If you want them, I have a few of your son's belongings."

She shook her head.

"Not my son. My nephew. He was the son of my older sister. I have no children of my own."

"I see. But, would you like the items?" We moved to where my bag lay, off to the side of the pavement.

"Yes, of course."

She knelt, her fingers flying over the surface like a flock of sparrows.

"So heavy," she said. "I'm so sorry to have caused you so much trouble. Let me help you."

"No," I replied, imagining her straining her back trying to lift it. "I've got it."

"My name is Komori," she said. "In Japanese, the characters mean 'Tree Tender.'"

"Komori-san," I said, then continued in Japanese. "Pleased to meet you. I am Neil Chase."

"Let me dash back and prepare the tea."

While she did, I hefted the suitcase. When I arrived at the entrance some ten minutes later she was waiting for me, her milk-colored eyes piercing me as if they'd been able to see. She held open the cotton curtain and waited as I stepped through. As I was taking off my shoes, as is the custom before walking on tatami floors, she knelt down and touched her forehead to the surface. This time, she spoke in Japanese.

"Welcome, dear guest, to my humble home." It was the old, formal speech, as done in feudal times.

I replied by uttering the book-learned phrase I'd studied, expecting to never use:

"Please forgive me for being rude to enter here."

The woman's knees popped as she lifted herself up from the floor. How hard it must be for her to live, blind, alone in this run-down old inn.

"This way," she said. "Let me serve you some tea."

We walked down an unlit, shabby corridor to a room with another hanging cotton screen, she moving so adeptly that it was easy to forget that she was blind. She ushered me into a small room that was a perfect Zen square. On one wall, a vase stood with an arrangement of dead sticks and spring flowers, a bird-

and-bloom tapestry hanging on a silk scroll behind it. In the middle, a charcoal brazier was glowing on a low raised table, above
which was an iron teapot that hung from a yellowed piece of
bamboo. A wisp of steam curled up from the mouth of the kettle
like breath on a cold day.

"There," she pointed. "Please sit."

I entered. The table had a hollowed-out area underneath it so that
one could sit. The wood was warm to the touch.

"I'll just be a minute," she said, leaving me alone. I smelled
straw from the tatami reed mats mixed with the fragrant charcoal
smoke. Outside, the chirp of a Japanese nightingale echoed
through the garden.

Komori-san returned with a small lacquer-ware tray, red and
black, with teacups and serving dishes and sweets made from
pounded rice. She knelt again and shook some green tea leaves into a
small ceramic teapot, then took the iron pot off the bamboo hanger
and poured in some hot water. Neither of us spoke.

I observed her movements, realizing how she managed to function
without sight and still accomplish so much. The tray provided con-
tainment for the cups, for example. By lining one cup in the upper
left corner before she poured, she knew where it was and could pour
in just the right amount of liquid. I did not see her spill a single drop.
Her hearing must have been as keen as a tiger's.

When the tea was ready, she held out a cup for me.

"What about your sister?" I asked, breaking the silence. "You said
Kenji-san was your nephew?"

"She passed away. When Kenji was just a few years old."

"I'm sorry."

"Kenji was like the son I never had."

"He spoke highly of you," I said. A white lie, as Kagoshima had
never mentioned her and only barely talked about his home. In fact, I
had gotten the impression that part of the reason the young man had
become a sailor was to escape certain things that had happened here.

"That's nice to hear," Komori-san said.

Another pause, long enough to again hear the nightingale.

"Delicious tea."

The next pause lasted until I had finished my cup. She raised herself up on her knees again and poured. A trickle of green liquid filled
the delicate vessel.

"May I offer you a room here?" Komori-san asked. "At one time this place was famous. While it's not like it used to be, we still have people who insist on bathing or staying here."

I put the cup down, unsure whether to be wary or warm. She was an innkeeper offering a weary traveler a place to stay for the night, and I would be a guest. It crossed my mind that perhaps she planned on sticking me with an exorbitant bill but that hardly seemed likely. And even if she did, it would just be a simple matter to leave without paying. More importantly, her sincerity and kindness and even her careworn yet noble face had made an impression on me. I trusted her already. Perhaps trust is unavoidable when people share a cup of tea.

"I would be honored to stay," I replied. "If you're sure that it won't be any trouble."

"Oh," she said, breaking into the first smile that I'd seen since my arrival. "That's lovely. Please excuse me while I ready your room. If you would like, please feel free to visit the onsen down at the river."

I remembered the ladies who had arrived in the small car and left.

"Were those guests earlier here for the bath?"

"Yes," came the reply, already from down the hall. "We don't have many overnight visitors these days but people still come for the bath. It's one of the best in the area."

It seemed unbelievable to me that this place would have guests at all, given the ramshackle exterior. But perhaps Japanese visitors were trying to help the woman get by in what was a difficult time, coming as a "donation" to help someone far too proud for open charity.

Or perhaps the bath was just inexpensive.

I stood up and stretched my legs, staring at the little altar where the flower arrangement was. The sticks were interesting, the bark rough in some places and gone in others, leaving just smooth white wood the color of bone. The little flowers at their base might have been a kind of aster, with bushy purple petals and a yellow center. I saw in the arrangement a juxtaposition of young life contrasted with old age, of love rising up out of heartbreak, of the beauty of spring as it overtakes winter. This was no mere bouquet of cut flowers, Western-style. It was a form of poetry, expressed in petals, branches, and leaves.

I thought of Marinne and how much she would enjoy being here at my side, seeing these same flowers, looking out on these same forests. What would she have to say about all these things? I resolved to write her that evening, tell her as much as I could about the past weeks' adventures. I did not realize it yet, but whether it was days or weeks or months, I had already accepted that I would spend a length of time here. I had been a rolling stone for too long; now I craved moss.

Looking at the flower arrangement and thinking back on the sum of my adventures, I realized that this entire chain, the unbroken string of random links that had brought me to stand in this very spot, all of it, would not have happened had I been with Marinne. I realized this because of the absurdity, even the danger, of the two of us spending a night sleeping on benches outside the Moon Island train station. Marinne, tender, sweet Marinne, would never have entertained the thought of a night spent outside. She and I would have been in a hotel. A careening chain of thoughts tore through my mind and ended with the certainty, the absolute certainty, that if I had stayed with Marinne I would have stayed in Boston. There would have been no journey, I would never have met Kagoshima or been with him in Panama, I would not have been entrusted with his effects and would never have gotten malaria. I would never have gone to the brothel. Nor perhaps even left the ship.

As much as there had been a sense of loss the moment I stepped onto the *Pandora*, it hadn't settled into me, become part of my core, until I stopped there with Komori-san. Stepping through that threshold disconnected me from the person I'd been when I was in Boston, as if the choice I'd made — the choice Marinne and I had made together — was a portal through time and space into some parallel world. Not merely a change in countries marked in miles and days of travel, but some kind of fundamental transformation. I was older, aware of the world, forever different even in these several months. The boy I'd been on the Boston dock was as strange to me as someone I might bump into at a street crossing.

So as much as I wanted to, I did not write Marinne all of what had happened after all. There was too much to tell, too much that she would not comprehend. She would worry about me, I'm sure, if she knew I had slept outside that night. Malaria too: How could she not read something like that and entreat me to come back and rest in her arms?

All of this flood of thoughts from a simple collection of four bent twigs and fresh forest blossoms.

"I've prepared your room," said Komori-san, reappearing at the doorway, so silently that she startled me. "Come this way."

CHAPTER EIGHTEEN

I followed Komori-san. The building was long and narrow, paralleling a ravine with the river below it, so that the front side where I'd entered was on the ground level, but most of the guest rooms had balconies and views looking out as if on a second floor. My room was at the end of a dark hallway, then down a flight of warped wooden stairs that had been burnished to a shine over the decades by slippered feet. The chamber was small and bare, with a lone bulb that hung down from the center of the ceiling, a tarnished pull chain like a tail. Here too was a small altar with a vase in front of a silk scroll. This arrangement was even more enchanting than the one I'd seen in the tea room: Out of the center of the wide, flat vase rose a smooth stone, off center, almost like an egg. At its base extended one tiny red flower on a stem so thin that the blossom seemed to hover in the air like some kind of butterfly. Behind the rock was a thick, gnarled branch with shaggy bark that was flaking off of wood the color of ivory.

More marvelous than the arrangement was the mystery surrounding it: Had Komori-san done these all herself? If so, was she — despite the apparent milkiness of her eyes — not blind? It seemed impossible that she could do such delicate works without the ability to see. But perhaps she was like Beethoven, composing symphonies while hearing the music only in his mind.

The best part of the room was its balcony, which though narrow, opened up with giant sliding screens onto a view of the river and ravine behind it. Moss and ferns dangled from crevasses in the dark lava bank, vines hung like church bell ropes, extending into a canopy of bamboo and cypress and deciduous foliage so thick it blocked out the sun. Rays of light pierced through here and there, as thick and solid as if made of steel.

Then there was the rush of the river itself: Shallow yet forceful, it foamed up over the rocks and sent sprites of white froth dancing into the air. I saw a water ouzel perch on a stone for a moment, then duck into the current as effortlessly as a pearl diver.

The difference between the shabby front side and the stunning majesty of this view seemed to fit, somehow, as the more I pried beneath the surface of things here in this curious country, the less sure I was of what I did and did not know. Again I felt that sense of having passed through some boundary into a parallel reality where not even the mysteries were what they seemed. The difference between looking at an oyster's unimpressive shell and eating one. Or opening it to find the dazzling pearl.

As I was about to close the screens and return my attentions to the room, I saw a dwelling of some kind on the opposite side of the ravine, almost hidden by the lush foliage. I realized that while this little inn seemed remote, it was just minutes from other houses and the appearance of its being in the middle of nowhere was, like much of the rest of Japan, carefully cultivated. To see the structure at all, I had to already be looking for it. Anyone in that building would be able to look down both into my room's window and to the open-air bath by the riverside. I hoped whoever lived there was not a voyeur. How ironic, for I was soon to become one.

I stepped away from the window and drew shut the rice paper screens. Tiny maple leaves were woven into the rice fibers, each leaf like a baby's handprint on the creamy white.

"Why don't you take an onsen before dinner?" Komori-san said, reappearing at the doorway. "We don't have any overnight guests tonight, and it's already past the daytime bathing hours. You can have it all to yourself."

"Thank you. Komori-san," I said. Onsen are similar to hot springs, yet elevated, like so many things are in Japan, to the level of art. The main reason the inn survived was that people came to partake in its row of relaxing, riverside hot baths.

"I'll ring a bell when dinner's ready. Perhaps one hour?" She turned as if to leave, then looked back. "You do know how we bathe in Japan, right?"

I shook my head. "No, I don't."

"You rinse off outside the bath first, then dip after you're clean. I had a group of Russians here once and they were splashing around in their filthy clothes! Can you believe it?! Their clothes!" She said "clothes" with such distaste that it sounded like a swear word.

"Are there towels down there?"

She opened a sliding panel in the wall and showed me a low dresser. A cotton robe, sash, and bathing towel set were neatly folded. "Just use these walking to and from the house. No need to wear clothes in the bathing area."

"But if someone were to come? Like that pair of ladies who were here when I arrived?"

"This is a mixed gender bath. Men and women bathe together. No need to worry. If you have a tiny one just hold the face cloth over it. But nobody cares. We're all naked under our clothes."

The light had disappeared by the time I reached the bathing area, which was down several sets of stairs and at the end of yet another long corridor. The moss beneath my feet was treacherous, but — as in the house — the center of the path was less slippery, the moss worn down by bathers' footsteps over time. The rush of the river was now more like a roar.

I dropped the robe and sash into a wicker basket and tucked it into a shelf in the men's changing room, then pushed open the door, revealing a series of four baths that lined the water's edge. Naked, holding the small washcloth in front of me as if someone were watching, I walked to a tiled area where some low wooden stools were lined up, one each in front of a small spigot and shower head. A bar of soap and bottle of shampoo was just to the right, within easy arm's reach. With a little experimentation, I found the right combination of pressure and temperature, sat down on the stool, and began to bathe. When I had soaped and rinsed off, I was ready for the best part: soaking in the baths, which were at the river's edge, down yet another narrow stairway and another slippery path.

Standing at the first steaming pool, I turned toward the river, with the clichéd, unmistakable sensation of being watched. I didn't see anyone, yet at the same time I knew someone was there. My subconscious was alerting me to something my eyes and brain still hadn't seen. I peered down both sides of the river, looking for fishermen or onlookers. Almost out of sight there was a small footbridge, I noticed, leading from one side of the bank to the other. But nobody was on it. In fact, as I scrutinized it, I could see some planks were broken, hanging down in the middle. Clearly it was not currently being used.

I turned back toward the hotel, expecting a curtain to draw closed or a flicker of motion from some far room. But there was no clear line of sight from any of the hotel windows to the bath. The inn had respect for bather privacy, and while the bath was open to the river, a series of well-planted bamboo and maple thickets obscured any direct peeking from anyone inside the hotel.

Telling myself I was being silly, I turned back to the onsen pools and approached them. Cautious not to plunge in without testing the water temperature first, I placed a foot into the nearest bath and removed it, a line of red skin going up to my ankle. Could anyone enjoy a bath in water that scalding? I wondered if I would have to turn around, put on my cotton robe, and return to the hotel.

But the other pools were progressively cooler, and the one farthest from the washing area was exactly right: nowhere near scalding, yet not so tepid that I would get cold after a few minutes. I stepped down into the pool, tucked my knees, and sunk in up to my neck, the penetrating warmth relaxing me. I felt my arms loosen, my legs becoming light and weightless. As the sweat beaded on my forehead I felt giddy. The sound of the river water became a lullaby.

I stayed in that particular bath for some twenty minutes, long enough to forget how unsettled I'd felt before, how convinced I was that someone was watching me. I was so calm that it took me a moment to realize that on the far side of the river, up high on the bank of the ravine, something was glowing a deep orange-crimson.

"Fire!" I thought, leaping up for a better view through the leaves. My foot slipped on the algae-covered rock and I lost my balance, splashing back down into the hot water. By the time I had gotten to my feet the forest looked green again. I waited, peering up at the spot where I'd seen the curious glow. After a few minutes, it appeared again. As the fire disappeared I heard the faint sound of cinder blocks scraping together. Stone against stone.

And then, for one split moment, in the only opening of foliage large enough for me to see anything, I saw the flash of a female face.

I was on the opposite side of the river, looking up at a bank that had to have been at least twenty feet high, and she was walking past on some kind of path behind the edge of the ravine. Yet there could be no mistake. It was the same girl. The one I had seen — spied upon, chased — at the temple.

Yes, you are thinking that I was just another foreigner who believes all Asian faces look alike. Black hair, almond eyes, yellow skin. One indistinguishable from another.

You would be wrong.

I was not imagining it

Could it be the very same girl?

I had to see the color of her eyes.

Chapter Nineteen

I stood still. My extremities felt strange, prickling, as if they had been asleep and the blood flow had only just returned. Despite the heat of the bath, I was shivering. I was simultaneously so certain that it was her and yet unable to imagine that it could be.

I looked back toward the inn, where my clothes lay folded on the bench in the changing room at the end of the long path. I did a quick calculus of what might be gained and lost were I to race back and dress myself. I would be clothed, a gain. But I might lose sight of her. I would also have to wade across the river either way, clothed or not, and were I wearing something, how would I explain sopping garments so wet they'd leave trails on the floors of the inn? I'd put on clothes just to take them off again before crossing the river.

I also knew Komori-san would not see me, could not see me, clothed or not. And I had no plan to be seen by the girl. So, taking a long look up and down the stream for fishermen, I decided to take the risks. Covering myself with only the hand towel, I scrambled across the slippery rocks as best I could. The icy water, fresh from the Kirishima mountain range and spring fed, made my feet sting, then numbed them, as I splashed and slid. Once I fell, submerging myself up to my waist, the cold such a shock that I couldn't breathe. But I sprang up, crossing the rest of the river in two great strides, fearful

that by the time I got to the cliff edge she would already be gone.
Had it not been for the noise of the river itself I'm sure she would
have heard me crossing, noises as loud as an elephant's.

I reached the opposite bank and began pulling myself up the
ravine by clutching roots and protruding branches. It was steep, but
not sheer vertical, and I scrambled up the loose earth, sending a
shower of dirt clods down below me with each foot step. Several
times I slipped, but each time I managed to hold on just long enough
to regain my footing.

I was panting by the time I reached the top. A small path led from
an outbuilding on my right to what I assumed was a house, about
twenty yards to my left. Though the bushes and vines were dense,
just a few feet of earth separated the walk from the ravine's edge, and
that left nowhere for me — clinging to vines like someone out of a
Tarzan movie — to hide.

I had not even had time to catch my breath when I heard the slam
of a screen door, followed by footsteps. Not knowing what else to do,
I crouched and froze, ducking as best I could. One of my toes was already hanging off the cliff. I hung onto the bush, held my breath, and
hoped that she wouldn't see me.

I was so scared that I even closed my eyes as she passed. I heard
her footsteps but don't remember anything else until several seconds later, when she reached the outbuilding. Through a break in
the foliage I could see the whole scene clearly, something I will
never forget.

First, it was indeed the very same girl I'd seen in the temple. No
mistaking that: the fiery green eyes that seemed so impossibly set in
an Asian's face. I inhaled, so loud that she heard me and turned my
direction. For a moment I thought she'd seen me, but after scanning
the bushes she shifted back to what she was doing.

Wielding a shovel, she was carrying the stiff, matted corpse of a
dead cat. As I watched, she took the animal's remains and set them
down. Then she went inside the building and I couldn't see her for a
moment. There was that same distinct stone-on-stone sound that I
had heard all the way down at the river, and the entire doorway of
the shed glowed as if she'd turned on a sunrise. She returned, picked
up the shovel and cat, and disappeared again. Another clanking
sound, the glow disappeared, and she returned to the door carrying
only the tool.

No cat.

As she closed the outer door, either I stepped back or perhaps the earth just gave out beneath me. I remember clinging for a split second to the strong bush branch as I tried to regain my footing, then my sweaty palm slipped and I plummeted down the ravine, scraping and sliding, branches slashing me in the face and other more tender places as I went down. I hit the bottom with a thud and heard my ankle give way with an audible pop, yet I felt — then, just for a moment — no pain. My face was still staring at the patch of open leaves at the top of the ravine, where the girl now stood, looking down on me with those eyes, eyes so bright they seemed to float in the darkness, wide and judging and afraid. Her mouth was open, one hand paused a few inches from her lips as if she were protecting them. For a moment our eyes met, and then she turned and ran. I could hear her footsteps on the path and the slam of the screen door.

Then the pain hit. I looked down at my ankle and saw a large purple stain seeping out across the skin. A throbbing heat began. I do not know how I managed to make it back across the slippery rock-strewn river, but I did. The icy chill of the mountain water kept the swelling down. Just as I had limped to the changing area and was putting on my robe I heard the voice of Komori-san calling me.

"Chase-san?"

Her head appeared at the top of the path. "Is everything all right?"

"Yes," I answered, glad that she could not see the bloody scrapes and the huge bruise on my ankle. "Everything is fine, but I'm afraid I slipped and gave my ankle a good twist."

It wasn't exactly a lie.

"I'm so sorry," Komori-san replied. "I should have warned you that the rocks get slick sometimes."

"It wasn't anything you could have prevented."

"Do you need help?"

"No, I was just finishing. It's a lovely bath. Such a marvelous view."

"Well when you're ready, dinner is waiting for us."

At the time I thought nothing of the "us" in her statement. People often use "us" in Japanese when they are being polite. I put on my *yukata* robe and limped back up the path to the inn.

CHAPTER TWENTY

There is a wonderful word in Japanese, *mottainai*, used when something — often food or a love interest — is just "too good to waste." One says this when, despite having just started a diet, one decides to finish the piece of delicious cake that's just been served. Calories be damned. Or when a smart, bright, beautiful girl one knows decides to ruin her life by marrying an unworthy guy. *Mottainai*. She is too good to waste.

It was *mottainai* that my ankle, swollen and throbbing, prevented me from enjoying the dinner Komori-san had prepared. It took me twice the expected time to limp up the long pathway to the building, and halfway up I had to stop and steady myself on the bamboo rails, barely able to take the pain. By the time I reached the dining room sweat was pouring from my forehead, and my ankle felt as if it were on fire.

We ate in a small, intimate salon with a low rectangular table in the middle, made from a kind of timber no longer harvested, a kind of cypress unique to an island off the southern coast of Japan. The table, stained with a lustrous varnish and sanded to a shine, seemed as if it were made of agate: glowing, alive.

In the center of this table Komori-san placed a platter of roasted, salted river fish, grilled whole, each done up on individual bamboo skewers. A constellation of different bowls and cups orbited around a central plate of sashimi, with a bowl of steaming rice placed at my left hand. Off to the side a hot pot held green tea, which Komori-san poured for me as I eased myself, wincing, down to the floor.

"Please help yourself," she said. "I'm sorry that it's such simple food."

"It's not simple at all," I said. "It's like you cooked for a king!"

"You flatter me."

I picked at the rice, dipped a slice of raw fish into the soy sauce, allowed it to melt on my tongue. I hardly tasted it though, for the pain in my ankle almost made me cry out.

"Delicious," I said. "But may I ask a favor?"

"Anything."

"Would you have a plate of ice by any chance?"

"Ice?"

"I've injured my ankle, badly I think. I'm sorry to inconvenience you … ."

"Inconvenience me?" She leaped up. "You poor thing. Give me just a moment!"

She rushed out of the room, returning a few minutes later with a wide enamel bowl filled with cubes. Kneeling next to me, she touched my thigh, tracing her fingers down the cotton cloth to the swollen ankle. Her hands, so soft, felt like a breeze on my hot skin. As she explored the damage I saw her stiffen, realizing how swollen it was. I watched her pick up one single ice cube and place it on my leg. The cold felt like a needle; I flinched.

"I'm so sorry," she said. "It must be painful."

"The cold surprised me."

She moved the ice cube around on my skin, so sensually that I felt myself almost hypnotized. I felt the embarrassing hydraulics of an erection and pushed my mind to think of other things. I thought of the river outside. Then the girl with the dead cat's corpse.

"If you're hungry, please feel free to eat."

I was not hungry.

I was embarrassed and exhausted, so I did nothing while this woman ran the ice over my ankle. As she did so, she shifted her weight and then, and I barely realized it at first, moved my feet closer to her pelvis. At first I thought it was nothing, a chance motion, a fluke of how she was sitting. But then it became clear that she was not only running ice cubes up and down my swollen foot, but also using my other foot as if it were a personal massage tool, pressing it into the fabric of her crotch.

I did not move. I was so confused by this, so overwhelmed by what the day — the entire trip — had for me, I closed my eyes and pretended that it was not happening.

At length, her rubbing stopped. For a long time neither of us spoke.

"Does your foot feel better?" she asked.

I nodded, forgetting that she could not see me, see anything. Was it possible she hadn't known, hadn't realized what had just happened? Or was I in denial about it, unwilling to admit what had just gone on.

She waited.

"Yes," I said. "My ankle is fine now."

"Good," she replied, and left the room, gathering dishes as she went.

CHAPTER TWENTY-ONE

Each time I sat down with the pen and paper intending to write Marinne I found it harder and harder to have anything to say. In the end I resorted to sending her the address of the Kawasoba-sō, detailing the weather, how the humidity turned paper soft and made one's clothes cling to the skin and how one hid from the heat in the cool cypress groves or inside the house until late at night when it was — and only with a fan — possible to sleep. When I wrote how much I missed her, it was as much to convince myself that was true as to profess my feelings.

> *You don't know how much I miss you, how strange these past few weeks have been, how deeply I wish I could share this journey with you. If you could see what I've seen with your own eyes you would understand me. I can't seem to put much of it into words.*
>
> *And how is my father, by the way? I hate feeling like you're burdened with his care. Please give him my love. And write soon, I should be at this inn for some time, though for how long only the journey will tell.*

As I wrote how much I longed to hold her in my arms, to kiss her soft mouth, to hear her teasing me, I would stop and daydream about those eyes looking down at me from the cliffside, eyes feral and wild and untamed and ineffably beautiful, and I would remember how I'd sprained my ankle that day. The enigmatic, almost evil incineration of a cat I had seen.

By the time I had finished my letter and was ready to mail it, the sprain had eased enough that I could walk on it. Yet Komori-san still went on using me as her own massage tool. As much as part of me felt captive, another part did not want to embarrass her. It seemed too insignificant to risk offending her. I was a guest in her house and in a strange and foreign country after all, so distant from my life at home that it might have been the far side of the moon.

And how would I broach the subject, anyway? In Japan things are brought up delicately and yet there didn't seem to be any indirect way to put this.

In the end I decided to bring up the topic of loneliness. It seemed like perhaps I could hint to her some of my confusion without causing her to lose face or feel shame.

One evening, at dinner, I broached the topic. She had brought me rice with a pickled plum and a tender piece of fried river fish and a bowl of miso soup. Beside the fish were some vegetables pan-fried in a soy-based sauce. A cup with a cube of tofu, simmered, and topped with grated *daikon* radish. Each dish she placed in front of me with a never-erring accuracy that made it nearly impossible to believe she was blind. The fish on a plate in back. The miso soup at the right, the rice at the lower left, closest to the edge of the table, and don't forget the chopsticks, on a little rest, closest of all.

I took several bites and then had to put my chopsticks down.

"Komori-san," I said. "This food is so delicious and you have been so kind to me."

"It's nothing," she replied. "You are my guest. No need to flatter."

"I was curious about your life before I arrived."

"My life?"

"Did you ever feel lonely?"

She paused. "I miss my nephew."

"It was difficult for you when he left?"

"I was already blind," she murmured. "But when he went away, I knew it was the last time I would ever see him. And I do not mean see him. I knew. I was like a mother to him."

Instead of confronting her about what on earth she was doing with my foot, I reached across the small square table and patted her forearm. She flinched like a startled horse.

"I'm sorry," she said. "I didn't expect your hand."

"You and your nephew didn't get along?"

"When he was a boy we were very close," she said. "But when he became a teenager, he was interested in girls."

"There's nothing unusual about that." I remembered my own tormented adolescence, those years of longing, pent-up frustration. I knew that somehow, if I could only flee Watertown I would find someone who loved me.

"I'm not talking about teenage girls, classmates, girls his own age," Komori-san said. "I would have been happy with that sort of thing. But my nephew, he was fourteen when someone told me he'd been seen at a whiskey bar. A 'Snack Club' as they say. With women in their twenties and thirties sitting on his lap. He'd saved up birthday and New Year's money. To throw it away on … filth."

She reached for her miso soup and spilled it. Any thought I'd had of approaching the subject of her inappropriate massages was lost. I took the bowl of miso soup from her shaking hands and wiped the table with a steamed towel, now cold and clammy.

"I'm sorry," was all I could say.

"It was as if a light switch had gone on and nothing I did could tear him away. He was like a pet there of course, a cute little boy and they all teased him fondly. The mama-san even made him show her his homework before she'd let him in — she was running the next-closest thing to a cathouse, but she would make sure the boy had done his studies. I wanted to kill her for letting him in there at all."

She paused a while before continuing.

"He was an excellent student and barely had to study to get good grades. If he were shirking I might have had more leverage, I suppose. I could have done something. He would have gone to Tokyo University or Waseda, maybe. If not for … throwing it all away."

I tried to eat my rice but it stuck in my throat. I sipped soup, trying to imagine a young Kagoshima, what he must have looked like as a teenager.

"I didn't know he was bright," I said, realizing too late it might come across as offensive.

"Bright?" the old lady answered. "Nobody knew. Because by the time he finished high school that's all he did, hang around with those women. And he left for the city the moment he was done with school. Assured me that I'd never have to pay for anything. That he'd make his own way. But I knew what he was really saying."

"What was that?"

"You'll never own me." Komori-san paused. "He never wanted me to tell him what to do. Or what not to do."

Into a lengthening silence I said the obligatory, "I'm sorry." But I wasn't sure whom it was for. Her, for the suffering she must have gone through? Or me, for myself, for being so unmoored in such a faraway place that even things that were happening didn't seem real. Or for Kenji, whose path had led to such a grim and unexpected end.

"He went to women the way a moth incinerates itself in a flame."

I remembered the brothel in Panama, how comfortable Kagoshima had been there. Watching this old woman tremble as she remembered the boy who'd been a son to her, I realized my hands were shaking too. Part of me wanted to hold her, comfort her, tell her that it would all turn out okay. Another part of me knew that being involved would draw me deeper than I could handle. I was a stranger here, orbiting this place and observing it like a satellite. So I sat there at the square table, most of the food uneaten, my hands cupped around tea that eventually went cold, the two of us frozen in thoughts we couldn't share.

Eventually Komori-san excused herself and went into the kitchen. When I stood up, my knees were weak, and after sitting in my room for a few minutes I decided that I would turn in early. There was just enough light for a quick bath, which is customary in Japan: Bathing in the morning is almost unheard of, but bathing to be clean before getting into bed is the norm.

I stripped, put on my *yukata* and slippers and shuffled down to the baths. As I descended I could feel the air become heavy with the moisture of the river, the green, slippery moss on the narrow walls glistened, as if excited that I was there. A white egret picked its way along the gurgling eddies and then stopped, cocked its head, and thrust its beak like an arrow into the water, coming out with a struggling frog. It was both beautiful and chilling. Nature, its winners and losers bonded and inseparable.

I dropped my cotton robe and knelt by the hot pool of water to splash myself clean. When I was wet I eased into the steaming water until only my head was visible. I closed my eyes and felt the heat sucking all the stress away. I gave myself up to the power of the pool, let it sap me, let it take everything it needed from my body, the minerals and salts and sweats that it craved. I don't know how long I stayed motionless in the bath, but eventually I was watching the stars. The inn above me had only one small lantern lit; Komori-san did not need light so it made no difference to her.

As my eyes adjusted I could still make out the egret, just a white fog hovering above the black brook.

I was just about to get out of the water when I heard a rock fall from somewhere high above on the opposite side of the ravine.

I looked up.

Even though it was dark, I could see someone's face for a moment before it disappeared into the bushes. I heard footsteps running back up a path.

Her face.

The green-eyed beauty. It had to be her.

I walked back up to the inn, casting furtive looks at the opposite bank, hoping to see her still there.

Curiosity could mean anything.

When I pushed back the sliding panel and made my way down the hallway in the dark, I had to feel the wall for guidance. When I found my room, I took off my slippers and fumbled for the lamp, then decided to leave it off.

I crossed the soft tatami mats and slid open the paper privacy panel that covered the window glass. I could see lights across the ravine, nothing more. But I watched them for a long time, feeling dizzy, feeling almost as if I were watching the stars scamper across the sky and seeing their movements like a navigator would, understanding everything from the dark sky and its stars to the currents that tugged at the egret's feet.

I stood at the windowsill staring across the void: at the night-cloaked river and ravine; at those lights above the embankment where the girl lived; at the lamps that twinkled through the leaves like stars. A boy with a good arm might have thrown a rock across the river and shattered one of the windows, they were that close. Yet it seemed those stars were as far away as the ones strewn across the night above me. Or perhaps the gulf was just the horizon line between the earth and sky? Those lights were not part of the earthly world.

When I turned to get my futon bedding out of the closet and prepare for the night, my knees buckled and I fell on the tatami floor. My temples hurt as if I'd been hiking at high altitude, and it was difficult to breathe. I pulled myself up and then went to the wall, tossing out my bedding haphazardly before collapsing like a poisoned man into the crisp, cold cotton.

CHAPTER TWENTY-TWO

It may have seemed as distant as outer space in the dark of the previous night, but when I woke up the next morning, squinting against the beams of sunlight, I realized that visiting the other side of the ravine was just a simple matter of crossing a nearby bridge. Not that dilapidated one I'd noticed earlier, but a real one. A mile, two, three in one direction or the other would surely have a place where cars could cross to the other side. Somehow since arriving at Komori-san's, I'd felt trapped, marooned. But that morning, after a breakfast of salted salmon, raw egg in miso soup, rice, and some root vegetables in a sweet ginger sauce, I told Komori-san I intended to take a walk and get some fresh air. I would go exploring.

"Could I bring you anything?" I asked. "There must be a store somewhere nearby?"

"There's nothing," she said. "Nothing for miles."

"Well, it would be nice to see the landscape then."

An expression crossed her face that baffled me, as if I had vexed her, upset her in some way. She seemed poised to say something and then didn't, and as the silence grew longer and louder, I traded my indoor slippers for my outdoor shoes, then hurried past.

"I'll be back in a few hours," I said. "By lunchtime. *Ittekimasu*." The ubiquitous Japanese phrase for I'm leaving.

"*Itterasshai*," she replied, the complementary farewell.

As I went up the long, twisting driveway with its somber cypresses and moss, I looked at the building below me. I wanted to feel something, more kinship, something of that "no place like home" feeling that one gets. The simplest of cottages can churn the heart into butter if there's connection there, but I felt more like a zoo animal escaping the confines of a cage than someone leaving his home. The place looked even shabbier and more decrepit. The roof seemed barely able to keep out the rain.

When I reached the highway where I'd first been dropped off, I stopped to appreciate the beauty of the place I'd found, or that had found me. A series of terraced rice fields stretched as far as I could see above and below, hemmed in on either side by dark cypress groves interspersed with that magical yellow-green bamboo. Visible to the south was Sakurajima, its bulk flattened by haze, making it look like a grade school movie prop, something two dimensional stuck with glue in the sky. In the foreground lay the glass-flat pool of Kinkō Bay, I knew, but I was too far up in the highlands to see the water.

A small road wound along each side of the river; I could see a car wending its way up on one side, and a small white truck going down toward the bay on the other. The sun, just peeking over the eastern mountains, cast long shadows and thick yellow light on the rice fields, making them glow greener and brighter than seemed possible. This town on the surface seemed perfect and it was all too easy to imagine that nothing dark lay beneath the beauty.

But as I looked up the valley, I was surprised to see what I first thought was a high-rise apartment building in the distance: an oddly shaped tower several hundreds of feet high, made of concrete and scaffolding. It seemed as alien in this peaceful, pastoral landscape as if it were a spaceship from Mars.

Another was going up even farther away. I could just see it rising up above the treeline. Komori-san would tell me that night that these were the supports for an elevated highway that was underway. When completed it would connect the city of Kagoshima with the capital of the neighboring prefecture, Miyazaki, cutting what had been an all-day drive through pastures and tiny towns into a zip of under two hours. It was progress, yet something about these strange "creatures" filled me with a sense of foreboding. They were like Orson Welles' aliens, descending on a peaceful, quiet land. Invaders.

I turned toward where I knew the river had to be, and by walking a few minutes I reached a simple bridge with a low railing. Another kingfisher with a bright orange beak was perched there, shimmering and iridescent. It flew away as I approached. Down below I could see a egret in the shallows. The same one, perhaps, that I'd seen when I was bathing. The mist from the rushing water was like natural air conditioning, making the bridge cool and pleasant. I breathed in and out, in and out, as if I were readying myself for a deep dive.

Then I crossed the bridge.

As soon as I reached the other side I noticed the landscape was different. More lush, thick, overgrown. Vines of differing sorts made a web of veins over the ravine walls. Even the bridge was being overtaken by tendrils that were wrapping around the posts, creeping up from below, reaching out into the airy spaces for anything to cling to and strangle. I considered turning around more than once, yet the thought of seeing the girl again enchanted me, mesmerized me, kept me walking despite those voices that were telling me "no."

It was that moment when I could have gone back.

We are presented with choices in our lives that we never get again.

We go one way.

We go another.

The paths we choose shape and reshape us, and sometimes cause us or the people we love great, irreparable pain. If I could have taken back one single moment of my life, it would be this one. I would have paused there on the bridge, looked at the dark, shadowy tangle of veins, I would have heeded that premonition, and I would have turned around.

But we don't get choices to relive or redo or take over. We have them presented just once, and whatever bridges are burned can't be unburned. We move forward through time and if we're lucky we can circle back to a place, revisit it, but never have that wasted time again.

How much simpler life might be if we were just to heed those warnings that we hear inside our heads. If we had the wisdom to say no to something before it took us for a ride.

I knew that despite all our distance, despite that I'd seen and experienced things I didn't think Marinne would understand, I had not at any point broken her trust as far as our relationship was concerned. I hadn't done anything at the brothel. Despite all my best efforts in high school, I remained a virgin, and Marinne was too. We were still planning on sharing that moment together.

Yet, I crossed the bridge anyway. Then I went left, walking up two mossy tracks of ancient tar, cracked and displaced by creeping vines.

As I wound my way up the narrow road, I heard something I couldn't identify: a deep, baritone *thud-thud, thud-thud, thud-thud* sound, as regular as a heartbeat. *Thud-thud, thud-thud, thud-thud.* Giant's blood coursing through these vine-tendril veins. It was a few minutes of walking before I reached the studio and discovered what was making that sound.

Four giant mortars and pestles lined the road just downriver of the studio buildings. I saw them first, strange spoon-shaped things carved whole out of cypress logs. If you can picture a children's playground teeter-totter, you have some idea of what this structure looked like: beams balanced across a central fulcrum, each with a trough-like cavity for water cut out on the river side and a large, downward-facing pestle peg at the other, which fit into a depression in the ground. The largest one was upstream, the peg part the diameter of a basketball. The middle one was nearly that size, and the two downstream were about as wide as grapefruits. The vase-maker had diverted the water upstream into a bamboo channel, which emptied into each of the four logs' chambers. When the hollow was empty the log would rest in the hole. But when it was full, the weight of the water would lift the beam up into the air for a few moments as the trough spilled and emptied, and the pestle part would slam back down into the hole, pulverizing whatever chunks of raw clay were there inside. Only two of the four were operating, and they were off sync, making that distinctive, heartbeat-like *thump-thump*. I laughed at myself for feeling something as simple as a seesaw could have sounded so sinister.

Over time, the clay would be pulverized and rise to the top as a fine powder. The beauty of the system was that it put the river to work doing some of the hardest manual labor: turning the dry clay into dust, which would then be mixed with water and become what was used for the vases.

The strange heartbeat sound affected me like a drug. I felt dizzy, off balance, out of body but not in a way that made me uneasy. In fact, it was the opposite: I felt more comfortable as I stood there, more sure that this side of the river, not the other, was the destination

I'd searched for my whole life. I felt at ease and calm and in control.

I walked on a little farther, passing some small bamboo thickets and outbuildings. Sheds with mossy tiled roofs. A calico cat shot across the road, stopping once on the other side to stare at me, its eyes wide and startled. I froze and waited until it disappeared in the bushes.

I kept walking until, around a final bend, I came upon a long series of buildings, many of them topped with corrugated metal, some built of bricks and mud that I would realize were the kilns, all set in a stunning series of Japanese gardens that someone had meticulously cared for. The quiet road cut right through the property, with the house and sheds along the river and the kilns going up the mountain on the other side. Lush moss clung not only to stones, but to vessels that I assume were from the discard pile: each one different, sentry-like, an army of forest gnomes. The heartbeat of the mortars had grown fainter but I realized it was my own heartbeat that was throbbing now, for the girl I'd seen before was getting off her bicycle, and as she turned, her eyes looked into mine.

It was as if she'd pushed me into the kiln.

CHAPTER TWENTY-THREE

Unexpectedly, she smiled at me, long enough that I had to drop my eyes to the pavement.

"Hey, Foreigner!" she said. The word can have many subtle meanings ranging from the descriptive to the very derogatory, depending on how it is used. Here, it was a matter of description. "Foreigner," she called again. "What are you doing here?"

"Here?" I asked. "I'm visiting Japan."

She laughed. "Not here in Japan. Here in the road. Why do you come all this way?"

I realized I'd translated her word wrong. "What are you doing there?" would have been better.

"I'm ... ," My voice trailed off. "I'm out for a walk."

"You didn't come for a studio tour?"

"A tour?"

"That's what foreigners usually come for. Though we haven't had any in several years."

"You give tours?" I asked, astonished that such an easy, facile excuse to be there had been dropped into my hands. "I'd love one."

"Then you'll have to come back later," she said, crushing my hopes. "My father's out. I don't know when he'll return."

"I'm sorry for the intrusion then. I can come back."

She smiled. "Your Japanese is very good."

"So is your flattery, Miss Local-san."

She laughed, a short sound like a pebble tossed in a pond.

"So is your teasing," she answered. "Mister Foreigner-san."

"Now you're the one teasing."

"No," she said. "In a way, it's the truth: You can stay here as long as you want and you'll always be a foreigner."

"Even if I marry someone? Raise a family here?" I had begun walking toward her. With each step I felt that I might spook her, that she would startle like wildlife and disappear.

She tipped her head to one side and lifted a shoulder in the universal sign of a careless, half-hearted apology. A grade school girl caughteating a forbidden cookie. A teen caught out back trying a beer on the patio when nobody's looking. A woman, unafraid and unapologetic, who knows she's bewitched the man in front of her.

"Are you ever going to tell me your name? Or will I always have to call you Foreigner-san?"

"I'm Neil," I said.

"And I'm Miyū."

"Isn't that what cats do?" I said. "Meow?"

"Funny." Her nose wrinkled, as if she'd smelled something bad. "Miyū. Like 'me' and 'you.' "

"Nice. Can you draw me the kanji?" I asked. "The meaning of your name?"

We were standing together now. She drew the characters with a finger on her palm.

"Mi."

"Green? Like '*midori*.'"

"Impressive," she said. "Your Japanese is good."

"I don't know 'Yū.'"

"You don't know me?" she laughed.

"I meant the character. Yū. What is the meaning?"

"It's hard to explain. Everything? The universe?"

"It should mean eyes," I said. "Miss Green Eyes."

"Don't make fun of me."

"I'm not. Your eyes are beautiful. At the temple, right? You were praying. The image stayed with me."

Her face changed. Her smile faded and she pulled away.

"I don't know what you're talking about."

"I saw you at the temple that morning. I'm sure it was you."

"All Japanese look alike to foreigners. It could have been anyone."

"I'll remember your green eyes for the rest of my life. Don't say it wasn't you, I saw —"

She ran to the steps of the house.

"If you saw someone praying it wasn't me. I'm not religious even."

"Your identical twin, then? How could I forget?"

She pulled open the door. "My father will be back soon, I'm sure. So if you want a tour or want to purchase something, please ask him. It was nice meeting you. Goodbye."

She slid inside and shut the door behind her. I heard the latch click, a small sound, but it echoed in my ears. I imagined her inside the house, peering at me through a drawn shade and wishing for me to leave.

After a few minutes I walked a bit further up the road and looked at the giant step kiln. It was different from the one I'd seen the girl using a few nights ago to roast the hapless feline. This was a massive structure that extended from the road halfway up the mountain in a series of "steps," like a staircase. Each room of the kiln was large enough to park a small car, and beside the walls were piles upon piles of cypress planking. It was not in use, but it seemed to me like some sleeping dinosaur, as if the slightest motion might enrage it, set it writhing and hissing upon me.

I walked over to one of the small doors. It smelled of smoke and wood tar and something else, an animal that died within the walls. Bending down, I opened the rusty iron latch that held a door in the side of one wall, a small window, far too narrow to put anything through, and I peered in.

My eyes adjusted and I saw what looked like an army at the ready, waiting there inside the kiln. Row upon row upon row of vases were lined up, each placed within millimeters of one another, yet none touching. There were racks, the largest ones near the lowest part of the kiln, the smaller ones closest to the top.

I was so intent on peering inside the kiln that I didn't hear the footsteps behind me.

"Can I help you?" a gruff voice shouted. A strong hand grabbed my shoulder and spun me around. "Or are you trespassing?"

CHAPTER TWENTY-FOUR

"Can I help you?" he said again. The man I assumed was the girl's father had returned. He was a full head taller than I and built like a mason, with wide shoulders and huge forearms and almost no neck at all. He had a bandanna wrapped around his head like a pirate; a thin wisp of facial hair on his upper lip and chin completed the cliché.

What struck me most, though, was that his eyes, like his daughter's, were nearly as green.

"I'm sorry," I said. "I didn't mean to intrude. I was just looking around—"

"Putting your nose where it doesn't belong isn't 'just looking,'" he growled. "Why are you in Japan?"

Why was I in Japan? The answer could begin when I was a boy climbing to the top of the water tower and staring across to Boston and whatever lay beyond. Each step I'd taken had led me here. Each crossed bridge, each road, each bend and turn and twist of fate.

"Pottery," I answered. "I've always had an interest in ceramics, but when I saw your work in the hospital in Kagoshima, I couldn't resist trying to come here." It wasn't the entire truth, but it was entirely true.

He released my shoulder and then looked at my hands. His were rough and chapped and calloused. Mine were like a baby's bottom.

"You've never worked with clay."

"I'm not a potter, no. I did a little work on the wheel in high school." As soon as I'd said it I regretted saying anything. The white lie would turn black the moment I was set before a wheel. I'd walked past the high-school pottery room a few times, that was it.

"Just a little," I repeated. "Many years ago."

He squinted his eyes.

"What were you doing peeking inside the kiln?"

"They don't have step kilns like this in America."

"You know what it is then? Most of the visitors from the West don't even know what to call it. Your Japanese is good."

"Thank you," I replied. "It's not so good. I make many mistakes."

"But to know the word 'step kiln' in Japanese? I'm impressed." He walked back to the road. "Did you come for a tour?"

I thought I saw a flash of motion at one of the windows and wondered what the girl was thinking about the foreigner now talking with her father.

"Yes," I answered. "Seeing how the pots are made would be lovely."

He nodded. "Get in the car," he said. "The story begins quite far away from here."

And with that, he led me to his truck, opened the door, and I got in. It crossed my mind that he could be taking me anywhere, perhaps, and that if he were the evil sort of person, I'd end up like that cat's corpse I'd seen Miyū carrying to the glowing kiln. Nobody would know. If anyone missed me it would be Komori-san, but I'd told her nothing of where I was going and she would soon just assume that I'd gone off somewhere, disappearing as suddenly as I'd arrived. I could end here just as Kagoshima had ended in that dirty gully in Panama.

"Let's go," I said, and hopped in the passenger's seat.

CHAPTER TWENTY-FIVE

The vasemaker drove as if chased by police, never seeming to acknowledge that the edges of the road were lined with open culverts that would devour a tire or topple the little minivan down one of the many ravines or hurl it into a dense thicket of bamboo. I lost count of the number of times when he lurched to the left after nearly colliding head-on with an oncoming car. I kept my hand gripped around the door handle, my knuckles aching as I prayed we wouldn't have an accident.

We drove for ten minutes up the winding valley road, along the river that turned this way and that, each corner seeming to surprise the driver and require emergency navigation. The rice fields were like huge steps that led up the fertile valley to where the giant pillar I'd seen rose hundreds of feet into the sky. Some vast vestige of a long-ruined pyramid, an obelisk placed at the top.

From a distance, and even quite close, it looked like a massive rocket on a launching pad, the same kind of thing I'd expect to see at Cape Canaveral. A thin network of scaffolding wrapped around a long cylinder of concrete that was painted a bright, moon-rocket white, ringed here and there with black, as if marking the stages of a booster. About three-quarters of the way up was a platform that spread out like two wings on either side. Then it continued up, all the way to another winglike area at the very top, where it widened and stretched in either direction where the road would be. It was so tall that only vultures, soaring on the thermals, were above it. Circling on the updrafts, tiny as specks, the great birds looked like cinders being carried up in a fire's plume.

The tower turned out to be our destination. Close up, the structure seemed less like a launch pad than the reverse — as if something had crash-landed, plunging itself deep into the earth after hurtling down through the atmosphere at a speed that would have made it glow like a shooting star. Scaffolding was attached at odd angles, white and orange bars that from where we stood were as small as toothpicks. A lone set of rebar rungs ran up the side of one of the channels, just like that stairway in the furnace chimney that had so defined my childhood. The thousands of steps got smaller and smaller until they just looked like a dark line as they neared the top.

At the base of the massive construction project the earth had been bulldozed away and pushed into ugly hills that were covered with weeds or eroded into jagged gullies. Water pooled in ruts made by the machinery, and the area was cordoned off by a tall chain-link fence that sported signs reading, "Keep Out! Government Property! No Trespassing!"

The potter pulled the minivan close to the fence, parking parallel to it, and hopped out. He opened the back door and put on a pair of heavy gloves. Then he removed a pair of industrial-grade wire cutters. He turned and began snipping the links in the fence.

"What are you doing?" I asked.

"This is where the clay is." By now he had opened a hole large enough for a man to walk through. He put the cutters down and grabbed the fence, fighting to bend it back and hook it on itself so that it would stay open.

"This is the only place to get the clay?"

He nodded.

"For centuries my family has made our vessels with clay from this hillside, in veins that are found nowhere else in the region. A special kind of kaolin. Perhaps nowhere else in the world." He walked back to the van and threw the wire cutters in, then pulled out several five-gallon buckets.

"Get the spade," he said. "I'll tell you more while we work."

"Work? I thought this was a tour."

I had left Komori-san's house hoping to meet a pretty girl, and now I was embarking on what for all I knew was an imprisonable felony. Yet I grabbed the shovel, looked up and down the valley road (For what? Oncoming police? What would I have done?), and ducked through the hole in the fence, following the vasemaker.

By the time I caught up to him, he'd reached the shadow cast by the highway construction. He walked to the base of the gargantuan concrete shaft and spat on it. Then he unzipped his pants and urinated, the thin yellow liquid dripping down, darkening the white cement. The Japanese language does not have profanities as vulgar or contemptuous as Western ones.

"They had this entire valley to build the road," he said. "The idiots. Imbeciles. The entire valley. And they had to plant this here. In the only place that provided us our livelihood. And why?" He turned to me. "Give me the shovel. Can you hold that bucket?"

Yes, why? I wanted to ask, but didn't. Why?

With a practiced hand he began filling the pail. While much of the earth was a sand- and stone-filled loam, here and there were ridges of hard, gray clay. The untrained eye would not have perceived any difference. In a few seconds the potter was done.

"Take this to the van," he said.

Not wanting to disappoint the man or embarrass myself, I hefted the heavy bucket, letting the thin wire handle dig deep into my hands. I had to put it down several times. When I got to the chain-link fence, I bent the mesh back and hooked it, leaving a small opening for me to squeeze through. But as I bent to move the bucket through to the other side where the car was, the fence unhooked and snapped back into place with the speed of a snare, whipping me in the face with the razor-sharp, freshly cut metal. At first I didn't realize I'd been hurt and kept carrying the bucket, but by the time I reached the back of the truck I saw drops of blood splashing on the pavement. I reached up and touched my face; when I pulled it away it was as if I'd dipped it in crimson.

"I'm sorry," I called from outside the car. "I've cut myself."

The man rushed over and sucked in his breath.

"Are you all right?" he said. "You're lucky — one of those scratches is right near your eye." He dabbed at me with a rag. "Just hold that on the wounds for a moment. Give it some pressure. They don't look very deep."

"The mirror," I said, moving to the driver's side. "Let me see."

When I took the rag away, for a brief second the five lines seemed insignificant, just thin red striations across my face, as if I'd been scratched by a tiger's paw. One went across my forehead, another cut from my left temple down through the eyebrows and reappeared on my right cheek, another began at my left cheek, crossed my nostril, followed my upper lip and ended in the hollow of my jowl, one cut my upper and lower lip, and the last one, only an inch long, went across my chin.

I was about to say they were nothing, as they looked minor, when blood began to gush out of all of them at once, five razor cuts that had closed from the pressure of my hand. I pressed the rag again to my face. Blood seeped into my eyes and stung them. I blinked, knowing that the stickiness was the liquid's attempt to seal whatever fissure it had erupted from. My own blood was trying to blind me.

"Sit down," the potter said, opening the door of his vehicle. "Keep your legs down, head back."

"Do you have any water?" I asked. The helplessness that blindness, even temporary, would bring was too terrifying to think about. I just wanted to rinse the blood out of my eyes. I wanted to see.

The potter shook his head. "We will go to the house." He squeezed through the fence, collected his shovel and buckets, and then jumped in the car.

I stayed in the back seat, bumping around as he sped along the narrow country road. The potter said nothing, his lips pressed together, his shoulders tense. Twice I was hurled forward as he slammed on the brakes, whether to avoid a car collision or a gutter I wouldn't know. We had driven nearly all the way there when he screeched the tires again and brought the car skidding to a stop.

"Sorry!" he said, leaping out of the car. "Just have to collect a dead *tanuki*."

I lifted myself up and tried to watch as he removed the same shovel and five-gallon bucket, and proceeded to scoop up a dead animal that looked like a soggy raccoon. The process took all of two minutes. As the car again pulled forward, the stench of rotting carcass hit my nostrils, so strong that I felt bile in my throat as I tried to breathe. I opened the nearest window but that seemed to just push the odor around, whipping it up more, so I soon closed it again and sat there, a few feet away from the bucket that contained the corpse.

At some point there was so much blood that I had to keep my eyes shut. Pressing my eyelids together, unable to see, I was at the potter's mercy. The car seemed even more out of control. I felt as if I were hurtling through space, deeper and deeper, the sense of what I'd lost by leaving Boston finally reaching me. I had to write Marinne. It had been too long. Now I wanted to see her, watch her lips turn up into that smile I so loved.

In those moments of fear, she was the one I needed.

When we arrived at the studio, the potter leaped out of the car and, holding me by the shoulder, led me to the door. I heard it slide open.

"Mi-chan!" he called. "I need some help!"

"Coming, Father." There were footsteps, then silence.

"What is it, child? Stop staring at the foreigner. Get a bowl of water and a fresh cloth."

Still a pause.

"Now!" he commanded.

"Yes, Father."

He helped me take off my shoes and I could feel the soft, yielding tatami mats under my feet. He led me down a hall. I felt him guide me downward to the small heated table, and nearby I heard the sound of water.

"Here," the potter said. "Miyū will tend to your needs. I have to return to the clay field."

And he was gone. For the second time that day, I was alone with the girl.

Miyū took a long time getting what I assumed was just a simple pot of hot water ready. I waited, my hand still pressing the rag to my face. At some point I heard the faucet squeaking and the water stopped. Soft footsteps approached. I felt and heard her slide into the low *kotatsu* table next to me, and I waited, waited, waited for her to speak. She didn't.

When she put the rag to my face, the cloth nearly scalded me. I flinched.

"That hurt?" she asked.

"Yes," I answered.

"Good. I told you to stay away."

"I was helping your father."

"That's your definition of 'stay away'?"

My skin had adjusted to the heat of the compress. Now it felt good. She continued to press and wipe in silence.

"Is it true what your father said about the highway?" I asked.

She dipped the rag into the bowl of hot water again, rinsed it. I smelled something astringent. An alcohol or antiseptic. When she put the cloth on me this time, it stung.

"What did he say?" she asked.

I told her.

"Yes, that's it. Only did he tell you the part about the corruption trial? How the farmers there paid the highway commissioner to plot it right through and drive us under for good? Because we're artists? Because they resent our ... methods? But it doesn't matter anyway. Everything ends."

I could understand why some people might think incinerating dead animals was outside the norm. But had these people harmed anyone? Didn't they just make pottery? What was wrong with that?

"It will be okay," I said.

At the time, I meant it, with an optimism I would never have again. Miyū was not looking for invented comfort or a shoulder to cry on. She did not answer me, but dipped the cloth into the water again, wrung it dry, then placed it on my eyes to wipe them.

"Try now," she said. "Can you see anything?"

I let them relax and the lids separated. Light seared them as the irises adjusted, squeezing the dilated pupils shut. The room and Miyū came into focus.

"Thank you." I said.

She didn't look at me. How many hundreds of years of her family history were coming to an end as I sat there, still wiping blood off my face, just wondering if there would be a way to kiss her.

Neither of us spoke.

She seemed to already know where she was going, there was something otherworldly about her, her cold eyes staring at a place out there, out beyond the walls that enclosed us and beyond the cypress forests and bamboo groves.

I thought of her lips that seemed painted on porcelain. Lips that were open slightly, giving her face an expression of surprise.

I would never know everything that was going through her mind right there.

I knew only what was going through my own.

And I leaned across the table and I put two fingers under her chin and tipped her waiting mouth up and brought hers to mine.

For a moment I felt her shudder. Or was it a shiver? Then she pulled me to her. I brought my hand to her neck and ran my fingers through her jet-black hair. I felt her body soften and lean toward me, before she pulled away again and shook her head. We looked at each other. Her eyes seemed gentle now.

"Go," she said. "Before my father comes back."

"I need to see you again."

"Just go," she whispered. "Please. Some things aren't meant to be."

"But some things are."

"You can't be a part of this."

"I can learn how to throw clay if you'll teach me."

"You think this is just about pottery?"

"What else would this be about?"

She shook her head, her lips pressed together. "Just go."

CHAPTER TWENTY-SIX

Going back to Komori-san that evening was a relief. Something familiar. Why did Miyū let the kiss linger at all if she wasn't enjoying it? Why push me away if she was? I find it odd that even now, in the age of emails and texting and saying what can be said in seconds, rather than the letters I'd write to Marinne that took weeks to arrive, people still find it so impossible to say what matters, and into the vacuums of what we cannot say, we insert our own words, write our own reasons, insist that this is the truth. We can transmit whatever we want in milliseconds, we can place a map pin and zoom in on anywhere in the world, yet the contents of the human heart remain as unfathomable as when Romeo sought Juliet. Cleopatra's burning kingdom. No two hearts are the same. What woos one person scares another. No latitude or longitude chart will map the way to what lies within a person's soul or what sets a heart on fire.

I tried to stay on Komori-san's side of the river for most of the rest of August. Miyū had told me to forget her, and I pretended to busy myself with affairs at the onsen, helping in whatever way I could. I weeded the gardens, trimmed the grass, using a towel wrapped on my forehead to keep the sweat from running into my eyes. A wobbly wooden ladder with a rung missing gave me access to the roof, where I cleaned the gutters and removed detritus from the thatching.

The leaves on the walkways down to the baths I collected and put in a compost pile I'd begun in the back of the property. Inside too, I assisted in wiping down floors with a wet towel and polishing the wooden furniture. Dusting, a chore I have always hated, never seemed to end. Usually in the mornings I'd spend a few hours doing the things that Komori-san couldn't, scrubbing down the walls of the baths or sweeping away leaves, then we'd have lunch together, and I'd have the remainder of the afternoon free. Often I spent it trying to improve my Japanese, but sometimes I took walks around the neighborhood, and by dusk I'd be ready for a bath.

Not seeing Miyū again simmered inside me. She'd asked me to stay away, yet nothing made sense but seeing her again. Having her lips on mine. That moment when she'd softened: As if for a split second she'd let me in, forgotten that she needed the walls around her. I wanted that moment again more than I wanted anything else.

I had to see her. If only to know that I would stay away for good.

First, I had to have a bicycle. Komori-san had one that was manufactured before the war, with a leather seat with springs in it made of white cowhide and cracked whitewall tires. Most important, it had a basket. Though the cycle had flat tires and a loose chain and brakes that didn't work well, I didn't need anything fancy. I spent most of an afternoon doing what I could to repair it and then, after Komori-san had retired for the night, I would sneak out of the inn with my bicycle and head off for the clay fields. I also had with me a plastic bucket and a small trowel.

Parting the fence where the potter and I had cut it, I slipped into the worksite. At the somber base of the giant monolith towering above me, I filled the pail with as much clay as I could find. With one hand holding the handlebars of the bike, I wobbled and glided back down to the studio and to the series of sheds near the clay grinding machines. I emptied the bucket outside the door on a clean slab of rock, then took the empty pail and returned to the clayfield.

I did this for several hours, until my legs were shaking and my palms had blisters from holding the thin metal wire on the bucket and digging with the trowel. Exhausted, I parked the bike back in Komori-san's, and then snuck into my room. I slept deeply and dreamlessly.

Night after night after night, I did this. Sometimes, when I was too worn down I would stop and soak in the baths before returning inside, warmed and relaxed to the the point of dizziness.

One night, as I was gliding down the hill with a batch of freshly dug clay I was planning to deliver, I saw a car parked at the studio. The headlights were on, the engine rumbling, and I pulled the bike over to the curb and listened. The glare prevented me from seeing any faces, but I could make out several voices. Three or four people were standing in the shadows. One person was talking with a rough, uneducated accent, a thick dialect that was difficult for me to understand.

Another was Miyū; I would recognize her voice anywhere.

"No," I heard her say. "I can't. Not right now."

"That's too bad," I heard the rough voice say. "Because I didn't ask you."

There was the sound of a slap. Then laughter.

I tore down the rest of the hill and leaped off as I reached the car, letting the bike clatter to the pavement.

"Leave her alone!" I yelled, reaching into the bucket and slopping the men with thick, wet mud.

"What the — ?"

"Get out of here!" I said, pushing the largest of them against the car. He had a thick, square face with pockmarked skin, a head that looked like a craps die on a pair of shoulders. No neck. He stood there, eyes wide open with surprise. Then he pushed back, a blow that sent me tumbling into the bushes. He wiped at the clay on his clothes and then turned back to Miyū.

"Your foreigner ruined a fucking expensive suit," he hissed at her. "I'll add that to your tab, whore."

He and the other two goons got into the mud-splattered Toyota Crown. I heard a chirp of the wheels spinning and the car headed back toward town.

"Are you okay?" I asked.

Miyū glared at me. "Just stay away from us. Can't you? We don't want your help. We don't want your clay. I don't want to see your stupid foreigner face looking at me." She broke into a sob and ran to the house. I heard the door open, close, lock.

I picked up the bucket and got back on the bike. One tire squeaked with each revolution as I rode back across the bridge to the inn. A long soak in the onsen bath did nothing to refresh me. But if Miyū'd expected that night would make me want to leave, it was the opposite. Now more than ever I had to know what she was doing, discover what was going on.

Like a ghoul in the night, I kept delivering clay. Every so often, I would take a break from digging and bike around through the darkness. I would take this road or that one, following it up or down the valley, rarely knowing where I was. My latitude and longitude were established by whether I'd gone down the valley toward town or up the other way, where the construction was, and to the mountains beyond. I could either be on the potter's or Komori-san's side of the river. Beyond that, I didn't care about my location.

If I happened to be really lucky and found a roadkill, I would scrape it up with the trusty trowel and place it in the basket, then bring it to the studio, putting it on the same slab where I put the clay.

Several weeks went by like this. And then one afternoon, as I was raking the Komori-san's driveway to remove the fallen cypress needles, I looked up and saw the potter standing there.

"How serious are you about learning the art of clay?" he asked.

CHAPTER TWENTY-SEVEN

Thus it was that I found myself again walking up the hill, hearing the heartbeat-like *thump-thump* of the river pestles growing louder, smelling the odd mix of fragrant cypress wood, glaze, and a hint of burning flesh. This time, I was the father's apprentice. Miyu came and glared at me, waiting until her dad went to get something inside the house before she spoke.

"You can't be here," she said. "I told you to leave."

"Right," I said. "I understand. Everyone's been telling me that. That I don't know what I'm getting into. That this is strange. That those people are this, that these other people are that. I've been pushed that way or this way. And I don't care what you think is right for me." I shrugged. "I just don't care. I'd like to learn more about clay and I find the process fascinating. And … ."

She waited. My eyes felt like they were burning, like I was too close to the fire, but I held her gaze. This time, she was the one to look away.

"And?" she said.

"And I find you fascinating, too."

Her head turned a little and her eyebrows came together. Not angry. She looked scared.

"I'm the last person you want to be falling for."

"Don't say that."

She looked out, away, into the forest as if somewhere deep inside the bamboo was the answer she needed. A Japanese nightingale cooed. Leaves rustled in the wind.

"You're not interested in pottery. I know why you're here. You're just using my father to get to me."

"I know why you think that," I said. "But you're wrong." I told her the story of Kenji on the ship, of the vase I'd seen in Kagoshima hospital, of how it had affected me. I told her of the strange coincidences. How everything in my life seemed to lead me here.

She was about to say something when her father called to us.

"Neil-san, let me show you how to prepare wood for the kiln."

I followed Miyū to where the potter was standing, the heat from the kiln blurring the air around him, giving him a halo. It felt as if I were standing under the exhaust from a rocket ship. Sweat was already beading on my forehead and I could feel the drenched cloth beneath my armpits.

"I'd love to learn anything you two care to teach me."

The father nodded, but Miyū looked at me, her lips pressed thin. She shook her head: Don't.

I carried wood for the kiln the entire afternoon. Miyū would load me up like a mule and I would trundle off, trying to avoid treacherous bamboo roots and the slippery moss-covered stones. We started close to the kiln, taking loads from what seemed like an inexhaustible supply of planks but which vanished after only an hour. I learned that was the staging area. So we focused on re-filling that, taking as much as we could from a spot higher up on the hillside. From there, if I could look away from Miyū long enough, I had a good view of the valley with its yellow-green bamboo groves, its winding roads, the series of low arches that bridged the stream cutting through the middle of it all. The steps of the rice fields widened as they neared the sea. Far off in the distance I could see the Sakurajima volcano.

It made no sense that this strange, alien landscape with its bamboo and cypress trees would feel as comfortable as the suburbs of Water-town with its leafy oaks and towering elms. I should have missed my father and Marinne, dear sweet Marinne, who I knew was waiting for me. I hadn't received a single letter from her yet, and had written her just twice since I'd left the hospital.

I felt peaceful and calm and it amazed me to have found such interesting people and to have a task to accomplish, something to do that was useful. With Komori-san, though I appreciated her kindness and wanted to help her, I never felt at home. Only in those luxurious baths did I feel relaxed, with the hot, sulfurous water pressing in all around me and the cool mists of the river muses rushing past.

That was a meditation.

This was meditation in its own way.

"It's lovely here," I whispered to Miyū, then looked right at her eyes. "The view."

"It's so-so," she said. "If you've been here all your life, you see it for the boa constrictor that it is."

"Boa constrictor?" I said. "That's an interesting analogy." I wanted her to explain, to open up, to give me more, but she sidestepped my invitation and brought us back to the task.

"Can you carry any more wood? A little?"

"I think so."

She placed a few more boards in my arms.

"There."

We started down the steep path. She had an armload of wood too, but smaller, and as we descended she called out to warn me of places where I might lose my footing. "There's a rock here," or "Careful. It's tricky footing here."

We worked together for several hours, long enough to be comfortable and relaxed despite the heat. There were even times when I'd catch her looking at me, always flicking her eyes away as if I'd burn her. She even laughed, a soft, musical gurgle, a chimera more songbird than human. Her footsteps were feather-light along the path, yet her stride was long, as if we were traversing a lunar landscape at partial gravity. At some point she stopped near the kiln and coaxed her father and me to share a break for tea.

We stayed at the side of the step kiln, feeding in the cypress planks and sharing green tea in little cups. Hot tea, but it seemed cool compared with the furnace when the door was opened. We chatted about the weather and I even caught Miyū smiling at me. Twice.

Carrying the wood was exhausting, but what struck me was that I'd traveled to the opposite side of the world to discover that I was home.

We finished our tea and got back to work. The sun started to set. As it grew dark the scent of cedar seemed to get stronger, the air heavier, as if we were in some alternative gravity or atmosphere.

Then it happened: All the details in my head like a photograph. Miyū had loaded me up with wood and we had just begun to descend. There was one treacherous spot on the trail, a place where with my arms full of boards I couldn't see my footing. The girl was right behind me, close on my heels, crowding me almost. I was feeling for my step when my foot hit something. A root, a branch, something was there catching my toe as I tried to move forward, and then I lost my balance and fell.

I toppled, sending the planks scattering around me. There was a strange electrical zing as I landed on the ground, one leg underneath me, the boards bouncing off my solar plexus. Some lay on top of me, some slid all the way down the hill like long skis that have left their fallen rider. Then a sharp, gut-wrenching pang made me call out, and the agony hit me in a tidal wave. I writhed, screamed, tried to get my hands to my ankle where the pain was. That same damn ankle, it had gone out again, this time far worse than in the river. Rough bark and splinters dug into my skin. The swelling in my leg was so intense I felt my heartbeat quicken, and a few seconds after that, Miyū's face faded; I saw it framed by blue sky and shimmery green bamboo right before I passed out.

CHAPTER TWENTY-EIGHT

For the second time I found myself injured and in the potter's house, in that same room where Miyū and I had kissed. I lay there, understanding the sounds of her feet on the tatami and the *woosh-slosh, woosh-slosh* of a teapot being swirled with boiling water in the preparation of green tea. The smell of the house, the old dusty beams, the grassy tatami, the scent of Miyū as she knelt close and adjusted the bags of ice that were wrapped around my foot; it was all familiar, an awkward déjà vu.

"Are you okay?" she said, when my eyes had focused and I'd attempted a smile.

"I've been better. How did I get here?"

"We carried you. My father left the kiln, came running. Perhaps the entire firing has gone bad."

"I didn't ask you to call him."

"You were passed out," she said. "What were we supposed to do?"

"Not my finest moment."

"You hurt yourself a lot when you're around me."

"I haven't learned to stay away, maybe?"

"You will learn." Her tone made it sound as if no one could learn to stay. I shifted, pulled myself up and then winced.

"Don't say that," I said. "What's not to like about you? Or about being here?"

The Japanese are masters at avoiding what doesn't need to be said. To mention anything about the kiss seemed impossible, yet it was all I could think about. How her lips had tasted, how soft they'd been, how she'd shivered, pulled me to her like a wave on the shore that sucks a piece of driftwood deep before spitting it out on the sand. I had held her the last time she'd cared for me, and now we were both pretending that it hadn't happened at all.

She looked at me for a long time without speaking and then nodded, as if accepting a challenge. She walked (bounced? floated?) to the other room and returned in a moment with a stunning lacquerware bowl. It was red and black and had an intricate gold leaf design.

"Looks beautiful, right?" she said. "Now pick it up. Use it. Pretend you're having miso soup."

I lifted the feather-light bowl and brought it to my lips, sipped imaginary soup, and returned it to the table. It was as airy as an egg shell.

She placed her hand on the bowl and in one quick motion pulverized it under her palm. Nothing was left. Just a few shards and a bit of dust.

"Rotten," she said. "Mold."

"So?"

"Beautiful things can be rotten inside."

"You're saying you're ... rotten?"

She got a strange expression on her face and I — perhaps becoming a bit more Japanese — decided that I would not ask her to define that any further.

"If you care about someone, anything is possible," I said.

"You're so naive," she replied. Then she leaned in and kissed me. On the mouth. A long, moist kiss that took me by surprise. As if I were on some kind of glacier that had just shifted, unbalancing me. My heart beat faster than a hummingbird's wings. A taste of fire.

"Miyū," I said as she pulled away. "You're all I'm thinking about. You're all I want. I love you."

"Hah. That's your little man down there talking."

"I loved you from the moment I saw you at that temple."

Her lips tightened.

"You didn't see me at the temple, because I wasn't there."

"It was you."

She said nothing.

"Fine," I said. "It wasn't you. I made a mistake."

Only then did she lean toward me another time. Her lips sought mine, our tongues traced contours across the galaxies of each other's mouths. She tipped her head back and I kissed her neck, ran my tongue down her milky skin. Pulling me against her, she sighed.

"Don't stop," she whispered.

I tasted her ears, her lips, ran my mouth along her jawline. My ankle should have been hurting, but I couldn't think of anything else but this girl in my arms. She ran her fingers through my hair, sometimes holding me in place and whispering "There!" before I moved on. I moved my hands to her breasts, our thighs entwined. Anything more intimate and we'd have needed to remove clothes.

Later, she lay next to me, shaking. Two stars had collided. We were two lovers looking into the fire, something so intense, so powerful, nothing could have pulled me away.

I realized she was crying.

"What?" I asked. "Are you okay?"

She shook her head. "You wouldn't understand."

"Try me. Maybe I can make you smile."

"I don't need to smile," she said. "If there's nothing to smile about."

"Lighten up."

"Japanese don't need to smile either. They need to think. They need to wake up. They need something that will shake them to their core. Everyone just goes around with their head in the sand, a whole country of ostriches, pretending things aren't happening around them."

"Plenty of ostriches where I'm from, too."

She looked at me. "In America? So it's just a human flaw then. Same everywhere?"

"Maybe more so."

She looked at me. "Want to know something ironic? I grew up longing for this. For exactly this. For something that would end the business and free me to go to Tokyo or be anywhere else than here."

"You can't be serious. I love it here."

"You 'love' it here. Beautiful. You've been here all of a few weeks and yet you feel like you're an expert in everything? Like you know it, what, as well as you know your home?"

"I didn't mean it like that," I answered. "But sometimes you have to be from outside to see how pretty something is. Maybe you take it for granted."

"You think it's pretty. It's all those things you say now. And it was, for hundreds of years. And now they're burying this beneath a highway. All those rice fields? They'll be shaded by the overpass. What happens to rice fields with no sun? The rice doesn't grow. The fields turn to mud." She almost spat the words. "It's not even for the town, it's for people to fly over the town. Not to have to think about us at all." She shook her head. "The beauty here is already long in the past. Everything you see, the river, the studio, the baths, the clay, the people … everything you see is already like milk that's soured. We're just marking time until it curdles."

"I don't believe you."

"Because you're American. Americans are stupid that way."

"Americans believe in hope."

Miyū stared at me. "You don't even know what you're saying. You have no idea."

As she said that I felt a tremor, the earth shifting, settling, moving underneath us. One of the thousand minor earthquakes that hit the island every year. Just enough to have vertigo.

"Was that an earthquake?" I asked.

She shook her head.

"I felt it. Dizziness."

"You got dizzy because you were about to lose an argument," she said. "Anyway, can't we stop talking? You always talk too much."

"I'll stop talking." And I took my fingers and lifted her chin as I'd done before until her lips were level with mine. I leaned in and kissed her again, and she pressed against me.

Later, I limped back to Komori-san's.

CHAPTER TWENTY-NINE

Miyū met me several days later at the bridge. My ankle was still tender, but healed enough that I could put weight on it. An overcast day, with a sky of cloud puffs that hung in the conifers like torn cotton. Mist collected on the branches over the river. To someone else it might have seemed gloomy but I would have thought anything was beautiful if Miyū were at my side. She looked troubled, though, and after a short greeting we found ourselves silently watching the water flowing beneath the river. I asked her what was wrong.

"The kiln failed. All the pots were ruined."

"Because of me."

She just stared down into the currents and let silence tell me everything I needed to know.

Later, feeling responsible, I helped them unload the still-warm vases. We moved in silence, the vasemaker examining each vessel, sometimes muttering under his breath, before taking it across to the river and dashing it to pieces on the wet stones. Underfired, the glazes hadn't melted as they should have and instead of smooth, glassy surfaces the vessels came out looking as if they'd been exposed to a pox: blistered bumps that flaked into razor-sharp edges the moment they were touched. Brown, none of the green iridescence that made them unique

Not a single piece was saved.

I would learn later that the firing represented half of their annual income. At the time, the only hint I had was that the potter himself took the afternoon off. I saw him down at the river bathing for an hour, floating a square wooden cup around in the steaming hot water as a baby would with a rubber duck. A few *kabosu* citrus fruits bobbed around him. When he came back up to the house he was red-faced and laughing to himself, and when he stumbled he put his hand through one of the paper-thin sliding walls. Miyū's lips were tight as she came back from putting her father to sleep.

It was still evening. Shafts of sunlight traced their way across the tatami floor.

"If I hadn't slipped—" I started to say.

"But you did," Miyū said, her voice far off, distant. "You did. We can't change what happened. The past is written and shapes our future. So each step we make right now matters."

"You're not making me feel better," I said.

"I'm not trying to."

I looked at her face to confirm what I knew already: She wasn't joking.Why should she be expected to make me feel better? Whether or not my intention had been to help, I'd been the cause of the kiln failure.

"Just because something isn't your fault doesn't mean you're not to blame," she went on.

"How could I have known I would fall?" I replied.

"It doesn't matter that you knew or didn't. You fell. It happened. And now," she paused. "This will be a very difficult year for us."

"Is there anything I can do? To make things better?"

"Blow up the bridge with me," she said. "That would help. Teach the developers and civil engineers a lesson."

I laughed. "Blow up the bridge? What would that do?"

"So that's a no?" She looked at me. "Come on. You wouldn't love to watch it fall? Topple like a tree into the rice field mud."

"It might hurt someone," I replied.

She looked at me. "That would be the whole point."

I must have looked shocked, because she laughed.

"I'm joking," she said.

"Doesn't feel like it," I said.

"So kiss me again," she answered. "Kiss me until I forget all about it. You're good for that. My father has his cocktails, I've got your kisses."

She traced her tongue across my neck and cheekbone, breathed heat into my ear. Our lips met. Just as I was about to kiss her neck, we heard the bedroom door slide open. She sprang away, off me and darted into the kitchen. I stayed at the table, pretending to be absorbed in the room decor as the potter kicked off his shoes, weaved across the tatami, and entered the living room.

He leaned toward me, his breath reeking of alcohol. "You're feeling better?"

I nodded. "It was my fault the kiln didn't fire properly." I bowed my head, the only way I knew to show my shame.

He stared at me, his face inscrutable.

"Bad things happen sometimes. If we cannot stop the bridge," the potter said, "it doesn't matter whether this kiln load or the one after that or the one after that will be the last. If something is to end, it can end sooner or it can end later, but it still ends. The 'when' is less important. It can end now, perhaps. Or next time. Or next year. But it ends." He slammed his hand down on the table. "Everything ends."

I felt an anger, a frustration, a sadness well up inside me that this curious, unique, hardworking family had been beset by such misfortune. I was angry at them, too, for accepting it, for not fighting harder. There was almost a sense that it was more important to fail, somehow, than to win.

"There has to be a way to work things out," I said. "Where there's a will, there's a way."

I heard Miyū scoff from somewhere in the kitchen. She came out and shook her head. "There's a difference between optimism and just being stupid."

The potter looked at me. His face was tired, the skin seemed stretched tighter across his cheekbones. I realized that he had lost some weight since I'd met him a few weeks before. A stripe of soot smudged his shiny forehead and I wanted to reach up and wipe it away, as I would do for my own father when he would come out of the tunnels so many years ago. A lump rose in my throat as I thought about him. It wasn't just that I wanted to stay in Japan, but a part of me knew I had abandoned him. Now here too, I was poised to lose another father.

A few days later the potter invited me to eat dinner with them and I used their telephone to let Komori-san know I would not be coming back until late.

"You won't need to prepare my dinner. But thank you for everything."

There was a long pause on the phone when I told her I was over across the river at the pottery studio.

"You shouldn't be there," she said. "They are dangerous people."

"They've been very kind to me."

"I will leave the light on. Please come back as soon as possible."

I hung up the phone, tired of this intrigue. My instincts told me that this beautiful girl and her father were goodhearted and believed in something they felt was important. It was Komori-san who had to be mistaken.

Americans ask questions when they shouldn't: "Why would Komori-san be afraid of you?" I said to the father, my fingers still on the black handset in the cradle.

Japanese avoid answering, even when they should: The daughter and father exchanged a glance and looked at me. The moment lengthened, stretched like Silly Putty going into a black hole, longer and longer and longer until I realized that they had no intention of answering. Either they didn't know what I was talking about, or my question was stupid, or perhaps they knew exactly why Komori-san would say that and didn't want to bring out dirty laundry that they wanted kept to themselves.

"Dinner's ready," said Miyū. "Let's sit down before the miso soup overheats."

"I still need to wash my hands," said the vasemaker, getting up. His knees cracked and he braced himself on the door for a moment before walking into the bathroom. He returned a few minutes later.

The meal was simple: miso soup, some pickles, a few small pieces of chicken Miyū had fried with garlic, and rice with golden millet grains in it. We ate in silence. Something shared and inescapable was between the father and daughter, a telepathy, a communication without need for words. When the food was finished, the potter stood up and went to a small cabinet in the kitchen under the sink. It was where my father always kept the trash, but here, instead of a bin, was a small collection of alcohol bottles.

"Do you drink?" the man said.

"Father, you could take it easy tonight."

The man ignored his daughter and looked at me. "Yes?"

"Sure," I said.

He took out three glasses and put two cubes of ice in each glass.

"Strong or sweet?"

"Strong," I said.

"You don't have to drink if you don't want to," Miyū said. She leaned close to me and whispered: "Sip me instead."

Her father stood in the semi-darkness of the kitchen, mixing the drinks. I heard ice fall into a shaker and the sound of a hard stir. When he returned, the drink he brought glowed green, the color of antifreeze. It could have been embalming fluid for all I knew. I remembered Komori-san's caution as I lifted the glass to my lips: These people were dangerous. If they were using roadkill in their glazes to create certain shades of color, who was to say they wouldn't use a nice, fresh, *gaijin* cadaver as well?

Why was I suspicious of these people? The first sip was all I needed to know that it was just a cocktail, a delicious one at that, though strong.

"You should live with us," the vasemaker said.

"Father, you're drunk."

"Why live with that old bat across the way? We have room, it makes sense if he's planning to learn the trade."

In reply, Miyū got up and left. A few seconds later a door slammed.

Her father poured me another drink and we talked. About my Boston life a bit. About my trip to Japan. About the vases and the steps that led me here. We talked and drank, and when the glass was empty he mixed another one. And another one after that.

Later, tipsy, I spilled out of the house and into the warm mouth of Japanese night. Cicadas thrummed their ecstatic throes; crickets sang love poems into the darkness; the river was its own song. I had kissed the most beautiful girl on the planet and even better yet, she had kissed me. That invitation to "sip her" tormented me. Love starts with being teased.

I was standing at the river when I saw the headlights of a car racing up the road. I stood in the shadows waiting for it to pass and realized it was the shiny Toyota Crown. Trotting after it back up the road, I saw it pull in at the potter's house. Moments later, Miyū appeared. The door opened and she got in. Then the car drove off, not back toward town but further into the countryside, up toward the construction site and the dark, foreboding woods.

I reached the bridge and took forever to cross. Each step sent pangs shooting through me. I no longer wanted anything to do with Komori-san and her strange foot fetish and her blindness and her decaying onsen. I wanted to be in the potter's studio, with its heartbeat of the clay pestles and the heat of the kilns and stealing love in the shadows from the gorgeous green-eyed beauty who had so indelibly branded me.

CHAPTER THIRTY

The next morning, I packed my belongings into the tired suitcase, the one with Marinne's underwear still buried in the bottom somewhere. I hadn't thought about the contents in months. Having the panties seemed cheap now, and I was glad Komori-san was blind so she wouldn't find me with them. Wondering how Miyū would react. I located them, wrapped them in a piece of newspaper, and dropped them into the trash. The late-September air was cool and refreshing, the sky overcast.

"Don't go," Komori-san said, interrupting my packing. "There's so much good you could do here." She reached out into the air, as if hoping to hold my arm, but I stepped back and she missed.

"I've enjoyed your hospitality," I replied. "But I need to move on."

Whether it worked out or not, I needed to follow the vasemaker's offer, despite Miyū's objections. I had to be close to her.

"You'll be sorry." Komori-san said, her eyes straining to see me.

"You're an old woman," I replied, in what was the first bridge I would burn. "Blind in far more ways than just your eyes." It was a cruel thing to say to someone who had let me stay under her roof for several months, and she inhaled as if I had slapped her.

"Are you so foolish?" she said, her voice collapsing in on itself as if the weight of the anger was too much to bear. It became grief, then silence. I picked up my few remaining items, grabbed the suit-case in my hands, and without even thanking her, I slid open the screen and went outside.

That choice, that moment when I left Komori-san was the first actual decision I'd made for myself since embarking on the voyage from Boston. Yes, it had been my decision to go, despite my father's objections and the love I felt for Marinne. Everything from the moment I boarded the *Pandora* to now had been, in some way, buffeting me around like I was a leaf in a windstorm. This was my own decision and though I wasn't proud of the way it ended with Komori-san, I felt good as I climbed the steep driveway up to the road, looking back just once at the aged bath-house and inn. It seemed smaller now, more tottery than ever before. Despite all the hours spent cleaning it, raking, weeding, it was hard not to see how decrepit the building was. The weathered structure with its mossy tiles looked as if it might blow over in a gust of wind. The flower beds I had spent so much time tending were already covered with tendrils of wisteria that seemed to have sprouted overnight. Up on the road, even the river where I'd spent so much time soaking and relaxing seemed smaller, less magical.

It was just a river now.

A light rain was falling as I walked toward the rows of cypresses that lined the other bank of the ravine, but I breathed in, relishing the moisture in the air. In the mist, the rice fields seemed even more vibrant than before, golden and pregnant with the season's harvest. Any day now, farmers would cut the sheaves. Puffs of wind played with them, rippling the grain in what I saw to be the "amber waves" that I'd learned in grade school. Ironic that it would be here in Japan that I would understand that bit of American patriotism.

I felt peaceful, calm, with a kind of slow, measured euphoria lapping in my blood like gentle ripples on a pond's edge. It was all a dream. This pastoral countryside and its quiet beauty. The simple needs of a rural life. I was oddly out of body, unconcerned about the future and carefree: If not with Miyū, I could settle down with some-one else here, become a potter in my own right. If not famous, then locally well-known.

There were two obstacles to this daydream vision. One was that giant spire that rose up from the earth like some sci-fi hypodermic r.eedle. The highway and everything it represented was poised to rip this mountain village apart.

The other was a letter to arrive, at Komori-san's, which I would not get for another ten days. A letter that Komori-san might have ripped up or burned, but instead chose to hold onto and deliver to me in person.

I saw her late one afternoon as I was walking down the path to the *kara-usu* shed, their constant *thud-thud, thud-thud* marking time as clearly as a clock. I'd adjusted to my new life at the studio and fallen into its routine. I was not allowed to make anything, but they were showing me skills for tending the clay and maintaining the kilns, giving me tasks that made me impatient to learn to throw vessels, but that I understood these were vital building blocks in the foundation of the craft. Miyū had avoided me for the most part, but I resolved to bide my time.

A stooped-over woman was coming up the road, pushing a baby stroller from the 1940s. Possibly one that had held Kagoshima in it. Big wheels with spokes like a bicycle's. Springs below the carriage. Solid, gun-metal gray leather stretched over the chrome frame.

Komori-san used the carriage to ascertain where she was in the road, forgoing the typical blind person's cane. She hooked one side of the wheels on the curb and then followed the pavement, letting the edge guide her It was a simple U-shape journey from her house, over the bridge, to the potter's. What took me ten minutes to walk might at her pace have taken her an hour.

I approached her.

"Komori-san," I said. "What are you doing here?"

"Neil, I have a letter. The mailman told me it was for the foreigner."

I could tell just from a glance at the envelope that it was from Marinne, her handwriting on a plain white envelope. I heard a noise and Miyū appeared behind me. She looked at me, her expression blank.

Komori-san waited. I tore open the paper and read the note inside.

Dearest Neil,
I hope this letter reaches you. I don't
even know how to say this, I feel empty,

> *worthless, saying it in a letter when I should be there to hold you, comfort you, ease the pain. Your dear father passed away yesterday. It was an accident, at least that's what the doctors are saying. To tell the truth I don't understand half of what they say, the medical words, the jargon. It's all above me. Something about his medications, mixing the wrong ones, too much of a sedative. But he's in a better place: I'm sure we both know how much he suffered.*
>
> *I feel numb, just numb. I know we're not married, not yet, but he was my father too ... as important to me as my own Papa was. There will be a service. I cannot believe you can't be here to say goodbye.*
>
> *And perhaps I shouldn't ask you this but have you decided when you'll be returning? It seems by now you must know. Know something at least. I haven't heard from you in so long and it's times like these that I need you the most. Not the idea of you, but you, the real person to hold and care for.*
>
> *I could make you soup. I could hold your hand. I know I could comfort you. Being apart makes me feel so lost and helpless ... .*

Miyū sensed that something was wrong and withdrew to the house. I felt my lower lip tremble and had to force myself to take long, measured breaths. For all our frustrations and differences, he was my father, a goodhearted man who had done nothing to deserve the lot that life had thrown at him. I had no idea that in getting on that boat I was saying my final goodbye. On the page in my hand, I saw the ink smudged in a large watery circle where a tear had dropped onto it, just above the signature. I imagined Marinne pausing, the tear dropping onto the still fresh ink. Her using her sleeve to blot it away.

I was destroying her.

But I was also gone. Helpless. Beyond the moon, spinning off past comets and into the deepest space. No tossed line could reach me not even the death of my father would make me return.

"I wanted to make sure you got the letter," Komori-san said. Then she wrangled the pram around so that it faced the other direction and headed back the way she had come.

When I went inside, Miyū was staring at me.

"Are you okay?" she asked.

"My father passed away," I whispered. "But I'm fine."

"I'm sorry, will you go back for the funeral?"

"He died months ago." I felt dizzy, needed air. "Where's a good place to take a walk? Are there any trails nearby?"

"There's one," the girl said, her green eyes piercing the shadows. "If you go up past the kiln."

"Where I fell?"

"Same place. Just keep going. It leads up to the top of a peak that gives you a good view of the valley."

I nodded.

"I'm sorry about your father," she said, as I left the room.

Chapter Thirty-One

I picked my way up the same place where I'd had that accident, I kept looking for the spot where I'd tripped, for the rock or root that had caught my foot, thinking about my father's death and about how the girl had gotten into the Toyota with those goons, then not thinking about anything at all. I took my time and chose my footing with care. The heat of late summer had dried out the soil and the path wasn't slippery now. Just like Miyū said, beyond the clearing where we'd gotten the wood the path continued — a rough, unmaintained track that cut through some scrub and a few bamboo stands before turning and rising to the top of the bluff.

It was not an imposing hill, yet everything seemed prettier to me somehow. Even the few large spiderwebs that crossed the path seemed like crafted works of art. I ducked under them to keep from disturbing the glittering threaded diadems, each web's creator hiding in the center, her work done, the trap laid. Then the path opened up to a little clearing that went right to the edge of a ravine, giving a lovely view of the village below, a vista every bit as head-clearing as I'd hoped it would be. I felt again that strange sensation of time passing faster, of my own time on the earth collapsing in on itself, of everything happening too fast.

From the little clearing at the summit, I could see the entire valley, how it stretched out below me southward, a patchwork quilt of rice fields and their greens and ambers and browns, now muted by the dusk. Lights were coming on in the valley the way stars appear in the sky.

Here and there a road cut through the quilt; the river lay like a silver ribbon across the fabric. The occasional tiled-roof houses stood like sentinel outposts, all but abandoned. The landscape was changing from green to rusts, browns, golds. I could see rows of tea hedges visible even from far away, always the color of dark moss. The peak I was standing on was just part of a larger range that rose up behind me and formed the eastern wall of the plateau that the bridge would span. To the west, the river and the full thicket of the town. A neon sign alerted aliens to the presence of the one convenience store. Next to it the red "T"-like symbol of the tiny post office branch.

I watched a lone raven carve a path through the gray-blue sky and thought of Marinne waiting alone for me, and I thought about my father. How long had he been planning the accident, I wondered. Probably ever since losing his eyesight. Never reaching out, never opening up, never wanting to pull me down into that helplessness more than I had to be, he had borne the weight of his disability with dignity and — by opting for silence — a degree of peace.

I hoped for his sake that there was more out there on the other side.

I stayed on the hilltop for a long time, looking southward, watching like an eagle over the little corner of the world that had become my new home, trying to make sense of everything that had happened. Whatever was going on with Miyū, looking out at this landscape, I decided that my relationship with Marinne had to end. Too much had changed now, I was too different to ever go back and be the same person I was when I'd boarded the *Pandora*. I hadn't arrived at this alien landscape by accident. It wasn't random chance. Destiny had pulled me there as surely as a deep-water fish feels the tug of a tuna line and — fight as it may — is drawn to the boat and what awaits it after it's gaffed and pulled onto the deck.

Boston seemed as tangible as fog. I was in Japan now. I loved these rice fields and their humble changing of the seasons. The serpentine river laughing its way to the sea belonged to me as much as any villager. The somber cypress stands like rows of sentinels, watching over the town, were watching me too. The grandfathers walking their toy dogs along the curbsides felt like my own family. A fondness swelled inside me, an all-encompassing understanding of how dear this village was. Just a few decades had passed since World War II had ripped this land apart. Yet even the war seemed buried and forgotten. I couldn't imagine life being anything but peaceful here.

Yes, for certain, if Miyū weren't here it would be a different landscape, more strange and more foreign, and I would feel more alone. No kiss Marinne had ever shared with me felt as intoxicating as those I shared with my new lover. That moment she'd seen me peering at her through the bushes. The caged look in those infinite eyes. Her praying at the temple. Her relationship with the man in the Toyota Crown. But none of that mattered: I was hooked, helpless and addicted to someone whose mysteries I'd only begun to unravel.

Staring out at the town I resolved I would become a part of this place. Live out my life here, let everything about Boston become the past.

I heard a rustle at the edge of the clearing and looked up, expecting an animal. Instead, it was Miyū.

"I wanted to see if you were okay."

"It's an amazing view," I said, touched that she'd feel the need to check on me. "You were right."

"It's okay."

"You're only blind to its beauty because you're from here. People never appreciate what they have until they go somewhere else."

"You can't really think that, can you?" She pointed. "That this … is beautiful."

"Yes, sure," I said. "It's when you leave that you see what you're missing back home."

"Oh, so is that why you left her, that girl who wrote you the letter? So you could know what you're missing?"

I didn't know how to answer that. "It's different for me."

She kept going. "And now that you know … what happens then? You go home, report your findings to the tribunal? Make a document?"

Her eyes flashed, deep and injured.

"I didn't mean anything like that."

"It doesn't matter. I'm not mad. Maybe sad, a little, because I'm finding myself fond of you and I didn't expect that, and it will be hard to say goodbye. But you haven't been here long enough to understand, see anything beyond the superficial. And you never will. The 'quaintness' of the country life and all that crap. It fades when you deal with narrow-minded people and their vindictive games from which you'll never escape, never, not unless you die. You can't see it because you're just a temporary visitor, someone passing through. If you're bound to it, then you'll be able to see it the way it is: a cage."

She was calling a bluff as calmly as if she'd read inside my mind.

"Miyū, what if I did? Would I be a part of it then? If I lived here the rest of my life?"

"No," she said. "Not even then."

"Then for how long do I have to stay … ?"

"If your ancestors stepped out of the heavens onto Takachiho mountain, then maybe you qualify as real Japanese. My family's been here centuries and there are people who will still call me a foreigner."

"You?"

"We weren't born here. We were brought here from Korea. Only our pottery is prized. Not our lineage."

I didn't know what to say. I remembered the museum curator's speech to me about this topic. She was one of them.

Miyū walked to the edge of the clearing where the embankment dropped away and for a moment I thought she was going to jump. Her whole body seemed poised, tense, coiled like a snake that sees something out there in the future it needs to strike at. But she turned around instead and looked at me.

"There's an even better view I can show you," she said. "Want to see? One that will blow you away."

I wanted to kiss her. I wanted to stay on the top of that little hill and hold her in my arms, crush her to my lips and make love that would set the mountain on fire. I wanted to be the one to save her from whatever it was in that future she was running from.

"Sure," I answered. "Anything you want to show me, I want to see."

CHAPTER THIRTY-TWO

She brought me to a shed near the kilns and pulled open the unlocked door, revealing hoes and rakes and some large bags of fertilizer that were marked "Poison" in Japanese, with the universal skull and crossbones. The air was stale and smelled of mold, but the bicycle she pulled out was serviceable enough. An old 1950's style shopping bike with a wide saddle seat and handlebars that curved up like antelope horns. It was similar to the one I'd used at Komori-san's.

"It's my father's," Miyū said. "He won't care if you borrow it. Hasn't ridden in years."

She walked with me back to get her bike, and then led me up a series of twisting, cypress-and-bamboo-lined roads that wound past farmhouses, small rock walls, and terraced rice fields. I could still feel the injury to my ankle, a tension and a dull ache that was never strong enough to make me wince, but enough to remind me of that fall. What pain there was, I pushed away, focusing instead on the beauty of the scenery and being able to share it with this girl.

Yet another kingfisher glittered in the air before dropping into a pool. Another white egret squawked as it flew away. The scenes felt frozen, like *ukiyoe* paintings. The art of the beautiful cliché. I watched Miyū as she pedaled, her taut, muscular calves straining on the uphills; her bobbed hair flipping behind her in the breeze when we coasted down.

Everything about the moment was perfect. The rush of the crisp air calmed me as we pedaled through the countryside. At one point we raced each other, first I passing her, then she passing me, then we were both laughing, the two bicycles parallel, our voices stolen from our mouths by the wind.

We reached the needle-like form of the bridge pile and dismounted. Standing at the base, looking up, it felt vast and immeasurable. Dusk added drama to the clouds that whipped by, making the column seem already in motion, already pushing its way from Earth to orbit.

"Ready to climb?" Miyū said.

"That?"

In reply, she let her bicycle drop into the soft soil and went to the base of the tower. The first of the iron rungs were just low enough for her to reach and she pulled herself up by hanging on them and then walking up the side of the concrete with her sneakers.

"You coming or not?" she asked.

Was I coming?

Of course I was.

But it was more than that. The moment my hands touched the cold metal rebar, I was transported back in time to that discovery of the ladder up the chimney at the factory where my father worked. I was a child again, full of that same wonder and excitement. As rung after rung pulled me higher, I left all the doubts and fears and insecurities I'd ever had and let the adrenaline take me. I felt the rush of wind that whipped down from the mountains — I was part of it all. My heartbeat seemed loud enough to burst my ribs each time I sneaked glimpses of Miyū's legs and white, cotton underpants as she climbed up above me. Once she looked down and caught me looking and laughed.

"Enjoying the view?" she asked.

She did not mean the scenery.

Each rung I climbed turned Marinne to memory.

And even now I have to stop and say, "Why not?" Isn't that what being young is all about? Discovering yourself in the experiences you share with other people? Finding out who you do and don't trust, like, and love? It's not as if we're obligated to anyone to remain true to whom we've always been. I was falling in love with her. And what young man wouldn't? The promises we make in one life don't always carry over to the next.

When we reached the top we crawled out on the wide platform, breathless with the excitement and the exertion of the climb. Miyū staggered away from the hole we'd entered from and lay down, arms and legs wide, the way children do making snow angels.

"Look up," she said. "The stars are coming out already."

I lay down next to her, staring up into the gorgeous celestial abyss. As night deepened, it was as if we'd stepped up into a nebula, plasma pink and glowing, the Milky Way so dense that it was a living thing, some massive phoenix rising up around us, twisting and moving and shimmering. I could feel the insignificance of all that happens on this teacup planet, the vastness of time and space and into that immense void I turned and pulled her to me.

No kiss that Marinne and I had ever shared compared to that moment. She opened her mouth and our eyes closed and if any farmers were tending their fields that night they would have looked up at the giant obelisk and seen it glowing, as bright as iron coming out of a furnace ready to be forged. Her hands were in my hair, on my cheeks, in my mouth, her legs and arms wrapping like tentacles around me, twisting this way and that. I laid myself on top of her and pushed up her blouse. I was about to take it off and she shook her head.

"It will blow away," she laughed. "My father likes you, but he'll like you less if you've lost my clothes."

Her white blouse stayed like a yoke as I licked her neck, kissed the soft line of her cheekbone, nibbled her ears, brushing them with my lips. Her hair smelled of honey and kiln smoke and melon shampoo. Each time I kissed her she sighed, shifting position in little twists and spasms.

My hands ran up the smooth raceway of her thighs. I kissed her breasts, her stomach, then shifted down until I found the wet nectar. I traced the contours of butterfly wings until she held my head with both hands and pressed it deeper, deeper, deeper and twisted her back up into me, wrapping her legs around my face and moaning. I could feel the sensations ripping through her, her body rigid and shaking, until the demons left and she fell away from me.

I kissed her neck again. Her skin tasted as if dusted with powdered sugar.

"Don't stop," she said, panting, pushing herself toward me. She fiddled with my fly and pulled my pants down as far as she could. Entering her was like thrusting myself into fire, sensation searing through me, our two bodies fusing into one. She drew me in, then twisted her pelvis around as if using me to stir her deep inside. I kept kissing her until she stopped me by biting my lower lip and holding it between her teeth, tighter and tighter until I thought she was going to split it. As the pain in my lip deepened, so did the volcano within me and it grew and grew until I couldn't hold it any longer and exploded into her.

We lay there, fused. I could hear her still panting, her breath in my ear. The fingers of my left hand were entwined in the fingers of her right.

At some point she lifted herself up off the cold concrete to one elbow and stared at me.

"I told you it was amazing." She turned. "It's like the stars are right there, like you could reach up and rearrange them. Make your own constellations."

"Scorpio." I said, pointing.

"Libra." She answered.

"The Big Bear. We call it the Big Dipper in English."

"Cassiopeia." She said it with emphasis on the "O" not the "P." Like the word "opium."

We stayed there, quizzing each other's star knowledge, falling off friendship into something else that for convenience I'll call love. I'd never met anyone who could look up at the sky like I could. It seemed impossible that we were not supposed to find each other. Two specks drifting through the galaxy that inexorably get nearer and nearer until they fuse with a flash of fire.

Finally, when the air hinted of winter's approaching sting, we dressed and descended and went back home.

CHAPTER THIRTY-THREE

Say what you like about potters, they know how to use their hands. Gritty raku. Stiff stoneware. Sensual porcelain. Wedging, twisting the pliable earth, coaxing out the suppleness and silk, until it becomes tame, smooth, all the air bubbles are gone.

Placing it on the wheel with a spank like a hand on a bottom.

A few drips of water before you center it.

A meditation.

More liquid, until it is slippery and wet and waiting for fingers to open it.

Then pressing into the warmth until it starts to yield.

The hole appears, the walls slick and muscular.

You shape it.

Tease it.

Lift it.

Caress the clay, pull it just to the collapsing point and then let it rest, then pull again, rest, each time it comes closer to arrival. And then, if you're lucky, something hidden within springs to life and takes shape, moves your hands, crafts itself and sudden a vessel appears that is more than shape … it is art. It is beauty.

A birth.

You slice it from the wheel.

Then it sleeps.

I spent winter, 1965, absorbing everything I could about clay. Miyū's father was the chemist. He knew every component of every glaze they used. The base had been handed down for centuries, though it changed, he said, when they'd been brought to Japan. Certain ingredients were not available and the substitutes, as is sometimes the case, only improved the vessels. Japan has historically had a gift for refinement, for perfection, even for the "imperfect" perfection. Asia has had green tea for thousands of years but the meticulous ceremony culture arose only after it had been imported through Hirado island to Japan. The ways or "roads" of tea, of calligraphy, of archery, of so many things began in other countries, but they were elevated to art in Japan.

I find it very tempting to attribute everything I knew about this town and this father-daughter family to "the Japanese," but to assume that is to buy into a lie: that there actually is something definable as "the Japanese." I don't believe that. Or rather, I think one could live for decades in a town or travel a country up and down and never be any closer to knowing what that is any more than there is an "American" or a "German" or a "Dane." The potter and his daughter thought of themselves as Japanese, as I did. Some in the town felt they were Korean. There was an independence, a stubborn "fuck you!" about them that felt to me comfortably American. Another side of them didn't fit in anywhere. Like me, they were alien creatures making their way in a strange planet, alone in the spaceship of their family generations as it coasted through time.

Again, I warn anyone away from making assumptions, from trying to extrapolate from my experiences and what happened to me and to them, into anything larger. Indeed, the true traveler knows that it is not a country, its borders, its culture, or even its landscapes and cities that make a country great, but rather the depth of the friendships that one discovers there.

A month passed. Then another. 1966 arrived. On the first day of the year a light snow had fallen, a minor miracle itself in a place that rarely saw snow. Children screamed and danced in the streets, trying to scoop up enough snow to have fights with. To me it was both comical and cute, as by Boston winter's end one had seen more than enough snow for the year.

We went, as did most of the town, to the main shrine and waited in a long queue to pay respects to the year of the Horse and bid farewell to that of the Snake. Monks in white robes sold fortune papers to tie in tree branches for luck. Children tugged at parents' sleeves for horse-shaped candies on sticks, the air was filled with the scent of roasted corn. Vendors ladled hot raw sake — unfiltered, white, and cloudy — into paper cups that warmed people from the inside and turned cheeks red along with the cold. Fireworks lit up the night.

It was peaceful except that I could tell people were avoiding my adopted family. No-one spoke to us. Other people would bump into a friend and burst into *"Hisashiburi,"* the equivalent of "Long time no see" or ask how someone had been all this time. That didn't happen to us. Once a boy, perhaps ten, said something that I didn't understand. Miyū raised her hand as if to slap him, then relented when her father said to let it pass. Another time, some drunk, his face beet red and stumbling, spat, missing us but only barely. The two ignored it and kept walking, and for all I know, perhaps it was indeed an accident of unfortunate aim.

It was a similar experience attending the flower-viewing festival in early March. We took the afternoon off and all went to a local park on a peak that was visible for miles. I hadn't known it in the late summer, but in the spring it was covered with cherry trees, now bursting with fragile pink blooms. Miyū had made up a picnic basket with rice triangles, sweet egg wraps, and a thermos of green tea. We sat on a blanket under the blossoms and chatted and enjoyed the view. I remember feeling included, even though my apprenticeship hadn't progressed past the very basics of clay. There too, we walked as if in our own orbit, never interacting with anyone else from the town.

It didn't matter to me. I wasn't there to make friends with anyone. I didn't care to get to know others. It was only the aloofness that tipped me off to the undercurrents of friction there.

In any case, soon it was spring, 1966, and there was still so much about clay and the art of creating it that I had yet to learn. While I now knew much of the pottery process, they had not taught me the glazing combinations and Miyū said even she knew only a few of them. She hadn't — despite working with him her entire life — been let in on all the secrets. Sometimes when I was alone in the studio, listening to that deep heartbeat-thump of the river mortars, I would stare at the rows and rows of chemicals and wonder which ones created the ineffable green of that giant vase in the Kagoshima hospital. On the floor was a row of large glass jars the size of five-gallon buckets, labeled with symbols: an equilateral triangle, a square, a circle, a red triangle, and so on.

Above that was a work table and about twenty gallon-size jars. Some had no labels, and many were not even full words. Japanese letters, such as "*Fu*" and "*o*" (to make "Fo"), for example. A capital "S" in English. A capital "B." Above these were three rows of what looked like spice jars that could have been McCormick racks in the supermarket. I realized later that these were often the jars where the ash from dead things was stored.

It took just a tablespoon of spirit ash, apparently, to shift a glaze from beautiful to supernatural.

I found it strange that the potter was so focused on making our trips to dig clay in secret. We would leave at three in the morning sometimes or two, or when it was pouring rain. It seemed absurd to me that he would care when there was not another potter for twenty miles. Everyone knew he was still accessing the construction site and why.

Yet still he persisted. I believe for him it wasn't that people wouldn't know, but that his honor required that he not be caught red-handed. If he were getting clay surreptitiously perhaps even the police could look the other way, even though the holes where we mined grew deeper and deeper. When I arrived they were small shovel-head-sized depressions in the ground.

By the time I left, they'd grown to something impossible to miss. Children could play hide and seek in some of them, they were so deep. As the potter dug ever-larger holes, they connected, forming a system of trenches and craters that filled with rainwater and then stewed with algal blooms. The place became fetid and rank, producing a noxious odor that seemed to infuse even the clay itself. In the mornings, as the giant mallets pulverized the dried blocks into dust, I could swear the odor of those pits was escaping too.

I wondered as time went on why there had been so little movement toward actual building of the bridge. It seemed like the spot were frozen in time, the painted backdrop of a low-budget science fiction film. Once or twice the machinery at the base moved. They had repaired the fence in two different places where we'd cut it to slip through. Other than that, the giant structure above the village was as incomplete as ever.

Winter became spring; spring blended into summer. The nightingales were replaced by thrushes and two species of wagtails, comical things that alight and then wag their tails up and down, as if beckoning one to follow. The cherry trees had dropped their pink blossoms and replaced them with broad, shade-producing leaves. Only the bamboos and the cypress forests seemed immune to the seasons.

Like a blob of different clay that's wedged so solidly into another larger piece that it vanishes, so my life blurred and blended with that of these two potters. Miyū had changed back to her more reserved, distant self the moment we'd come down from the Needle, but that was her personality. I wanted to feel close to her, connected, but instead she gave me the sense that I was oafish, some kind of large toddler that needed to be looked after all the time. They gave me tasks like carrying the bags of powder from the mortar area up to the buckets where they sifted and re-hydrated them. For nearly a month the closest I got to shaping clay was wedging it, which is much like kneading bread dough. Stiff, heavy, resilient bread dough. At the end of the day my shoulders and wrists ached so much that I had to sneak back down to the river and soak in Komori-san's bath before I could sleep.

Chapter Thirty-Four

I will not go into boring detail about the months that brought me from ceramics novice to someone who could create a vessel worthy of that studio. From that day the potter took me to the wheel until this morning, all these decades later, I have done nothing other than work with clay. It has consumed me, devoured me, destroyed me.

There was no magic "system" for learning, only trial and error and work. The potter would not let me fire a piece for nearly five months. Instead, he taught me centering the clay: the process of shaping a wedged cone into something symmetrical and smooth.

"Without centering," he told me, "there is no form. You cannot be a great potter without that basic foundation."

If I were in high school I might have been furious that all I did from morning until night was tuck my elbow deep into my stomach, make a stiff "arm" and pull the slippery, lumpy clay against it until it reshaped into a smooth cylinder. But from the moment my hands touched that first cone of clay on the throwing wheel, I was hooked as deeply as when I'd seen Miyū's face for the first time. I ate, drank, slept, breathed clay. I wanted to listen, to learn, to soak up as much as possible, so it excited me even to do such mundane work as centering.

Had I stopped, had I gotten tired or complained or been frustrated, I suspect the potter would have given up on me. But at the end of the fourth week he nodded.

"You are ready to learn to open."

"Opening" is the process of forming the hole in the middle of the centered, perfectly balanced clay, an act that is as sensual and delicate as placing your fingers inside someone. Slippery, smooth, silk. The clay sighs, separates, relaxes into your hands and you push deeper, feeling it close and pull, flexing against your fingers. Yet push too deep or too strongly or too fast and the clay veers off balance, spins out of control.

If you do it right you see a shape appear where before there was nothing. A form. A coelomic cavity. It stretches, expands, rises, pulls, defies gravity. The walls thin down and down and down and this is where the expertise of a potter truly shows. I would finish a vessel that seemed near perfect to me and the potter would nod, then slice it in two with a wire, pulling half off and showing me the cross section. Instead of even walls from base to lip, the walls would be like rings: thick in some places, paper thin in others. In comparison he sliced through one of his own works, a two-foot-tall vase, a beautiful cylinder form.

But he sliced it up and tossed it away without a second thought, for the clay was merely the surface for the glaze, and only a few of the pots would truly turn out to be magical. He could do a hundred identical forms a day for a decade. Mud was just mud, as meaningless to him as a sperm that never reaches an egg.

The same applied to my own vessels, too: I would labor to raise the walls as high and as thin as possible, achieving something I thought was flawless — only to have the potter bisect it with the wire and immediately point to the ripples and thicknesses I hadn't seen. The two halves of clay, dark and slumped on the stopped wheel, looked like an organ freshly cut by a butcher. The air pockets like the valves of a heart.

"See?"

How could I not? His vessels were indeed perfect. The walls looked as if they'd been measured by a micrometer, the exact same thickness from the base of the vessel all the way up to the mouth. The problem, I realized, was not in my learning the process of how to throw, but in the hubris of thinking I'd become a master overnight.

He was not a talkative teacher and preferred to show me things, or rather, to let me make my own mistakes, than to yammer on about some aspect or other. When he felt I was ready we moved on. He showed me how to pull a scrap of deer chamois between my fingers, how to wrap it on the lip of a pot to smooth the rim.

I can't say with any sincerity the phrase, "when I had mastered each skill," because I am a septuagenarian now and still feel there are times when I haven't mastered anything. On such days I wake up feeling as incompetent as I did those first weeks when I'd begun to learn the craft. Clay has always been surprising me, talking back, forcing me to reevaluate and rediscover it.

But I did, I assure you, improve. Perhaps faster than some apprentices might have. Even Miyū, who had avoided me much of this time, pulled me aside once and said, "My father is amazed at how much you've been able to learn."

We had been getting firewood for the kiln, the very same path where I'd slipped and twisted my ankle and, consequently, destroyed their livelihood for months.

"It's for you," I said. "I want to be here forever."

Her expression changed. "Don't say things like that. You'll just make it harder."

"What do you mean? Why would it be harder?"

"You know you don't belong here," Miyū said, looking sullen. "You're a *gaijin*." An alien. The word can be said in any context, from affectionate to derogatory. It's all in the tone of voice, and Miyū's matter-of-fact, unembellished use sliced a chasm between us.

"What do you mean, I'm an alien? How? What part of me isn't fitting in here?"

"Just focus on getting firewood," Miyū said. "You'll understand. Someday."

In some ways I was like one of those up-and-coming Japanese wrestlers who lives in the sumo stable night and day, eating and drinking with other athletes, forgoing a life of his own for the chance to be a *yokozuna* someday. I never left the studio except to accompany the potter on our midnight runs to excavate more clay in the dead of night, stopping, as we had the first time we'd met, to collect any roadkill we'd find. Whereas I'd been revolted at first, when I realized that he was turning something disgusting into beauty I saw him as a visionary, an alchemist. He became more than just a mentor to me. I began to understand how important these vessels were, how they cheated death by marrying a part of it.

After nine months I was nowhere near a master of the craft, but I was competent, and I began experimenting with glazing on my own. I used grasses and dusts and raw chemicals, then animals too, as my mentors did. I underwent a kind of hypnotism: I began to see the world in terms of colors that the object would produce when fired — a snake, a raccoon dog, a frog, the delicate balance of the minerals, the quantity and ratio of this to that, all of it affected the outcome of a kiln firing. Take away the soul and the body is just a body. Fire it and it turns to carbon, the molecule all life on earth shares.

It became difficult not to imagine the flares and nuances of hue that a human corpse would offer. The intensity. Though the practice had stopped long before the tradition had ever been passed down to this potter or his daughter, centuries before, the vases had been fired alongside royal corpses. The vase in the hospital contained in its aurora-like glaze, the final resting place of one of the Kagoshima nobles and his wife. They had been arranged around each side of the vessel, arms and legs intertwined. I came to understand that these vessels were not glazed with mere elements of earth.

The potter and Miyū's tradition was glazing pots with human souls.

"If you ever look at that vessel again," the potter told me once, "look near the foot. A few centimeters above the bottom you can see where a bone left its imprint in the glaze."

Had I just arrived, this macabre detail would have revolted me. But just as the mortician adjusts his nose and soon can't notice the scent of death, I too adjusted to not seeing a corpse as something to be feared. In this calm, quiet pastoral landscape I had become someone different. An egg dropped into boiling water, the protein chains hardening irreversibly. Now I thought nothing of death, of bodies incinerating in the heat of a kiln's flame. It seemed a shame that we could not try that technique on a vessel ourselves. The intensity, the release of a fragile person's essence into something as permanent as glaze, it was a rush, an intoxicant. I wondered about my own body: the signature that would paint itself in flame and smoke onto a vessel were I to be that person.

In fact, there was a point at which that was all I thought about as I went through my day: Everything alive was a repository of chemicals that could be used for glaze creation, a little moving pouch of glazing ash. A scampering squirrel would — in my mind — be wrapped tightly around a teacup, vaporizing into the melting glass. The little brown fox that I would see in the mornings trotting through the rice fields would nest among a family of vases, each one burning with the fox on one side, the rest at the mercy of the kiln.

Looking back at this apprenticeship, I can see that not long after I fired my first pots, I was like a novice swimmer who had plunged into a river not understanding how strong the current could pull.

Marinne's letters would languish for weeks before I'd find the time to write something. And when I did write back it was always short.

What could I say? How could I tell her about Miyū? When ever. I didn't know how to describe what we had together. There were days when she seemed desperate to have me inside her, and other times when she hardly spoke to me. She'd tease me by sliding into my futon long after her father had passed out, then the next day treat me as if I were a total stranger. Or be chatty and inviting dur-ing the day, yet I would lie awake waiting for her until the moon sank behind the hills without hearing the creak of her footsteps on the hallway floorboards.

But either way, the person Marinne knew and loved was gone. I had no plans to return to her. If it sounds horrible that I would be so callous, remember that I was under a kind of spell. As Komori-san had said, I did not know what I was getting into and even less how to get out of it. I simply envisioned my life there. Days spent making pots, nights spent sipping cocktails and adjusting the rabbit ears on their fuzz-filled black-and-white TV. I was Odysseus without beeswax: The siren call kept me entranced there and I would have done anything to stay.

Chapter Thirty-Five

It was June 26th, two days after the one year anniversary of my stepping onto the *Pandora*, that Komori-san visited with a package for me. The potter and I were out at the riverside adjusting the log troughs that pulverized the clay. We were collecting the finest dust, which would be mixed with water and then dried until it was suitable for throwing. A small X-shaped crutch held each log up and immobile while we scooped out the earth. At first I'd reached in with my hand and the potter had chided me.

"These machines should be thought of like loaded firearms," he said. "Just as you never point the barrel at a person, even unloaded, with these you never trust that they won't come crashing down on you. If somehow that crutch gets loose at the wrong time it will mash your hand as if it were made of cabbage leaves."

He taught me to use spoonlike instruments on long bamboo handles to remove the clay, so that if by some freak chance the support did fall out from under the giant crushing arm, only a tool would be lost, not a limb.

That morning, I was scraping the fine kaolin powder from one of the holes when I saw the woman coming up the road, carrying a package about the size of a football. This time she was using a white and red cane, tapping it beside the edge of the road to guide her instead of the baby carriage.

She paused above the pestle-logs and waited and it made me realize that she was far more aware of her surroundings than I'd ever known when I was living with her.

She seemed to sense that I was down there. Or that someone was.

"*Konnichiwa*," she said. "I'm sorry to trouble you, but I've got mail for the foreigner. Is he still living with you?"

"It's me, Komori-san," I answered. I hoisted myself out of the trough and went up the hill to the road.

"It's nice to see you again," I lied. "*Hisashiburi*. It's been a while."

"I've brought you a package and a letter," she said, then handed it to me.

I took them, surprised at how heavy the box was. They were both from Marinne.

"They got delayed," she said, reading my mind. "Lost in the mail. The postal worker was very apologetic."

"Thank you."

She lowered her voice. "Come back across the river. Please."

"I'm happy where I am."

"You shouldn't be—"

"Komori-san," I interrupted. "They treat me just as kindly as you did. They are hard-working. They don't harm anyone—"

"They would destroy the entire town if they could. Just for their own selfish—"

"It's the town that's being selfish!" I said. "They're the ones who allowed the expressway, who paid officials to plant it right through the potter's clay field."

Komori-san pulled herself upright at that point, then took a step backward, then another, then a third. "I am sorry for interrupting," she said.

She turned and after several tries found the edge of the road with her cane.

"Do you need help getting home?" I asked.

"I've gotten this far," she said. "Getting home will be easier now that I don't have that to carry."

I watched her proceed, tapping the stick at the curb to mark the way. She seemed much older than I'd remembered, even though less than a year had passed.

I put the package and letter down and went back to work. Together, the potter and I bagged two hundred pounds of clay that afternoon.

Later, in the evening, over a bowl of hot *udon* noodles and some rice and grilled scallops that tasted fresher than the ocean, I remembered. Excusing myself I went outside, found the package in the damp night dew, resting against one of the structure's pillars like a square garden gnome. The letter had blown onto some nearby leaves.

I brought them inside and placed them on the table.

"Aren't you going to open it?" Miyū asked, pointing to the package.

"I can wait."

The potter brought over his cocktail and handed it to me. Antifreeze green, it glowed like a cup of electricity.

"Open it," he said. "What did your girlfriend send you?"

If that word bothered Miyū, she didn't show it. Her face was glass, as frozen as the surface of the moon.

"Open it," she repeated.

CHAPTER THIRTY-SIX

I tore one corner of the wrapping and the rest slid away. A sheet of paper slipped out, but I couldn't take my eyes off the box inside. I knew what it was. There was no mistaking the somber color and the one piece of satin ribbon that held it closed.

Ashes.

The paper enclosed with the urn, undated, said only, "*Dear Neil, I am so sorry for your loss. And sorry if this somehow feels like I've failed you, but I can't. I just can't.*"

The separate letter read:

> *Dear, dearest Neil,*
> *This is almost too much for me to bear: Your father's accident with his medication, you know, the stuff he took for the pain. It's so complicated to explain. The doctor said that — oh, Neil, why aren't you here? Why are you so far away when something like this has happened? — the doctor said that your father wasn't using just the prescription*

pills, but taking laudanum as well, secretly. And he just ... took too much. Mixed up the dosage somehow. I can't write much because I don't know more than that and it is too agonizing to write.

I was the one who found him, Neil. As I wrote earlier, he and I were closer with you gone. We both missed you so much. He missed you, though he would never admit it. I know that's why he objected to your dodging the draft so much. Because it would mean you had to stay far away in Canada even if you came back. He talked about you a lot. He told me stories of you as a boy. He said how brave you'd been during the accident and afterward. How proud he was of you. He told me how you and he put constellations on the ceiling together.

The letter went on, and at some point I stopped reading and stared out into space. Because I knew my father. I'd seen him torquing pipes within a fraction of their tolerance. I'd watched him put his medication pill by pill into little cups so he'd always know which day of the week it was. The idea of him casually "making a mistake" seemed impossible to me.

My father had decided, at some point after I left, that there was a time for all things to come to an end. Like what Miyū said. Things end. All those years we'd lived together, it must have enraged him to be an invalid, to be so helpless. Never able to teach me to play ball or to drive, always needing me. And to have his son so full of teen angst, lashing out at him.

I looked at the date the letter had been sent. It was postmarked two months, just two mere months, after I'd boarded the *Pandora*. Just about the time I'd arrived in this tiny village.

The date confirmed it for me, but opened another floodgate of doubts and confusion: Why had Marinne opted to send me the ashes at all? Why not just keep them there for me? The date on the urn was in May, but there was no explanation of why they'd been sent from Watertown.

It made no sense. Nothing did anymore.

All I knew was that holding that heavy box in my arms I felt far away from her, farther from him, farthest from everything that had ever once been "home." If Marinne had sent the urn in the hopes of guilting me into returning, it had exactly the opposite effect.

It would take several months, and the arrival of another letter that had (along with the one from Boston) a postmark from Portugal (clearly a postal mistake and of course at exactly the wrong time) to finally piece together why Marinne had sent me my father's ashes in the first place. A letter dated May 1, 1966:

Neil, my dearest,

I cannot keep waiting forever to hear from you, and waiting for you, keeping up a false hope that you'll be back tomorrow and we can continue our lives hand in hand. Your father's ashes need to be scattered, and I cannot accept that task. Being entrusted by you to care for him, of course, I was happy to. But I'm not a mortuary. You need to come back and accept the duties of being your father's son.

Having this urn prevents me from sleeping. It haunts me. It's a symbol of everything we've failed to have together. I tried putting it in a closet, but now I don't even want to dress myself with the clothes that are hanging there. It's horrible. I know I shouldn't be superstitious but I can't, Neil.

I just can't.

If I don't hear from you I will just ship them to you. You should be the one to decide what happens from there.

And with us, if you do want to share a life together with me, please know that I'm

> *waiting for you as patiently and as faithfully
> as a lover can. But I don't want to wait for-
> ever, or in vain.*
>
> *Please come back, dearest. Come back
> safely, and soon.*

Later, the potter slid a cocktail in front of me. The green liquid glistened in the glass. I lifted it to my lips and sipped, letting the sweet, strong liquor warm me. I could see my father deciding to take his own life and making sure that he'd prepped Marinne beforehand, that he'd told her stories of me, that it would look like an accident. I knew that as much as he'd hated to burden me with his lack of independence, he was too proud to burden anyone outside the family with it.

This was his way of freeing Marinne.

Freeing both of us.

That night I lay on my futon, staring up at the ceiling, feeling that expanding darkness that death of a loved one always brings, and listening to the cacophony of sounds that late August nights hold. I could see each and every constellation my father had made for me as clearly as if it were in this house as well. I traced the thousand paths our lives might have had if not for this one, the one we were on. He was a good man; I missed him. But unlike Marinne's dreams, his death didn't make me pine more strongly for home. I needed to be here.

I heard footsteps, soft and quiet, outside the door. It slid open.

"Miyū?" I whispered.

"Shh," she said.

In moments she'd slipped under my blankets.

I pulled her to me, we shed our clothes, and I pressed her warm skin against mine. We kissed; her lips tasting like salt and clay, soft and moist and electric. I turned her over on her back and she sighed, arching herself up toward me. Her fingernails scraped across my skin. I shifted position and felt the tip of my penis slide into the hot wetness between her thighs. In one smooth, slow stroke I buried myself inside her, felt her body quiver. She lifted her legs and locked her ankles around my buttocks, holding on to me as I slid back and forth, back and forth, each thrust bringing us closer to incineration. Tighter and tighter, as if I were winding up a spring inside her that reached a breaking point. Her body shook and she gasped for air, then relaxed. I felt the contractions build inside me and exploded.

"Marry me," I whispered, lying next to her after, stroking her hair. "Marry me. I'll stay here; we'll be potters together."

"It's a dream," she said. "You could marry me and take me home with you. What about that?"

"I don't want to go home."

"I don't want to stay."

"Where would we go if we left?"

She looked at me. "I'm not expecting you to take me. At some point this will collapse around you and you'll have nothing holding you here. I'll be a memory. Just something nice in your mind."

"You don't understand me at all," I said. "I love you. If I leave, we'll leave together."

She kissed me, kissed me again, kept kissing me. I thought it might lead to more sex, but she slipped out of the covers and started putting on her clothes. "You don't know anything, do you? I am gone. Lost. If I leave for anywhere it'll be in an urn."

"I'm already lost," she repeated, as she opened the door and left.

Chapter Thirty-Seven

In the morning everything seemed different. Dappled. Sparkling. A high-pressure front pushed through, cleansing the air, making it possible to see beyond Sakurajima, not a bit of haze in the sky.

I'd had a deep and dreamless sleep, content in everything that had happened so far. Relief. That's what it was. A vast, overwhelming sense of relief. I decided to tell Marinne where my heart was and that this was the only way for her to be able to begin her life again, as hard as it would be initially. It should have been a difficult letter but as I wrote, as I put down what had happened to me — the seasickness, the voyage, the death of Kagoshima, the green vase and its inexorable pull to this idyllic mountain town — I felt more and more convinced that I was doing the right thing. For her and for myself, too. It was unfair to toy with that girl's heartstrings any longer, keep her waiting for me. And I was so integrated with this family that I couldn't imagine anything forcing me to come home. My father was gone, his ashes were here, and I had never liked Boston or Watertown. I'd spent my life longing to leave and now, finally, I'd found somewhere I felt comfortable, a place where I didn't want to look to the horizon.

I'd landed.

At breakfast, Miyū was talkative. She sat closer to me than she ever had before. She hooked her foot around my leg under the *kotatsu* and kept it there. Miyū looked older that day, more mature. Something seemed regal about her and I couldn't define why. Just that she was everything I could have ever wanted.

We took bags of clay to the storage shed. We brought wood for an upcoming kiln firing. It was a bisque firing, a way of hardening the thrown pots to make them withstand the handling and become more porous before glazing.

When the potter left, I leaned over to Miyū.

"What would you say if I wanted to use my father's ashes in the next glazing?"

Miyū looked at me.

"There might not be another glazing," she said.

"Of course there will be."

"You really want to use your father? Would he approve?"

"I'd love to tell you that he'd be honored."

"But you can't tell me that?"

"No," I said. "I never knew him that well." The thought of those ceilings of stars came into my mind. I loved him. I was fond of him. I'm sure he loved me too.

"You don't need my permission," Miyū said. "Or his. It's your box of ashes. Do whatever you want."

The dead are gone, I thought. They don't get to choose what happens anymore.

"Your father," I asked. "Would he mind?"

"Hell no. He'd be thrilled. The two of you can go off grave robbing, hand in hand."

I looked at her. She was staring at the ground.

"What's wrong?"

"Nothing."

"Miyū, what happened?"

She was crying.

"I hate this place and I hate pottery and I hate corpses and I hate ... you."

And she turned and ran inside the house.

I started to follow her, then stopped. This was how she was. Hot one moment, cool the next. I loved her for it. Why did I have to control every whim or bonfire? She would calm down.

With the potter gone, and no immediate chore to do I decided I'd take a tour through the valley. I hopped on the dusty shopping bike that was resting against the bags of nitrites and soon was gliding down the road that followed the river. It was a slight downhill, so I was far away in minutes, and despite what had happened, the minor quarrel we'd had, I felt carefree.

The road ended in a T and I turned right, crossing over the river and in a little bit I was on a narrow street that led into the center of town. From there it was not too hard to find the train station, and I stopped in front of the bench where I'd slept that very first night, before I'd met Komori-san. The memory was so distant that it felt more like déjà vu than something real.

Then I remembered that I'd seen the girl here too, that she'd been praying at the temple, just about a year ago. Feeling a swell of nostalgia, I began walking my bike on the pavement, passing people who craned their necks to look at me, until I came to the temple. I stopped before entering, looking at the inscription on the temple gate. The religious writings had unfamiliar vocabulary and were thus much harder for me to read, but in them I could pick out enough to know that this temple was dedicated to the souls of lost children.

I left the bike and went inside to where the rows of *ema* prayer boards hung. It was easy to read many of them: requests for forgiveness for children unborn. Then, almost without searching for it, I found the board that Miyū had written. I would have known her handwriting anywhere, and I remembered almost like a photograph her reaching up to tie it on a particular pole at exactly the height I was looking at now. The bag she'd left on the ground beside her. All of it was as vivid for me as if I'd been seeing it for real. Other details of the temple were fuzzy, but I was staring with one hundred percent certainty at what she had written so many months ago:

"Grant me the power to end a dynasty; forgive my soul for what I'm about to do."

It made no sense. I read it once, twice, three times, searching for some meaning I'd overlooked, something I'd known about her, or for Japanese readings of these characters that might add context. It crossed my mind that perhaps if she had been at this temple she had wanted forgiveness for a child that never came into the world. Had that been it, I would have felt nothing but warmth for her; my heart would have gone out to her.

I wished I hadn't seen it, but I couldn't stop reading it. I stood there, reading it again and again, scouring my brain for characters, trying to see if I'd incorrectly translated it somehow. But I hadn't.

Feeling the cold of approaching autumn, I returned to the bike and went home.

CHAPTER THIRTY-EIGHT

Summer returned for a few days as if to tease us before chilly nights began. Days were warm, even hot, but at night we were using blankets in addition to cotton sheets. It took me several weeks to confront Miyū about the *ema* board. Partly I was a coward and partly I had internalized that Japanese trait of not wanting to make a scene. Every night I would resolve to bring it up with her the next day.

Each morning I would wake up certain that I'd find a chance to ask her what those words meant. The invocation haunted me. And why had she tried to pretend I hadn't seen her there at the temple?

It struck me at that time that perhaps Komori-san was right, that I hadn't known — perhaps ever — what I was getting myself into when I crossed the river and started my unofficial apprenticeship there with the potter and his daughter, racing against time to make as many vessels as possible before the bridge was completed.

We had just completed another firing. My father's ashes had been scattered on the pots that I had made, and Miyū had sprinkled some of him like salt onto hers. The potter had kept his pots glazed entirely with charcoal from roadkill that he'd collected over the past few weeks. A few squirrels. A Japanese badger that had gotten hit. Even a few large birds had made their way into the animal crematorium and were now dust mixed in glazes, dust on the pots, some of their minerals mixed in with the wash and slips that he used. There was no calculated certain ratio that created beauty. Sometimes we fired the kiln and what it produced was earthen browns and blacks. In fact, more often than not, the results were not spectacular.

But that time, that time was.

When we opened the kiln after a few days of letting it cool, we could tell that something was different. Almost as soon as we pulled the first bricks out, still too hot to touch, we could see the pots inside were shimmery and glowing almost as if they were lamps lit from inside. The glazes were so brilliant, so intense, such an entrancing shade of greenish-blue, that we stood back and cheered.

"That!" the potter said, over and over, when the vessels were cool enough to remove. "That! And that!"

He seemed to have surprised even himself. Knowing him, knowing the workmanship, the process, the details of creating these, I knew how perfect they were, but I think even a lay person, someone with no interest in ceramics would have paused for an extra moment gazing upon any of these vessels in a museum or gallery.

"This," the potter said, as much to himself as to me. "This pot will last ten thousand years."

I do not know if other artists all struggle for the same goals, but I am sure that the greatest of the world's potters all strive for immortality. Miyū's father saw in these forms what parents see in their children: a way to place something on the planet that will remain long after they're gone. This was his lineage. I suspect Miyū understood that too, that as much as he loved her as any parent loves a child, she was just a temporary ghost as we all are, a flicker on the planet, and her candle would snuff, as would his, as would mine.

But these vessels, they would sail on through years into decades, decades into centuries, centuries into millennia. They would span countless human lives and survive wars and floods and who knows, perhaps they would still remain at the end of it all, when our dying sun swells up and devours Earth before collapsing. Pottery: permanent beauty that could outlast us all.

I would read decades later that Jōmon-era shards had been found in an industrial park excavation on a bluff close to Kinkō Bay. It is not hard to imagine those potters of ten thousand years ago pulling an earthen vessel from the fire, tapping it for timbre, and nodding with the same mix of humility and pride as the potter had. Long after we are all forgotten, after the island of Kyūshū no longer matters and there is nothing people remember about Japan, these vessels will still be here, testament to a culture that created mastery.

The few vessels that I had thrown myself were less hued and less spectacular, both in shape and color, but they were not bad. The flaws were ones that potters would notice only if they looked for them, but even these would sell to collectors. Miyū kept nodding her approval and at one point she squeezed my hand.

"You've got it," she said. "I didn't think you did but you do."

I leaned in and kissed her. Her father could have seen us at any time; whether or not he knew we were lovers, I didn't want to surprise him, yet I couldn't stop myself from kissing her every moment she would let me. This is what love is, I thought, pulling away and seeing the mix of embarrassment and joy on her face.

This.

Doing something you love with someone who admires you.

This.

We knew that for a while anyway, these pots would keep the income steady and while we would never be out of the woods, most of them would sell. A few of them would sell for thousands, perhaps tens of thousands. A kiln firing was like the big hauls fishermen had a few times a season. You just set your lines and hope that when you pull them up again there's a good catch.

This was a good catch.

We celebrated that night by driving into town and going to an *izakaya*, one that specialized in a wild boar meat *shabu-shabu*, where strips of pork are dipped into simmering soy milk and vegetables. It was a high-end place, with individual rooms for groups of four to six, and artful silk paintings on the walls. In the center of the establishment, charcoal embers glowed below an iron tea kettle that hung from a lacquered bamboo pole. I recognized one of the potter's works sitting behind the bartender, along with bottles of high-end whiskeys and *shōchū*.

"One of yours," I said to the potter, as the maitre d', a tiny, birdlike girl dressed in black, led us to our section.

"Here," she said, fluttering her arms like wings as she pointed to our booth.

"We eat here free," the potter said. "About fifteen years ago I gave him that vase. In exchange, we come here once or twice a year and celebrate. On him."

"Nice trade," I said.

"We could come here every night if we wanted," the potter added. "But I don't like to take advantage of a debt."

"Here you are," the girl said, placing steaming hand-cloths in front of each place setting. "And you will have the owner's suggestions?" In many high-end places in Japan, there is no menu. Because why would you come not wanting to eat whatever the chef thought was best?

"Of course," said the potter, opening a towel and wiping his face and fingers. "We'd be honored to."

Our booth was a low table with a sunken area for feet. The potter and Miyū were on one side; I sat on the other.

The meal came in courses, one after another after another. We drank sake and ate morsels of boar so delicate they seemed to melt like butter on my tongue. Each dish came in its own meticulously crafted preparation. The potter's vase floated above the table like Mount Fuji, "borrowed scenery," above a Shizuoka tea garden. The eye moved from the near to the far and back again, the food tasting all the better for the incredible view.

Eventually the potter stood, nodded to us, and put on his shoes. His face was flushed from drinking.

"I'm tired," he said, steadying himself with one hand against the cypress-wood threshold. He stayed there for a moment before excusing himself.

"Is he all right?" I asked.

"Drunk," Miyū said. "I don't want to go home yet. You?"

"I want to do whatever you want to."

"Let's look at stars."

The taxi dropped us off far enough from the Needle that the driver wouldn't suspect where we were going, and the two of us walked hand in hand, listening to the chirping of the season's last crickets and the far-off gurgle of the river. Somewhere in the distance a heron squawked. The night pressed in around us, drew us closer together. I moved my hand to her waist and she didn't pull away. In the darkness the tower pushed, oppressive, up against the canopy of stars.

We climbed in silence, reaching the top breathless and exhilarated and numb. The wind whipped against us and we clung to each other, kissing, hurriedly undressing, finally pressing ourselves together as if trying to fuse into one. The hum of the wind as it passed across the iron bars was like an instrument, hollow and otherworldly.

Still standing, she opened her legs, letting me slip deep inside her. Her lips bit my neck, my shoulder. She was liquid and fire, clinging to me, pulling herself up me, slipping down, riding me with purpose. Her head tipped back and moonlight spilled across her perfect neck; her breasts' cupped curves shone. Her eyes closed as if she were entering a trance and her breathing quickened. I pushed, holding the two of us upright, oblivious to the edges of the platform or the possibility of what might happen if we came too close to the precipice. With my chest bare and my pants at my knees, I should have been cold in the near-autumn chill, but I was part of some slow, controlled fission, a nuclear heat burning upward and leaving everything I'd known far below.

Her body began to tighten, the muscles contracting around me, pulling at me, fighting to hold off the climax, to let it build and build until it would rush through her like a bomb blast. I waited, holding to something earthbound as long as possible before allowing myself to fill her. She writhed and twisted and shivered until finally she relaxed. Limp, she seemed to float, as if held in the air by a parachute, back down to the ground.

She pulled her clothes around herself and stared at me, silent.

I stared back.

Wordlessly, we struggled to breathe again. The stars seemed too close, as if they'd been watching us, hovering, a billion sparkling voyeurs that expanded outward again, resetting themselves in the sky the moment our bodies unfused.

As we climbed down the long lines of rebar rungs to the earth again, Miyū seemed more distant, remote. By the time we touched the muddy clay she seemed to be angry with me. Several times I asked what she was thinking, tried to get her to talk, even about something meaningless, but she either didn't hear me or just didn't care to answer. She walked ahead of me, her chin up, her gait strong, looking like some kind of warrior marching determined into battle.

Holding hands as we had on the way up seemed impossible.

Did she regret what had happened?

Had it embarrassed her?

Did she want me to do something differently?

Should I just let her be?

We walked and walked, not speaking.

"Miyū?" I asked, when we were nearing the house. "You in there? You seem so angry, is everything okay?"

She turned. "I'm not angry."

"You're quiet."

"Just thinking."

"It must be pretty deep thought."

She nodded. "I have a big decision to make."

"Is it something connected to me?"

"Why would it be about you?"

"What we did up there—"

"Don't read anything deep into it. It was just sex."

"I don't 'just have sex' with anyone."

She turned back and kept walking. "Anyway, this has nothing to do with you."

I remembered the message she'd written on the ema board.

"Does it have anything to do with 'ending a dynasty'?"

She whirled around. "Where did you hear that?"

"You."

"What are you talking about?"

I told her about the *ema* and how I'd gone back to the temple "What does it mean?"

She stared at me, her lips a tight line. I tried to take her hand and she leaped back, as if I were attacking her.

"Stay away," she said.

"Miyū, whatever it is, whatever it is, please know that I'll understand it. I'm in love with you. You can tell me anything."

She laughed, shaking her head as she spat out the words. "How can you promise me anything when you don't even know what you're talking about?"

"I know that I love you."

"And that's it? Because you're in love, anything is possible? What if I were an evil person about to do something terrible? What about that? Would you still be in love?"

"You're not an evil person," I said.

"You want to know something about evil? Your fall carrying wood was no accident."

"What do you mean? I tripped —"

"I tripped you." She looked at me. "Now you still love me? Still think I'm your little gem? You know nothing about me."

The weight of that statement still hits me sometimes, even now, remembering it. I stopped as if I'd seen a chasm open up in front of me. She kept going, striding into the darkness. Somewhere far below us, a car crossed the bridge and turned up toward the studio, its headlights cutting through the night like search beams. Something made me uncomfortable about letting anyone pass by and see the two of us walking alone in the dark together. Or if not together, close enough that the astute driver would understand that we were not just randomly on the same road at the same time. I was near the path that led up to the hill and slipped onto it, expecting the lights to pass by in a few moments.

When they didn't, I had a strange feeling that something was wrong.

CHAPTER THIRTY-NINE

Instead of going to the house, I went farther up the path, picking my way through the darkness, until I got to the place where I could look down and see the studio. Not one, but two cars were there. I could see people with flashlights walking around the grounds. I heard the potter's voice several times, soft, then louder, and someone else too: a man, firm and commanding. It was in these sorts of situations — when I wanted my Japanese to be its most fluent — that I found the Kagoshima dialect the hardest or the words they used unfamiliar. Something about a discovery. Or a secret.

Then I heard Miyū, her thin voice clear and unmistakable.

"He's done nothing to you. You can't! You can't!"

I skidded and scrambled and slipped back down the path, not feeling the cuts or scrapes. All I could think of was that I had to be there, had to get to her. I remembered the unsavory characters that she'd been talking to in that car a few months before and thought maybe they had returned.

I reached the road and dashed down to the house. When I turned the last corner I stopped, my eyes flooded with light. The men Miyū was pleading with were the police.

"Let him go," she begged. "He's done nothing. Take me instead."

I arrived just as several men were taking the potter to a small van. His hands were bound behind his back with chrome handcuffs that glinted in the searchlights. Policemen were inside the house; others were methodically searching the outbuildings and kilns, ant-like in their uniforms, helmets, and demeanor. I walked down and tried to move toward Miyū but she hurried inside, shaking her head. Get out of here, she mouthed to me. Go while you can.

The men let me move around freely in what, presumably, was their crime scene. I suspect they just knew what they were looking for and thought I didn't speak Japanese. A young man with a blue helmet eyed me cautiously, as if I might bite.

"Did they do something wrong?" I asked.

He waved his hand in front of his face.

"Please go," he said. In English.

"Over here," someone called. "Found it!"

It was the outbuilding that Komori-san had been near when she'd passed me the urn with my father's ashes inside. I remembered that when the door had opened it had contained a few very old bags of glazing materials. We had kept the bicycles there.

Now the shed contained several new blue oil drums. I didn't need Japanese to read the symbol painted on the side: a skull and crossbones. Poison.

On top of the barrels were some additional containers about the size and shape of river sandbags. The one who had found them was on the radio.

Soon, far in the distance, I heard a police siren. A few minutes later, a large vehicle with gray metal sides and large tires pulled up, lights flashing. A team of five men in white coats, pants, and helmets with face shields spilled out and went into the shed. They loaded the materials into the back of their truck.

All this time the potter had been at the squad van, talking to an officer. I was close enough to overhear something about the shed, the officer seemed to tell the old man what they'd found there. When he heard, the potter slumped. He took a moment, his fingers went to his face, picking at his skin. His lip trembled.

"Yes," he said. "I did it. I confess."

"We'll take your confession down at the station."

They put him into the car and closed the door.

Just then Miyū came out, saw her father, and screamed.

"You can't take him! He's innocent! He's done nothing wrong!"

She started to run, but two policemen caught her by each arm. She hung there struggling, yelling at them to stop as they drove her father away.

I stayed in the house. The rest of the investigation took a few more hours. The policemen took dozens of things from inside: receipts, money, a camera, everything labeled in evidence bags. They took some of the glazing chemicals along with what the crime scene team had removed.

Miyū sat at the table, sobbing. I tried to put my arms around her several times but she just shook them off. "I need to be alone," she said. "Can't you understand that?"

"I don't think you do," I said. "You need to talk to someone."

"Ugh!" she said. "Fine, I'll talk. I'll tell you everything. Tomorrow. But please just let me grieve in peace right now."

I went to my room and turned on the light. I didn't know what had happened but I knew that I had put off telling Marinne about my feelings for so long out of laziness, out of a sense of ... of what? I didn't even know. I'd strung her along, taking the easy path, and I resolved that night to tell her everything.

I wrote Marinne a letter, long overdue.

I told her about the voyage. About Kenji "Kagoshima." About the brothel. About the hospital and Miwako and the vase that I had fallen in love with. About Komori-san and her strange foot fetish. I wrote in detail of seeing Miyū at the temple. How strange it was to meet her again, how predestined it felt. That first journey across the bridge to the studio. How everything alien was familiar now. About how everything seemed to be leading me here, to this town, to this person, to this strange, beautiful girl with whom I had fallen in love.

I wrote how I knew it was love. How could it not be? I had shared everything with this girl, physically and emotionally. I settled into this place, knew this family, felt as home here as I had been anywhere. This town was where I was meant to be.

Not Boston.

"*... and not,*" I wrote, eventually, my fingers shaking,

> *... and not with you. Marinne, you*
> *meant everything to me once and if I thought*
> *I could ever bring that back I would, I would*

do it in a heartbeat. I love you dearly, but Miyū simply burns far brighter for me than you ever will. In writing this I probably will break your heart, and it breaks mine, too. But I will stay here in this little village in Kagoshima and make the most of what comes with this girl. She needs me, and the potter does too. I am part of this family now.

Perhaps you will hate me for the rest of your life. Or perhaps you can forgive me despite how deeply this will hurt you. I hope the latter, as I wish nothing but amazing things for you. I just can't be a part of your life anymore.

I will always love you, Marinne, but we met by simple chance.

I love Miyū with a sense of destiny that nothing can destroy.

By the time I was done with the letter, there was light coming in the windows, and the outline, ever so faint, of bamboo thicket outside. I had to massage my hand, it ached from writing so much. Fourteen pages, both sides, and even then, I felt like there was so much that I'd left unsaid.

I went into the kitchen where Miyū still sat at the table, staring at the wall as if in a trance. Rummaging through the potter's jumble of pens, pads, bills, unopened mail, and chemical catalogs, I found an empty envelope and tucked the missive inside.

Not wanting to disturb Miyū, I slipped out and hopped on the potter's bicycle. Pedaling as fast as I could, I flew over the bridge, down the narrow lane that paralleled the river. The farmhouses gave way to smaller lots and then I reached the center of town. I swerved into the post office parking lot and leaped off my bike, letting it crash to the ground behind me as I rushed up to the doors. Pushing them open, I went to the clerk, a prim girl of perhaps thirty in a spotless uniform, who looked at me with a mix of wonder and concern.

"Are you all right?" she asked.

"I need to mail this," I said, pulling out the letter.

"Of course," she said, smiling as I wrote the address.

"Oh, America!" she commented. "How lovely. Are you from there?"

"I was," I replied. "But I'm from here now."

"Regular or express?"

"The fastest one, please."

She took the envelope and smiled again and wished me a nice day, the way people always do to be polite when neither they nor any of us know the enormity of what is about to happen.

Certain actions you can never undo.

Realizing I was hungry, I stopped at a roadside *yakitori* shop and stood, chatting with the cook-owner about the weather as he grilled the chicken skewers, basting them with soy sauce and syrup. When they were done he handed them to me and motioned for me to eat at the stand-up table on one end of the tiny stall. There was only room for a few people, but as I'd gotten there before the lunchtime rush I had the spot to myself. The meat was cooked perfectly and I decided I'd make a point to patronize this place more often in the future. I thanked him for the food, paid, and went out to my bicycle.

CHAPTER FORTY

When I got back to the potter's house it was afternoon. I pushed open the screen that separated the kitchen from the rest of the house.

"I'm back," I said. "*Tadaima.*"

Silence.

"Miyū?"

Quickly I went through the other rooms, pausing for a moment outside her bedroom just in case she was asleep — as she could have been, after such a horrible night — and not wanting to wake her even though it was almost lunch. But her room too was empty. Something in my knees began to ache.

"Miyū!" I yelled. "Are you here?"

I went outside and rushed down to the studio.

There, attached to the potter's wheel with a blob of clay, was a short, handwritten note. The ink smudged when I pulled it out and read it. She'd written it just minutes earlier.

> *Dear Father,*
> *I am so deeply sorry for the embarrass-*
> *ment and shame that my actions have caused*
> *you. You should never have sacrificed your-*

> *self for me. I am to blame for everything, and*
> *I will do what is necessary to free you. My*
> *kind of confession will be impossible to ig-*
> *nore. Even if the bridge is completed it will*
> *bear the stain forever.*
> *With deepest shame,*
> *Your devoted daughter*

I read and reread the message, a feeling like icy water dripping up and down my spine. Then everything hit me at once, and I knew what she was planning to do, and where, and how.

"No," I said to the empty room. "Miyū! No!"

I leaped on the bicycle and started pedaling toward the Needle. My hope was to overtake her before she'd even gotten there. At each turn I would crane forward on the bike trying to get a glimpse of her small figure on a bike in front of me, and each turn left me desperate to round the next one. Once I nearly rode off into the gutter, I was going so fast. The tire was just inches away from sending me hurling over the handlebars into the ditch.

When I reached the last turn I could see her: a blue-green dot ascending the gray cement obelisk. By the time I'd reached the base and slipped through the wire she was at least a third of the way up.

"Miyū!" I screamed. "Don't!" But the wind whipped the words sideways, scattering them across the mud flats and the roadway and the rice fields beyond. If she heard me, she ignored it and kept on climbing. She was halfway up now.

I climbed like a demon, leaping up the rungs, taking them two or three at a time. Gusts buffeted me, making it hard to keep my grip, and once my feet slipped and I hung there, many stories above the earth, swinging by just one arm until I could pull my feet back onto the rungs. The wind was howling, making the cement vibrate like a living creature, but it didn't slow me down. Up and up I climbed.

She had a long head start. If the Needle were twice as high I could have overtaken her, but I could tell she was going to reach the top before I would. When she pulled herself up and over the lip and disappeared I had only thirty more feet to go.

"Miyū!" I screamed.

I was almost at the lip myself when she looked down at me, her eyes wild and wide. It seemed for a moment that she wasn't even recognizing me.

"Miyū … stay right there. Please —"

"No," she said. "You stay there."

"You can't be … thinking about … ." Even though she was. I couldn't say it. I felt dizzy, my heart hitting my chest, rattling inside my ribs like a caged animal. I realized my hands were covered with blood where the rough iron had scraped them. My legs were shaking uncontrollably.

"I'll do it right now if you come any closer."

I stopped.

"Why?"

"Isn't it obvious?" she asked.

"You can't gain anything by killing yourself."

"I gain everything."

The words of Komori-san came back to me: There are so many things you cannot understand.

"Please. Let me come up there. My legs are about to give out. I could fall."

"We could fall together. Like lovers." She said it like a taunt. Daring me.

"Maybe," I said, willing to say anything to get a chance at being close enough to grab her. "We could. Let me come up before I fall alone. If I fall I want it to be with you."

"Make any move and I'll leap like a rabbit."

"I won't touch you," I lied.

She stepped away from the lip and I pulled myself over the edge and onto the flat expanse of what would eventually be the highway surface. She was at least twenty feet from me, watching.

"Tell me, at least, what you solve by killing yourself. I don't understand the logic at all."

"The logic is simple. It was me. Not my father. I thought I could show them something. I had enough explosive to send this hunk of cement to the moon."

Her eyes looked dark, not the green color I'd fallen in love with. They were all pupil even though it was bright daylight. I wondered if somehow she'd been taking something. Overdosed on sleeping pills just before starting the ride out here. Her face twitched a little as she continued.

"My father, this town has done nothing but try to destroy him. He knew the moment they found the explosives who had hidden them there. Me."

"How did you get them?"

"That 'ex' you were so jealous about. Not an ex. It angered me so much that you'd even think I'd date someone like that. Even you. For all your talk of love and understanding, you don't know me at all. At all! That hurt as much as what the town did."

Her voice got softer and then she stopped, looking out at the countryside. She spread her wings wide and looked at me. "You're a sweet guy, Neil. A sweet, stupid guy."

She took a step toward the edge.

"Wait!" I said. "Let me jump with you."

"You're a terrible liar."

"If you're going to jump, take me too."

She looked at me, her eyes boring their way into my chest, gauging the sincerity there. I waited, holding my breath.

"Okay," she said. "If you want to jump too, let's do it together." She walked to the platform's edge, where the tangle of rebar waited for its chance to mate with the road from the other structure, far away on the other side of the valley. She put one foot onto a bar and balanced there, testing to see if it would hold her weight. It bounced slightly, as would a diving board.

"Kiss me one last time," I asked, inching closer. "Please. Then we leap like lovers."

She stepped back onto the cement for a moment and for a split second softened enough that I thought I could hug her, hold her, then somehow talk her down.

The instant I had that thought, everything changed. She stepped back, her eyes black and glittering.

"You lie," she hissed. She had read everything, knew what was going on inside my mind. I was there to trap her, to throw myself onto her and keep her from dancing off that edge.

She took two steps.

One back onto the protruding rebar.

Then another, into space.

For a moment, she seemed to hang there as if gravity itself were refusing to pull her down. I lunged toward her, managing to catch hold of her hand as she fell. Her weight pulled my arm into the piece of metal she'd been standing on. The rebar sliced deep into my forearm. The pain made me cry out. Even now I have a deep scar.

But I had her. I'd caught her in the nick of time.

I was looking down at her; she was looking up at me. My hand was on her wrist, and that's all I could do. I just wasn't strong enough to pull her up. Reaching down with two hands would have meant we both plunged together, but she was far too heavy for me to lift with one injured arm alone.

Then the blood, gushing everywhere, slick and slippery, covering us in crimson.

I was still holding on to her.

She looked at me.

I was holding on to her.

She smiled.

Still I held her.

Then she twisted her wrist. One easy, deliberate motion. There was a sound. Suction broke.

And she fell.

I watched her grow smaller and smaller as gravity pulled her earthward, we were so high up, but the optical illusion was that she was staying in the same place and just shrinking like a star does when it dies, collapsing inward on itself until it is no bigger than a pencil dot. But what I remember most is her eyes, how bright those two stars were, that gaze so intense it seemed as if we were linked physically, as if it were tangible, something I could grab onto and pull her back.

Her eyes, brighter and brighter as she dropped, flashed a final beacon of green and then went out.

Numbness. A heavy numbness filled me. I climbed down rung by rung, barely feeling anything at all. I pulled her to me and just held her there, frozen. At some point it was pitch dark and I was cold. Covered in blood, I stumbled onto the street and walked in the direction of the studio, hearing only the blood pumping in my ears. A set of headlights passed. Then sirens. Everything after was just a blur.

I remember giving a statement to the police about what had happened. They got an English translator even though I was still able to speak in very coherent Japanese. A useless ambulance raced up, sirens blaring, to the hill where she lay. The next morning they released the potter and expressed deep sorrow for his loss.

It was when we were going back to the house, the potter and I wordless the entire taxi ride, that I remembered the letter I'd mailed the day before. Everything I'd written about, the dreams I'd had, the life I'd envisioned, it was all a fantasy. From the start, I'd never been a part of this town or this family. I wasn't making roots here. I was just a comet that approaches close enough to be visible for a time and then is flung back out into deep space.

When the car pulled up at the potter's house, I didn't get out.

"Take me to the post office," I told the driver. "I need to get there as quickly as possible."

My hope was to just beg them to take the letter out of their delivery pile, to have them hand it back to me. When I burst back in, the same girl looked up at me and nodded.

"Welcome back," she said.

"I'm so sorry, do you still have that letter? I need to get it back."

"It went out yesterday."

"There has to be a way."

She shook her head. "From here it goes to Kagoshima City, but even if you caught it there, they couldn't legally give it back to you." She lowered her voice. "Technically, I'm not even supposed to. But since I know it's your letter, I would have. But you needed to have been here yesterday."

"Are there any other options?"

She thought for moment. "Maybe a telegram? Tell them not to open it? We can do that here. I can take it for you, if you're ready."

My telegram was short and simple:

> MARINNE STOP YOU WILL GET A LETTER
> FROM ME STOP PLEASE DO NOT READ IT
> STOP BE HOME SOON STOP LOVE YOU.

The postal girl smiled. "That will get delivered today."

I paid her, thanked her, and left. When I got back to the house the potter was in the studio, already working on a vase. A bottle of *shōchū* was at his side. We didn't talk. I kneaded and wedged the clay and put it on the wheel but couldn't throw it. My focus was elsewhere.

"I have to leave tomorrow," I told the potter. "But I need money." I hesitated to ask him for a loan.

"Pick a pot," he replied. "Sell it in Kagoshima and you will have all the money you need."

CHAPTER FORTY-ONE

There is not much more to tell. The next morning I took one of the nicer vases we'd made together, then the potter and I said goodbye.

"What's your address?" he asked. "We should stay in touch."

I told him how I didn't know yet, as I could not return home and had decided to move to Canada for the time being. In the end we agreed that he'd send any letters to the central post office in Toronto, to be left until called for. They could do that back then: accept mail and hold it indefinitely.

We spoke nothing of what had happened. It was too vast a gulf for words to do anything but wound.

I took the taxi all the way to Kagoshima City, to the same place where I had gone more than a year ago, the museum. The curator recognized me, and we spoke inside the cluttered little office.

"I need to sell this vase," I said, uncovering it for him to see.

"My god, it's stunning," he answered. He looked at me. "It's not stolen, is it? We cannot accept anything stolen."

"It's straight from the potter's studio. I worked there. I helped make this vase."

I again had to assure him that I hadn't stolen it, as he didn't believe that I'd made it myself. Only when I showed him the foot, my own *inkan* seal embedded in the bottom, did he nod.

"You have a gift," he said. He took it and ran his finger inside, checking the thickness and how evenly the inner surface matched the outside.

"I cannot offer you its true value," he said. "Were this to go on auction it would —"

"Whatever you can do," I said. "But it has to be cash."

I don't know the value in today's dollars, but he paid me more than enough to book a flight to Toronto and have money left over to begin my life anew. I would not make it home to Massachusetts until after President Carter pardoned draft dodgers shortly after being sworn in on January 21, 1977. Instead, Marinne would join me in Canada.

The curator took me to the bank and in minutes I had a satchel full of money. In any other country in the world I would have worried that I'd be mugged and the money taken, but in Japan, no. Even then, long before it became the economic superpower it was to be, it was safe. A value most people living elsewhere cannot fathom.

After bowing goodbye to the vase's new owner, I took a taxi to the airport in Kamoike, just outside the city center. Eventually, even this airport would vanish, to be replaced by one that stood on a bluff high above the city about thirty minutes away. I would never return to Kagoshima.

All I wanted was to flee back to Marinne and her arms and her smells and bury myself inside her, burrow into her strength and her comfort and let her push away all the bad stuff I'd seen and done. I wanted to get to her fast enough so that when the letter arrived I could be there, could explain it away. If she didn't read it, I could bury everything that had happened forever and still return. It could be okay again, as long as she didn't read the letter.

I barely noticed the silver water of Kinkō Bay as the plane took off for Tokyo. From there I'd head to Gimpo, Seoul, then Calgary, then Toronto. My last views of Japan were of the giant volcano Sakurajima and an ash cloud seeping out across a perfect blue sky.

I pulled my shade down as we bumped up through the clouds into the stratosphere. I was back in a rocket ship, hurtling this time toward home. I only opened my window shade when the pilot mentioned that Mount Fuji was visible to the left of us, rising in splendor up through the clouds.

Each time my eyes closed I saw a girl getting smaller, shrinking into nothing as my bloody hand clawed at air. If I let my eyelids droop even for a moment, I'd see her eyes, fierce and defiant and untamed, refusing to let anyone tell her what to do.

I'd never broken through the walls she'd had around her. I'd never understood her. Every moment we would ever have already had happened.

By my own definition, I'd never even been in love. How can you love someone you don't understand? Someone who pushes you away at every opportunity?

All that I'd felt about destiny, that sense of connection, the intricate web that had pulled the two of us together, it was fiction. The mind will grasp at anything, convince you of what you want to believe. Right, wrong, it doesn't matter.

It is good we are human, fragile, and mortal.

It is good that we have the chance to die.

PART IV:
HOME

CHAPTER FORTY-TWO

Marinne came to meet me at the gate at Toronto Airport. She walked right up to me before I recognized her. She wore a stylish bob now, the exact cut of Miyū's. The two of us stood awkwardly together, realizing the full enormity of what the time away had done. It felt almost like meeting a stranger. Then we embraced, a deep, long hug.

"It seems impossible that you're here," she said, still clinging to me. "I've missed you so, so much. Neil. My Neil … you're in my arms, you're really here … home."

"You changed your hair," I said, when we'd stopped embracing and could look at each other again. "It looks lovely, but so different from before. "

"It's the style now."

I looked at her eyes, and they seemed so pure and wide and full of hope and wonder and love that I brushed off the doubts I had. Would she even be standing here if she'd read the letter? How would she want to still be with me after all that I'd done, the mistakes I'd made, the awful way I had treated her?

"Did you get my telegram?" I asked.

She nodded.

"And the letter?" I held my breath, praying she would say it hadn't arrived.

"It came."

I looked at her. "And?"

"I burned it."

She looked at me. A hardness flickered around her lips that any-one else might have never noticed, and it vanished quickly enough that I could tell myself that it was all in my imagination.

She threw her arms around me again. Then she was crying, and I was crying, and we stood there sobbing in the airport, touching each other's faces and running our hands through each other's hair as if proving to ourselves that we were standing together again. I bent down and kissed her and felt her pull into me.

"You're home," she said again.

"I'm home because I'm with you. I'll never leave again."

CHAPTER FORTY-THREE

We were married the next month in the Toronto courthouse by a justice of the peace, and found an apartment near a community ceramic cooperative, where I worked for nearly a decade before we returned to the United States in 1977. I was in Toronto when my namesake took his giant leap for mankind; however, I chose to stay in the studio instead of watching the event on our thirteen-inch, black-and-white television. I was in Toronto when Bonnie Raitt released a cover of that same song, "Runaway," and even now, decades later, it seems that song was written exclusively for me.

When we could return, we moved to Scituate, where we purchased several acres of land and an old farmhouse with what remained of the vase money. It was the yard that sold it for Marinne; she had always dreamed of a garden and trees to put a hammock under.

"Maybe we could have a horse, someday."

I loved it for the cellar: large and airy, with several rooms with heavy wooden beams from the eighteen hundreds and porous cement floors. I put in several wheels and a wedging table and racks for drying the greenware. An electric kiln for bisque firing. A bulkhead opened out to the garage that would, eventually, be where I built my gas kiln, and where I would keep freezers for the animals.

I am the last living person to make this Moon Island-style pottery. When I die, this art will cease forever. I have had no children, Marinne and I for all our lust-filled beginnings remained more like friends than lovers. Though many youths have inquired about apprenticing to me, I've never seen the need to be a teacher. The art that I've created pales in comparison to that of Miyū's and her father's, and what has driven me has been a sense of duty.

Or survivor's guilt.

Months after we had settled in Toronto, checking for the first time at the central post office, a package was waiting for me. The crate was packed with straw, then newsprint, then another layer of straw. Around that was a wooden box that was nailed on all sides. Inside was a vessel that was eighteen inches high. As perfect a cylinder as you could imagine. Looking at it was like watching a dolphin riding the crest of a wave. Graceful, delicate, playful, yet strong and fearless, too.

The glaze was the same brilliant green as Miyū's eyes.

Inside it was stuffed with newspaper, and a note was tucked into the top.

It was written in Japanese.

> *To my Son,*
>
> *I am sending you this vessel because I know only you will keep her safe, as you would have done if she had lived. Inside this vessel you will find both her ashes, and my own, in separate bags. I hope this will release you to be the potter you know you must become.*
>
> *I do not know of anyone more innately talented at the art of clay. To think of you returning to your country and never throwing again is as difficult for me to bear as the loss of our Miyū. I have done what I was meant to do on this earth and left beauty behind me. Now it is your turn.*
>
> *I am sending you my ashes because you know what to do with them. If you do*

not use them to bring your own vessels to life
I will have sent them to you in vain.

Miyū, what did not become the glaze on
the vessel you are holding now, is there too.
Wild as she was, she loved you.

We all struggle to carve our way in
this world. The life of a potter is not easy.
But it is that road that you must follow or
you will always be unhappy.

I would get a letter later from the postal worker who had ridden his red moped up the winding road by the river, past the turn where the path led up to the overlook, past the series of sheds where the explosives had been found, to the place where the clay mills pounded out their heartbeats. I could see him stop at the top, looking down at the odd shape at the base of the largest of the mills.

A human shape.

"He must have slipped," the letter said. "Perhaps he was leaning in to clear away some clay and the support became dislodged. It killed him instantly." His will made it clear that he wanted to be cremated, and the remains sent — whatever the cost — to his "son" in America.

I folded the letter. My first bags of clay had already arrived a few days before. And I had made arrangements with an artist friend who taught at a university to use the department's ceramics studio. For a project, I told him. Just for a few weeks. A favor for a friend.

But the potter knew.

I am a potter. I have brought beauty into the world that will long outlive me and everyone I've met or known. It will carry on through time, generation after generation. My name will be remembered for the beautiful vessels that will sit in museums. When aliens land on this planet long after the human race is gone, they will find these creations and they will know what magic the human species was capable of.

I am a potter. But I am also an addict. In pursuit of perfect celadon, I have destroyed everyone I ever loved.

Marinne, I cannot imagine how it feels to have lived your whole life with someone who could toss you away, be so transfixed, so selfish, so completely consumed by a place — a person, a color — and not see that you were the only good and true and healthy thing that he'd ever had. I wish you had burned the letter. Even after you'd read it. Is this your message to me?

To watch me become a potter must have filled you with something akin to hatred, yet you never let me see it.

Perhaps you always meant for the letter to stay burning there, a present you knew would arrive for me only after you were gone, untouchable. Your last word. To remind me of the awful things I'd done, the things that could never be washed away. Was that it? I could toss and turn for the rest of my life trying to decipher that answer, but it doesn't matter. Wherever you are, I'll be there soon.

Please understand that my mistake was in leaving you in the first place, in thinking that I could leave the girl I loved and return unscathed, unchanged.

Some things, once done, can never be undone.

To the person reading this, there is a green vase on the table in my studio, one that I have protected ever since my return from Japan. Take care not to spill its contents when you add my ashes to those resting inside. Cover it and shake it well, and when the contents are completely mixed, take it to Professor Knightsbridge, the Asian art chair at Boston University. The vase and its contents are to be sent by him to the curator of the Kagoshima Prefectural Museum, in Kagoshima City, Japan.

My final vase.

THE CELADON BEAUTY

(Original recipe used by the vasemaker himself, with suggested substitutions for those readers outside of Japan)

2oz Kagoshima *shōchū**
½oz plum wine
½oz melon liqueur
½oz *kabosu* liqueur **

Stir ingredients in shaker with ice. Serve straight up or on the rocks. For a sweeter drink, reduce *shōchū* to 1oz. For a more martini-style beverage, increase *shōchū* to 3oz.

*Can substitute gin for *shōchū*.
**Can use citrus liqueur such as triple sec or Cointreau.

THE END

Author's Notes

The elements relating to pottery and ceramics I have tried my utmost to keep as accurate as possible to truth, be it present or historical. I have opted not to include a glossary for the Japanese words that are sprinkled throughout. In most cases, the meaning can be gleaned from context, but for those who need more there is a wealth of online dictionaries that will get the job done. While some places in this novel are set in real locations and, for example, Japan and Panama and Boston do still exist (at least at the time of writing), this is a work of fantasy and muse-whispers, and the characters, conversations, and situations are fictional. Any similarity to real people or events is coincidental.

Acknowledgments

I would like to thank so many people for their help in writing this book, from family to random people on the Internet I've never met in person but who kindly shared their thoughts, insights, or expertise. Among them, in no particular order, many thanks to: Akiko T., Kazue, Jim, Meg, Amy, Yuko, Danniel, Missy, Eir, Martin of Diesel-Duck.info, Mike Smith, Sachi, Yuki, Andri, Julie, Ayoung, Devon Ellington, Kim at The Barn Pottery, my wonderful family, and my editor extraordinaire, Al Waitt, of Barrel Fire Press.

www.ingramcontent.com/pod-product-compliance
Lightning Source LLC
Chambersburg PA
CBHW021651110726
47902CB00007B/1917